LOVE, HATE, LOVE

DONNA AUGUSTINE

CHAPTER 1

Leah

KADE HAWK. HE'D BEEN MY FIRST LOVE, PERFECT AND ALWAYS just out of reach. I'd skinned my knees with him as a child and then dreamt of him as a teen. He'd been everything I'd thought a man should be—until he hadn't. He'd turned his back on me when I needed him most. He'd taken a blowtorch to those feelings, leaving nothing but burned ash in their place.

Now he was inserting himself back into my life at the lowest point of my existence and there wasn't a damned thing I could do about it. I didn't like it. I didn't trust it, and damn anyone who told me he was just trying to help.

"*Leah.*" My brother Monroe's voice jarred me back to the present with an underlying urgency that made it clear this wasn't the first time he'd called my name.

My attention jerked back to the present, the one place I didn't want to be.

"We need to get out. It'll look weird if we just sit in

the car in his drive." He let out a sigh while I struggled to breathe at all.

"Looking weird is the least of my issues," I said.

The ranch house loomed ahead, nothing like the run-down house from my childhood. It could make the most hardened soul want to burst out singing "This Land Is Your Land." It oozed charm with its thick log walls, swing on the front porch, and even a damned weather vane on the roof. The Montana hills gave it a storybook setting, autumn colors making it look more idyllic than a Kinkade painting, and I still wasn't sure this was better than prison.

"It won't be that bad," my brother said, getting out of the car and letting in a gust of biting, cold air.

He dug my luggage out of the trunk and came around to the passenger side, opening the door. I had a fleeting thought of locking myself in the car before I got out.

"I'm telling you, it's not going to be bad," he said, standing beside me, feeling more like a jail guard than my best friend and the only blood relative left I wanted to speak to.

"Can I have a minute to enjoy my last few breaths of freedom without having to endure your unrelenting optimism?" If he kept talking to me like Glinda the Good Witch he was going to get a black eye. That would take the glow off his rainbow. Sometimes when you were wallowing in a pit of despair, cheeriness tasted like the bitterest of pills.

"You know, you used to be an optimist," he said, that *cheery* tone still clinging to his words like a bad case of mange.

"*Used* to. I'm reformed. Optimism is for the delusional."

"Are you implying I'm delusional?" he asked, his *all is good* tone still firmly in place.

"If the ruby slipper fits."

He snorted and then shook his head. "It won't last. You can't be a pessimist, or at least not for long. It's not who you are."

I loved him to death, but all I wanted right now was for him to shut the hell up.

"I didn't used to be a thief, either and I managed to change that up nice and quick," I said.

That bought me one second of silence before his rosy outlook kicked back in.

"I know there's more to the story. You've never stolen so much as a stick of gum and you'll tell me what really happened one day."

"You keep on believing that, just like how Kade is a great, stand-up guy."

Other than our both being blessed with blonde locks and good looks, me and my brother were nothing alike. Monroe always thought the best of everyone, and somehow that seemed to have been working out for him. His wife, who was incredibly wealthy with family money, thought he was the most perfect specimen to walk the earth and they spent their lives flitting around on vacations and parties, with their endless list of friends.

It didn't seem to matter where he was or what he was doing—he was the one who would take my call any time, day or night. More than my mother, or my father when he was alive, I'd do anything for Monroe.

"He's got his flaws, of course, but so does everyone," he said. "We're all a mixed bag. You two just don't click as adults. Sometimes that happens as we get older."

I rolled my eyes and then glued them to his face.

After a couple seconds of my laser stare, he shrugged. "Fine. Maybe he's not always the most pleasant person, but he's doing us a huge favor by letting you come here and keeping you out of prison."

I glanced over my shoulder at the rental car behind us. How much gas was in the tank? Had Monroe left the keys in the ignition?

He followed my line of vision. "Don't even think about it. You'll only get caught, and you know you won't make it a day in prison."

Did I, though? Was I really so sure about that? Could it be worse than this? Than *him*?

"You know they have those white-collar prisons. I've heard they let you play shuffleboard, take cooking classes. I'm way behind on my reading list. I think I could make it work."

My brother gave me a push on the back, like a broken toy he was trying to get moving.

My legs might've been frozen, but my elbows were working just fine.

"Ow," he grunted, moving his arm to shield his ribs from another blow. "You don't have to hit me."

"Then stop shoving me." We'd only been kicking, hitting, and shoving each other for the twenty-eight years I'd been alive. He knew the rules by now.

He reached out as if he were going to try to shove me forward again but stopped short. I might be barely over five foot, but I gave as good as I got.

"Leah, no part of me likes this. Just go in and get it over with."

He was right. I wasn't ready to go to prison, no matter how nice it seemed in comparison to *him*, the man who owned this ranch.

I might've made a groan similar to Big Foot dying as I nodded.

My brother picked up my suitcase and walked toward the house.

He stopped after a few feet, looking back at me. He tilted his head toward the front porch, his eyebrows raised.

I would've followed if I could've gotten my lungs to fill with air and the crushing sense of panic to ease up. This man who had once been my childhood confidant was now going to relish being front and center, watching my fall from grace. And wow was I doing it in the most stellar way imaginable. I'd tried to work hard my entire life to become someone, and this was definitely not the someone I imagined I'd become.

"I'm *coming*." I forced my legs forward, the gravel walk eating up my stiletto heels like it was trying to suck me under. Or save me? Just because I was walking across a gravel drive that had seen torrential rain within the last twenty-four hours didn't mean it was science or gravity at work. One might imagine it was Mother Earth, trying to warn me off and leave this hellish man's ranch.

Monroe had almost made it to the porch. I, on the other hand, had only made it another few feet, continuing to fight Mother Earth for my shoes.

I was actively trying to keep my heels on, walking like a drunk duck, when Kade stepped out onto the porch, the wind howling right at that moment as if even nature would do what he commanded. He'd surely known we were out here for a while. But yeah, that was Kade Hawk. Never one to rush himself on behalf of anyone else. Nope, he'd leave us lingering in his drive for an hour if that fit his schedule. He'd show up when he was good and ready, and the world could like it or shove it. For some reason, that behavior seemed to have worked out for him, considering the upgrades to this place.

I'd hoped he'd gotten paunchy. The only place his clothing was snug was where it stretched to accommodate his biceps. He was wearing jeans that were broken in at all the right places, roughed-up boots, and a t-shirt that hugged his body like it couldn't get enough of him, just like all the girls had. I guess when you were born with a jaw that chiseled and hair so dark and thick that even the Kardashians were envious, you didn't have to spend too much time on the frills.

I used to think he was an angel sent from heaven to protect me. Now I thought his looks were to cloak his black soul from the naïve prey he stalked. That was how it went with the evil ones. There were perks to selling your soul to the devil. Although I might've been underestimating him. For all I knew, he might've been the one collecting the contracts.

Those whiskey-colored eyes turned on me and my breath caught. It was the first time we'd laid eyes on each other in years, and in spite of the fact my opinion of him had nosedived worse than a fighter plane in WWII trying to bomb the Germans, my body hadn't gotten the memo that we hated him. My stomach clenched and my heart stopped beating when our eyes locked.

He turned his attention to my brother, as if my presence was insignificant, but the vein bulging in his neck told a different story. I still got under his skin, as much as he did mine.

My steps slowed as they were gripping hands in greeting.

I couldn't make out what they were saying, but the

low timbre of Kade's voice carried, sending a hum through me that settled all the way in my gut and warmed me up better than half a bottle of whiskey on this chilly autumn night. I could attest to this, since I'd drunk close to that last night and all I'd gotten for it was a wicked headache today and a touch more nausea than I'd probably have had anyway.

I forced myself a few steps closer. Kade wasn't looking at me, but he was clocking my every move. Last thing I'd do was give him the satisfaction of appearing afraid. But I liked it here, safe in the shadows, where I could let my eyes adjust to the sight of him before every reaction would show on my face. When we were kids, everyone had known I had a crush on him from the way I looked at him. I couldn't risk any remnant of that popping back up. Even if I didn't like him anymore, I wasn't sure how my body might react. This situation was degrading enough without his thinking I carried a torch for him, or worse, a bonfire, as they used to tease. I had to blank out my face, the way he'd always been able to.

I took a few more steps.

"Thanks for doing this," Monroe said. He sounded so grateful that listening to him was like chugging a gallon of honey.

Luckily Kade was there to cut the sweetness with his vinegar. If there was one person who wasn't all apple pie and whipped cream, it was this man. He might've had a soft spot for me once upon a time, but he'd ripped that part out and run it through a meat grinder. Or maybe that had been the fantasy of a googly-eyed teen?

"Don't worry about it," Kade said. "I owed you one."

It was way more gracious than I'd expected—and a tad unbelievable, since I'd never heard of this debt to my brother. Kade cut his gaze to me, looking at me like a rodent he wanted to run off his land.

Yeah, what a *great guy*. Top of the line. Just *super*.

My brother laughed awkwardly, as if Kade's look was some sort of joke. He didn't know Kade the way I did. That man didn't have a funny bone.

"Leah, I should get going," my brother said, drawing my attention back to him. He let out a low sigh, his relief valve working overtime.

"Yep. Have a good trip." I didn't smile. We were all too far along for false pretenses. I couldn't pretend Monroe hadn't just dropped me off in the depths of hell and was now about to climb out and take the ladder with him.

He gave me a fast hug and whispered, "It'll be over before you know it."

The last time he'd used those words was when he was convincing me to climb through a patch of poison ivy because he'd been too lazy to walk around. It hadn't been good then, and it would be even worse now.

Not to mention he was hugging me. We didn't hug it out. We were more the hitting variety of siblings. If he was hugging me, I was about to die, and we all knew it.

He gave me a last pat on my back before hightailing it out of there. I stood there, listening to the sounds of his steps on the gravel like it was a funeral dirge. The car door shutting sounded like a gunshot hitting my heart. I watched the taillights disappear and forced myself not to chase after his car like a flea-ridden dog abandoned on the side of the road.

"You plan on moving, princess? I don't have all night," Kade said from the porch.

Yep, I was truly screwed.

CHAPTER 2

Leah

MY NEW WARDEN STOOD ON THE PORCH, HIS EYES BURNING UP my form. I ignored him for a few more seconds. I wasn't sure if it was because I was too stunned by my new reality to move, or because my heels had become permanently stuck in this damned gravel drive. If questioned, I'd swear it was to prove I wouldn't jump to his command.

I lifted a foot, the ground making a little popping sound as it finally let go of my heels. Seriously, he couldn't get this shit paved? He'd clearly come into some money.

I made my way to the porch, grabbing the suitcase my brother had forgotten as soon as he spotted Kade. I was under no illusions that this man would carry it for me. I shot him a look, making it clear what I thought of his manners.

"You're not here on vacation, princess."

Princess. He just loved saying that. I'd been doomed to

that nickname the second my mother decided to name me Leah. I'd begrudgingly lived with it, but it had never annoyed me as much as it did coming from this man's lips at this moment. He'd never used it when we were younger, because he'd known how I felt about it. Now he was using it for that exact reason. He might as well have poked me in the eye.

I walked the final few feet, dragging along my rolling suitcase, whose wheels were also rebelling over the gravel. By the time I got to the porch, my suitcase looked as roughed up as I did.

I glanced toward the front door of the house, wanting to get this torture session over with and find my bed. The past twenty-four hours had felt like a fifty-round bout with Mike Tyson.

Kade shook his head. "You don't go in there unless you're invited by me, which won't happen."

"Don't worry. I'm not looking to spend any more time with you than necessary." Claustrophobia or not, prison would've been better. *Hell* would've been better. I'd spotted some new buildings on the property, so it wasn't like I'd be stuck in a tent or something.

He turned and headed down the length of the porch, assuming I'd follow. I did because I had no other choice.

A breeze blew, dousing me in his scent. I had to stop myself from breathing deeper like a dog sniffing for scraps. He'd always smelled this good. It had been like his pheromones were concocted to tug at my insides and draw me in like a stupid, hormonal teen. I was older now and refused to let his smell suck me in again. I'd stamp out those feelings fast, even if I had to yank out my ovaries.

Farther down the porch, he opened another door.

"This is the only room of this building you are allowed to enter, and only when I'm present." He pointed to my suitcase. "You can leave that out here. No reason to bring it in."

He walked into an office that was overflowing with paperwork. It was piled high on every surface that lined the room. Someone needed a secretary, or an assistant. Even a few baskets or another filing cabinet. *Something.* I felt like the entire place was on the brink of a paperwork avalanche that might bury me alive. How did he function in here?

"Is there a problem?" he asked.

I jerked my gaze back to him. "Why would there be? You can run your business however you deem fit." I didn't hold back the judgment in those words. I'd never been the type to take a punch and not swing back. Being stuck here wasn't going to change that. Being stuck in prison probably wouldn't have either, so my odds of living through the next year were probably better here.

He watched me for a second, his face unreadable, before he took a seat behind his desk, letting the dig go. So far I'd score this round as a draw.

"Sit," Kade said, like I was his dog. At least he pointed to a chair and not the floor.

"I'm fine," I said, refusing to give up any points. We were still at a draw, but sitting would cost me. Even if my feet were killing me, I was not losing this first round. It set the tone for the rest of the fight to come.

I glanced at the top of his desk, which was one of the only areas not stacked a foot high with paper. A gossip rag sat front and center, with *The Devious Debutante Dodges Prison* in big, bold letters.

Who came up with these stupid headlines? Did they

not know about the internet and how to do a basic search on someone? If they'd bothered to look me up, even for a second, taken a glance at where I'd grown up and *how*, it would become shockingly obvious that was a load of bull. Unless there was a new category that included former welfare recipients, I was as far as you got from a debutante.

Kade didn't look like a regular follower of the trash mags, but he'd probably made an exception for me, the *Devious Debutante*. Knowing him, he'd picked it up and left it here to welcome me.

"Want to borrow it?" he asked, glancing at the magazine. "I'm finished with it."

I could feel my first-round score slipping.

"Not really my genre. Didn't know you were a fan of those types of magazines, but I guess reading something is a better than not reading at all." I shrugged.

"I found this edition quite entertaining," he said, not even flinching.

"I guess when you don't have much going on, it scratches an itch. I'm quite tired, so if we could wrap up this reunion? I'd like to get some sleep tonight."

He leaned back, settling in instead of speeding things up. "Before I bring you to your room, we need to be clear on a few things."

I made a point of sitting and said, "Then please, get it all out of your system." I rolled my hand in his direction.

It had been bad enough to be told these things over and over again by lawyers who spoke to me like I was a toddler. I wasn't sure I could stand to listen to them again, from *him*.

"I signed a lot of papers agreeing to a load of shit to save your ass from going to prison for that painting you stole. You are going to follow those rules to a T." He straightened and then leaned forward, his chest rising and falling visibly. "That means no cell phone. No leaving the premises. You work a full day, *every* day. Other than that? You don't take a single step unless you have my permission. Do you understand?"

"Why did you agree to this? Are you getting paid or something? What's the deal? Just tell me so we both know the angle." At least the pretense of whatever game we'd been playing was dropping.

There was a flicker in his eyes, a quick moment where he didn't look quite so sure of himself, before he resettled and said, "I owe your brother."

"No, you don't. You don't owe anyone anything." Even when he was barely a man, it had taken him months to decide to try to get a loan to keep this ranch going. He'd stressed so hard over that decision that it had kept him up nights. He wasn't the type to owe anyone anything, including my brother. "So what is it? You just get your rocks off bringing me here to torture me for some imagined slight a decade ago that you're too petty to get past?"

"Imagined? It must be nice to rewrite history, but that's not why you're here. Watching you suffer is just a minor benefit to repaying your brother, who is a *very good person*." He put such emphasis on those words that it was impossible to ignore the slight.

"As opposed to me, who is the scourge of mankind?" Yes, my saintly brother who always saw the best in everyone, including Kade. I'd been measured against him my entire life, but that splinter felt more like a stake right now.

Kade shrugged and threw up a hand. "If that's how you like to define yourself."

"You..." I shook my head, refusing to get pulled into a ridiculous argument. "Forget it. Say whatever you want. Get it all out of your system. You get a year to torture me all you want, and then I'll go back to having a happy life and you can continue doing..." I glanced around, and then lifted a brow as I ran my eyes over him, pretending I found something lacking. "*You.*"

He smiled. "A year can be quite a long time."

This was exactly what I'd expected from him, and I'd get through it. I would because I had to, and I'd be damned if I let him know he could get to me.

"Make the most of it, because it's all you're getting from me." I had to bite the inside of my cheek to not tell him to fuck off.

He got up and sat on the edge of his desk, his hand out. "Give me your phone."

My brother had said I'd have to hand it over, but this was the toughest thing I'd done yet. I was relinquishing my ties with my world.

"Per the agreement I signed, you'll get thirty minutes a week for a monitored phone call every Sunday."

He dropped my phone in a drawer and then walked to the door, waiting there. The only reason he held it open for me was probably to make sure he could close it behind me.

"Grab your suitcase and follow me."

"Where are we going?" I asked. The farther we walked from the house, the more I was reminded that nothing about me was gravel friendly.

"Showing you to your cabin, since the courts didn't

think the tent option would work," he said, pausing for me to catch up.

For a split second, I thought he was going to reach for my suitcase. It had probably just been a twitch in his arm from some evil spirit that had rethought trying to possess this particular man and was trying to make a break for it.

"A cabin?" That wasn't how I'd have described the larger building we were approaching.

"Yes. I can't have a thief staying with the rest of my staff in the bunkhouse. It's not fair to them."

Didn't matter how many times the word *thief* had been hurled at me. It still burned like a fresh brand every time. At least I'd gotten better at controlling the urge to flinch, hiding how hard it hit. I'd always detested thieves, and now I was walking around as one of the most infamous of them all. I'd gone from getting an invite to every hot party there was in New York City, being courted by the handsomest and most successful men, to being a pariah in one of the smallest towns in the U.S.

I'd really hit my lowest.

We walked around the larger building I'd spotted before, and that was when I saw it.

He stopped beside what could only be described as a shed, and I realized I hadn't quite hit bottom yet.

CHAPTER 3

Kade

What the hell had I been thinking? I hadn't seen her in years. That should have dulled something. After what had happened? It should've dulled *everything*.

Instead, her presence hit me like a tsunami. No warning. No mercy. Just Leah, reaching into my chest and getting a grip on me like she always had. Touching at something I'd thought untouchable.

I wasn't sure what I'd expected, but it hadn't been *her*, the girl who had always been able to undo me. The Devious Debutante might be a woman, but the girl who'd lived in the house across the creek was still there. She might've grown up since I'd seen her last, but Leah was still there. I hadn't been counting on that when this plan had been getting ironed out. Her blonde locks weren't the wild mess I remembered, and she looked thinner than she used to, more *sophisticated* than she used to, but she still fidgeted when she was nervous. She still tried to hide in the shadows as soon as attention shifted her way, like the wallflower she could never be.

Those sky-blue eyes were just as bright when she looked at me. For a second, they'd been almost hopeful when they met mine, until I'd quashed any chance of a cordial relationship, let alone anything close to what we'd had, with a swift dismissal. If she'd known it had taken all my restraint to not carry her suitcase for her, she'd have worked me around her little finger. How was I possibly going to have her here for an entire year? What the hell had I done? What did I do now? The only option I had at the moment was to get her situated and get away fast.

I opened the door to the cabin and flicked on the lights. Elijah, the stable manager and all-around fixer, was supposed to have had this place cleared out, cleaned up, and livable. A quick glance around made it clear that our standards on what was considered livable might not have matched up this time. At least she had it to herself and it wasn't a prison cell. That was something.

Damn it was cold, though.

I knelt by the wall, fidgeting with the controls on front of the electric baseboard heater. It wasn't on? No wonder it was so frigid in here.

"You need to turn the heat up manually when you come in." I made sure to keep any concern out of my voice. Damned if I'd let her work me over. She'd burned me when I was barely a man, and it wouldn't happen again.

"Where's the thermostat?" she asked, looking about the small space as if in disbelief that this was to be her new home.

"It's on the baseboard, down there." I pointed to where I had just been kneeling.

She walked into the middle of the room and shivered as she looked around.

"Wait, where's the bathroom?" Her tone was even, but she was chewing on her lower lip.

She was taking it better than I would've expected, at least pretending to be calm.

"The bunkhouse has bathrooms and a kitchen you can use." I motioned to the building no more than ten feet away, visible through the cloudy window.

We were about at the end of autumn, and the temperature reminded you every night if you happened to forget. Was it going to be miserable to traipse out in the cold in the middle of the night every time she had to pee? Most definitely, but I didn't trust her enough to have her stay in the house with me. And I sure as hell wasn't putting her in the bunkhouse surrounded by men so she could stir up trouble there. This would have to work, even if it wasn't ideal.

"It's"—she let out a sigh, as if she were coming to terms with the place—"exactly what I expected from you."

I caught her shivering again. It might've been this place or the temperature. I had to get out of here before I forgot who she was, what she'd done. She wasn't some wronged innocent who needed protection. She didn't need me to take care of her.

"You can go next door to the bunkhouse until it warms up. Everyone is expecting you. Chuck is the ranch foreman. He'll find you tomorrow and show you the ropes. Elijah is the stable manager and also handles a lot of the maintenance if something breaks or you need something."

Great. Now I'd made it sound like she had one of those New York supers she was used to at her beck and call.

"No one will be waiting on you," I added. "If it's light when you get up, you're late." I gave her shoes a pointed look. "And I hope you've got some sturdier clothes in that suitcase. It's going to be hard to shovel shit in those."

Her chin lifted an inch as she stared right back at me. "As much as I appreciate your experience in this area, I'll be just fine. I don't want you worrying about me when you've clearly got your own issues going on."

She'd be fine here. I wasn't her protector. I wasn't even her friend, not anymore. And this was Leah. She'd give as good as she got, which might've been why she could crawl under my skin the way she did. She was one of the toughest people I'd ever met, even when she'd just been a kid.

I walked back into the house and went immediately to the cabinet, pouring myself a whiskey. I threw it back and poured another before settling onto the couch, resisting the urge to drink until I was numb. I'd never been an alcoholic, but her being here felt like my brain had gotten tossed into the spin cycle.

My phone lit up, my brother's name flashing on the screen. The only thing surprising about the call was that he'd waited this long. I'd expected him to start rapid redialing hours ago, before she arrived.

"How'd it go?" Alec asked the second I answered.

"Don't you have anything better to do with your life than caring about this?" I certainly wished I didn't. Why had I done this to myself? Nothing good came

20

from feeling bad for others. I was positive of that right now.

It was too late to get out of it, though. Even if there were a chance to renege, could I really send her to prison? The Devious Debutante probably belonged there, but Leah wasn't just *that* woman, no matter how much I'd hoped that was who would show up. Little Leah had also come. No matter how much she'd tried to hide her, I'd seen her just beneath the surface, and *that* person I could never send to prison. I couldn't even evict her from my heart completely, as I'd learned tonight. She was still in there, with a grip so tight I could feel her nails biting inside of me.

"Someone is awfully testy. I guess all those denials of feelings aren't holding up?"

"You have no idea what you're talking about." I hated when Alec was right. Worse, he was laughing as he spoke. If he were here, I'd be punching him in the face already.

"I want to know every single detail. I'm still trying to figure out how this deal came to be. You've never really explained that, no matter how many times I ask."

He'd asked at least fifty time and I still wouldn't tell him if he asked fifty more.

"It doesn't matter how it happened. Monroe needed me and I helped out because I could. There's nothing else to say."

"Where's little Leah now?"

Unfortunately, he knew this place almost as well as anyone, and I was going to sound like the biggest dick going. "She's settled in a cabin."

"Cabin? Which one? I thought Missy was in the only livable cabin."

"Elijah fixed up the other one for her."

Alec groaned. "There was no fixing up that dump. The only thing that could fix that scenario was a dumpster. I can't believe you—"

"It was fine. She's fine. It's better than a cell." It wasn't like she couldn't spend her free time at the bunkhouse.

With the guys.

I needed another drink. I needed to rewind the clock a month, back before I'd agreed to this.

"Oh, I get what's going on. You didn't want her too close to *you*, so the house wouldn't work. But you were always a jealous fuck, so you weren't going to put her in the bunkhouse with the guys, either."

"I've never been jealous in my life." That was usually a true statement.

"Maybe not with other women, but no one could go near Leah, even though you weren't even banging her. Were you even kissing her?"

"You're a sick fuck, you know that? She was a baby, and I wasn't jealous; I didn't want anyone taking advantage of her."

"You're trying to tell me you were only protecting her? She was sixteen and you were nineteen. Not exactly robbing the cradle."

"I think it's time you found a hobby." I was resisting a third whiskey, but he wasn't making it easy.

"There's nothing as interesting as this. Is she as hot as she used to be? She looks even hotter if you go by her mug shot. She looked better in that than the covers of those mags on the newsstand."

If he only knew. The pictures I'd seen of her through the years, the memory of the shy teen, none of it did anything to prepare me for the stunning woman who'd arrived tonight. It had taken everything to act cold and aloof, and it was only because I couldn't let her know how she undid me.

My mind flashed back to her standing inside the cabin, giving me one last look, every line of her body stiff, her eyes flashing rage. She was such a force to be reckoned with that my dick stiffened just at the thought of her.

I had to stop thinking of her like that.

"Whoever she was, it isn't who she is now. Who steals a painting like that? It wasn't just the money. It was a priceless religious painting that's been missing since WWII. You realize how morally bankrupt you have to be in order to do that?" I'd have to keep repeating this to myself every time I softened.

"I don't care what the news says. There's more to this story. I know you don't want to hear this, but I'm telling you, she didn't steal that fucking painting. You weren't the only one who knew her."

"She's not the girl we grew up with. She was a kid then. She's different. I don't know if it was the money that got to her or—"

"You're wrong," he said, digging in. "People with hearts like hers don't change. Remember how she used to save all the abandoned bunnies and every other damned little critter who was hurt or sick? You don't go from that to a monster. I think you want her so much that you'd rather think the worst to dull any feelings because the world might burn down around you if you cared."

"Except I don't care. We both know who she is, who's she's always been, and nothing will change that." There was a short pause as I dragged up the past again. "She could've cost me this ranch." Alec had never wanted anything to do with this place, so of course he wouldn't care.

"You've always blamed her for that situation, and for the record, you're wrong about that too. Even if you aren't, she was a fucking *kid*," he said, rehashing the argument we'd had many times. "And while we're on the subject of the ranch, I'm clearing my schedule for a visit."

"This is not a sideshow. Do. Not. Come."

"Fuck off. I'm coming." He hung up before I could beat him to the end button.

How the hell I was going to make it a year with her here?

Distance. That was how. I'd delegate all my interactions to Chuck. If I didn't, she'd ruin me.

CHAPTER 4

Leah

THE SHED DIDN'T LOOK ANY BETTER IN THE MORNING, everything looking like it had come out of a Goodwill clearance sale twenty years ago. The sunlight, even filtered as it was through a thick film of grime, showed every stain on the green carpet, and how long the spiders had been tenants. The place had so many dust bunnies that it was as if they'd been banging like the real things. My suitcase was in the middle of the room, looking like a safer bet to store my clothes than the swelled particle-board thing in the corner, trying to pass itself off as a dresser. The twin bed had a mauve comforter and a pillow so flat that my back felt like it had aged fifty years in one night. I wasn't a stranger to roughing it, but this wasn't just frugal. This was *I don't give a shit*.

I'd sweep it out, borrow some glass cleaner, and go on. I was here for a year. I could survive anything for a year, including *him*.

Worse than the discomfort of this place, my bladder felt like a water balloon with a pin poised at its surface. This was what I got for wanting to avoid meeting my new coworkers last night.

It wasn't barely dawn. Did I bust in there now and sprint to find the bathroom?

Too awkward. I'd risk the bushes instead. I walked around to the side, hiding behind a nice, tall row of hedges.

I was squatting down, feeling a relief I hadn't imagined possible, when I heard footsteps.

I scrambled to stand up and fell over instead, my legs getting tangled in my pants at my ankles.

"You okay in there?" a man called out.

I froze. There was no ignoring him. If I didn't answer, he'd think he had to climb in after me and save me.

"I'm good," I squealed, my tone indicating pure humiliation.

"I'm Chuck," he replied. "I'll be over at the bunkhouse making coffee when you're done."

"Okay." I was already done. Now I was just hiding.

Oh noooo, did he think I was pooping? I scrambled to my feet so fast that I banged into the hedges as I scrambled out, rushing to get to the bunkhouse as fast as possible now.

I stepped into the bunkhouse. There were couches around a large, rolled-down screen on one wall. Several doors were closed and another was open, hinting at a bathroom.

An older man with a gray beard was in the kitchen area of a large main room, brewing coffee.

I smiled hesitantly.

"You're Leah, right?" He had a gruff voice and crinkles

near his eyes, which made him look like he was quick with a smile.

"Yes."

"Nice to meet you. I'm the foreman here."

"Nice to meet you, too."

"Want a cup?" He was already grabbing a mug and filling it up for me before it finished dripping.

"Thank you so much." I sipped the coffee, and it might've been the best cup I'd ever had. Or maybe it was because it marked the end of my worst day and a new start, of sorts. Well, at least it *was* a new day. I had to take what I could get at this point.

"Do you live here?" I asked, wondering how little Kade paid if his foreman had to live in the bunkhouse with the hands. When I'd known him, if I'd *ever* really known him, he'd been too poor to pay anyone. He'd had his hands full not losing this place.

"No, I've got a place down the way. I just come and get the coffee on and make sure the boys are up so they don't start slacking. Come on, take your coffee and I'll give you a tour before everyone else gets up—unless you want to get something for breakfast first?"

"Not really hungry."

"Yeah, me either. Give me one second and we'll head out."

He walked to the first of the closed doors and gave it a pound. "Get up!" he yelled before doing that two more times and then lapping the room, back to me.

His eyes shot to my shoes. "You got anything a little sturdier than those?"

He was looking down at my designer combat boots. They were more for looks than work, but they *were* still boots. Wardrobe hadn't been high on my list of concerns this past month.

"You don't think they'll be okay?"

He made a humming noise before he said, "I'll have someone pick you up some things to make it a little easier to get by."

"Thanks." I wasn't used to having to depend on anyone to get my things since I'd been in grammar school, and even then it had been sporadic after my dad had passed.

Chuck pointed to some buildings I hadn't noticed last night, farther away. "Those are the first stables, and then the newer stables are behind it. That one is only about half filled, but with Kade's breeding plans, it'll be full soon enough."

"That's a lot of horses." More than a decade ago, there had only been one. Kade had used to talk about how he was going breed a dynasty of cutting horses. I'd never even heard of a cutting horse until Kade explained how they were used in ranching to "cut" a cow from a herd. I'd never have imagined how much money they could be worth, either. He hadn't been kidding about building a horse dynasty.

"Considering you're new to ranching, I'll probably have you mucking out stalls and tending the chickens initially," Chuck said with a kind voice, as if apologizing in advance.

"Understandable." He was looking at me, spending an extra couple of minutes staring at my boots. Maybe the embroidery was just too much for him to handle? I might've looked like the princess Kade called me, but I'd never had an aversion to dirt or hard work.

I might've been living in a high-rise apartment in

New York when I rose to infamy, but I hadn't grown up with a silver spoon. There was no point in telling him that, though. People tended to believe what they saw, not what they heard.

It didn't matter much to me anyway. At this point, as long as I wasn't near Kade, I'd be more than happy shoveling shit. I'd actually consider it an upgrade.

"You got any other clothes? Those look like some fancy jeans you've got there." Chuck was eyeing them up, and not in the way most men looked at me in jeans.

"They won't work?" I mean, jeans were still jeans, right?

"They'll work fine, but they're going to get ruined. I'll get some stuff ordered for you. I'm sure Missy has some stuff she could lend you in the meantime. You look close to her size. I'm going to have you shadow her for a while until you get used to the place."

"Thanks. I appreciate it." For as rough as he appeared, Chuck had the feel of someone who'd been weathered by a lot of sun and fresh air and it had left his soul clean and bright, and a little soft around the edges.

"Oh, speak of the devil. Here she is now."

Missy was walking toward us, bright red hair up in a messy ponytail that was more of an authentic mess, than being intentionally styled that way.

"Leah, this is Missy. She'll show you the ropes."

"Nice to meet you." She had a smile that hit as fresh and open as a flower field and had gone extinct in the big cities. Although I'd grown up here, I wasn't sure I'd ever had that bright a look in my eyes. She reminded me of a Rockwell painting, ice cream sundaes and rolling up your jeans for a wade in the creek.

"You too." I tried to muster up a fraction of her fresh-ness and enthusiasm but was fairly certain I fell short.

"Maybe you could lend her a couple things to get by for a few days?" Chuck asked, as if instinctively knowing I never would.

Missy gave me a quick once-over, as if measuring my size, and nodded quickly. "Yeah, sure."

"Okay, I'll check in later." Chuck was already disap-pearing, as if he had no real concern over how I actually performed on the job, making me wonder what Kade had told him. Was I supposed to be useful or just keep busy?

"So you're from New York?" Missy asked.

"Yes." It wasn't clear whether she'd hold that against me or if it would play in my favor.

"I've never been there, but it looks amazing. I haven't been more than a few hundred miles from here. My fami-ly's been here for generations, and we kind of like staying put. Not that any of us have the money to go somewhere like New York." She wasn't holding my gaze like she had been, as if I'd hold her lack of travel against her.

"I didn't have much growing up either, and the way things are going, I won't have much going forward. My business pretty much tanked in the last couple of months."

"I kind of heard." She was shrugging, in an apologetic way. "I like to read the gossip pages. You were a marketer of sorts, right?"

"Yep. I used to help businesses come up with launch plans, or relaunch plans when they were tanking. No one wants a felon attached to their brand name, though. Isn't a strong selling point."

"Looks pretty amazing there, though, so it was prob-ably fun."

"You know what looks amazing to me right now? That." I pointed to the sun rising over the mountains, sunlight spreading out before us. I'd forgotten how much I'd loved this view as a kid. Or the smell of the crisp air and the sounds of the birds. I'd been surrounded by cement for so long that I'd forgotten how nice this place really was. How much I'd never wanted to leave.

"I'm sure you have sunrises in New York," she said, even as she stood beside me taking it in.

"Not like this, or at least it sure didn't feel like it." How could I forget how beautiful this place was in the morning?

"Come on. I'll give you some stuff real quick before we start," Missy said after a few minutes.

We walked past the bunkhouse to another small cabin about fifty feet or so away. It was about twice the size of mine but nothing that looked too elaborate, until you got inside.

It was set up like a studio, but it had a bathroom, and a small kitchenette against the wall. A loveseat and living room area was in the center and a bedroom area on the other end. On top of having modern conveniences, she'd decorated it in an eclectic, cozy way, with plants near the windows and paintings on the wall, furry throws, and plush area rugs. It made you want to curl up on a couch with a cup of tea. It was a penthouse suite in comparison to my hovel.

"This place is adorable."

"Thanks. If you want, I could lend you some stuff for yours? Make it more comfortable?"

"No, I'm fine." It was bad enough I was taking her clothes. Plus, my shack would need a lot more than a few pieces to make it livable.

She pulled some jeans out of her closet and a few flannels and handed them to me. "I've got some old boots so you don't have to ruin those. They look expensive."

"That would be great. Thanks. How long have you worked here?"

"A couple of years. I knew Chuck and he put in a good word for me. He's a bit rough sometimes, but he's as solid a guy as they come."

Rough was welcome. I was used to dealing with smooth-edged sharks who smiled right before they ripped your life to pieces.

"These should hold you for a bit." She handed me some boots that looked broken in but way better than what I was wearing.

"I'm going to be here a little while," I said, not sure how much she knew.

"I heard," she said, shrugging.

"I wasn't sure if they covered that in the gossip mags."

"They did," she said, giggling. "Okay, well, the chickens are going to be waiting. I put out some extra feed at night but they'll be wanting out of their pen so they can wander around for a bit."

"Chickens?" Kade had chickens? I'd thought Chuck had said chickens but that I'd misheard.

"Yeah, Kade likes fresh eggs. You didn't hear those roosters carrying on?"

"Yes, but I thought maybe they were the neighbor's."

She laughed. "Next neighbor ain't for miles. Kade bought up all the land surrounding this place. You won't see anyone, let alone hear anyone, unless they work here. Okay, well, let's go let the chickens out and then we can grab another coffee before we hit the stables."

We did a quick detour, letting the chickens out before heading back to the bunkhouse.

"Did you meet any of the guys?" she said.

"Only Chuck."

"Some of them live here. Some come in like it's a regular day job."

We walked into the bunkhouse, and three sets of eyes turned to us.

"Hey, all. This is Leah. She's going to be working here," Missy said, as if I'd been hired like a normal person and not sentenced to forced labor in order to dodge a federal sentence. It was a kind effort, but I wouldn't kid myself into thinking they didn't already know. The world seemed to know. "Benny there works with the horses, and so does Adam."

Benny didn't seem older than twenty and looked as if he were going to trip over his own feet as he nodded at me with a goofy, lopsided smile.

Adam, on the other hand, was pure man, and broad in all the places a woman, me included, tended to like. His smile was confident as he tipped his hat to me.

"Nice to meet you," he said, and I was pretty sure he probably didn't have to say much more to get most women in bed.

The way his eyes settled on me, I was fairly certain I'd just received an invitation too. I gave a small smile, not RSVPing.

Elijah fell somewhere in between the two, with sandy-brown hair and a demeanor that was easy and inviting, but did not lead to his bed. "Nice to meet you. Let me know if you need anything."

"Missy, we need more eggs," Elijah said.

"You know you can go get them, right?" Missy said.

"But you go there a couple times a day. You can't just bring them?" Elijah said.

"Fine, we'll go get them, but we want some of that bacon when we get back," Missy said, watching what Elijah was pulling out of the refrigerator.

"I'll make you both omelets if you go get them."

"You good with that?" Missy asked, as if I had a say in anything.

"Sounds great to me."

"See? Leah's easy. You should be like that," Elijah said.

"Oh, Missy can be pretty easy too," Adam said.

"Go screw, Adam," Missy said at the same time Elijah chucked a roll at his head.

"I was only kidding around," Adam said.

"Come on, let's go get the eggs. Adam usually leaves early, so by the time we get back he'll be gone."

We left the bunkhouse and all the dread I'd been feeling about my first day was fully gone. I could do this, with these people, for a year. Not only could I do it, I might even enjoy it.

CHAPTER 5

Kade

IT WAS AFTER TWO IN THE AFTERNOON WHEN I PULLED BACK UP to the ranch. If I could've stayed out all day, I would've, but there were things that I had to do around here. What I wanted to do was be away from her until I beat these feelings back into submission. Seeing her after so long had shocked my system. It felt like I'd stepped into a time machine and my body felt the jolt of a rough landing. I just needed to reset.

I got out of my truck and immediately spotted Leah. Gone were the fancy clothes and the smooth blonde perfection. Instead her hair was up in a ponytail and her fine clothes were swapped out for worn jeans and rough cowboy boots. Her face was lit with laughter as she perched on a fence beside Missy.

Chuck strolled over and stopped beside me, leaning a forearm on the hood of my truck. He turned to where my eyes were glued.

"She's settling in just fine. I don't think she'll be anywhere near the trouble you made her out to be."

"I never said she'd be a problem." Maybe she wouldn't be *for them*. It was only me she could take out at the knees.

Chuck adjusted his hat. "You might not have said it to me, but that's exactly what you implied when you dumped her on my lap. Plus I heard some of the other things you said."

I shrugged. "Maybe I did. Either way, I'm glad she's not causing you problems at the moment."

Leah glanced across the field, and our eyes locked for a second. She looked away first, and I forced myself to turn to Chuck.

He threw up a hand. "See? You just did it again. You make it sound like there are going to be problems."

"It's not a figment of my imagination. I do remember telling you why she's here. My concerns are not unfounded," I said.

"And I'm an old man who's seen a few things in his time. I can tell a good apple from a rotten one. I don't know why she did what she did, but that girl there is not rotten." He pointed in her direction, as if I needed the reminder she was right across the field, or in the cabin only a few minutes' walk away last night. I might as well have a tracking device on her with how aware I was of her movements, whether I wanted to be or not.

As long as I kept my distance, maybe this wouldn't be the five-alarm fire I feared. Standing here talking about her wasn't helping, though. I was already thinking about her every minute of the day.

"I'm not here to debate her situation. I've got to call Marvin," I said.

"Do you think you can get him down on the insemination doses? That stallion? He's got some good bloodlines, but Marvin is pricing his semen like he is shootin' golden bullets."

"I'm trying to negotiate." I tilted my head to where Leah was. "Just keep her busy and not too close to the house if you can help it."

Chuck laughed. "Go hide in your office. I'll try to keep the scary little girl away from you."

Sometimes I loved that old guy and sometimes I wanted to strangle him.

I might've argued, but she *did* scare me, to my absolute core. How was I going to make it a year like this? I'd have to take some trips, break it up. I'd basically have to figure out a way to escape my own ranch on a regular basis.

I LEANED BACK IN THE OFFICE CHAIR, HAVING JUST HUNG UP with the last call I'd had to make. The sun had just set and I'd barely been outside all day, let alone checked on my pregnant mare, which was my habit. I grabbed my jacket and headed out to the stables.

The horses were all bedded down for the night, and the lights off. I didn't need them on, though. I'd been out here every single day when this place was getting built. The only thing that threw me was hearing a soft voice as I walked the length of the stable.

The door was cracked open when I got to the mare's stall and slowed my step.

"It's all right. You're all right," Leah was saying softly.

I crept up slowly, staying in the shadows as she came into view. She was running a hand over my horse's neck, whispering softly to her as the horse nuzzled her shoulder.

Leah stopped speaking, spotting me out of the corner of her eye.

"I'm surprised you're still up," I said when she didn't appear inclined to speak.

She didn't turn fully toward me, even now, as if she were trying to avoid my presence as much as I was hers.

"She was restless earlier today. I wanted to check on her before I called it a day."

"She looks calm enough now," I said, not sure why I couldn't stop myself from talking to her. Even as I told myself to leave, I was walking closer instead.

"Princess?" she asked, raising a brow at the mare's name that was clearly written beside her stall.

"Chuck's granddaughter picked it," I said.

Chuck didn't have a granddaughter, but she didn't need to know that. I'd already made enough of a mistake by bringing her here. I wasn't doubling down by giving her the impression that there were any feelings between us. The only thing going on was a leftover physical attraction, a crushing need to kiss her that was nearly all consuming, and that was only because she was beautiful. I wouldn't be a straight man if I didn't want to kiss her.

If she was disappointed, it didn't show.

The time stretched out silently, my urge to touch her growing to an alarming level, and I forced myself to take a step back out of the stall before I stepped all the way forward.

"Don't stay up too late. We rise early here."

She glanced over, her face a mask, any glimpse of what she was thinking securely locked away from me.

I backed out of the stall wondering why I had to

constantly take a jab. Why I had to poke at her, trying to dig for that girl I knew, see what was really still there when it didn't matter.

I picked up my pace as I made my way to the ranch, knowing the worst thing for both of us was having any contact at all.

CHAPTER 6

Leah

"LEAH," MULTIPLE VOICES CALLED OUT AS I WALKED INTO THE bunkhouse. There were some new faces I didn't recognize among the group piled in front of the big-screen TV for Thursday night football.

It was the close of my fifth day here, but everyone acted like they'd known me since grammar school. Even if these people were concerned about my being a convicted felon, they acted as if they didn't know anything about my circumstances here. It was so different from the crowd I'd fallen in with back in New York, most of whom cut me as soon as a hint of suspicion became attached to my name.

I gave a wave. "Just coming to use the bathroom." I walked out a few minutes later.

"Come on, hang out with us for a few and watch the game," Elijah said, several others chiming in as well.

"Yeah, come on," Missy said, having come in. She

walked closer and then looped an arm through mine, locking me to her side and whispering, "I need you. I'm tired of drowning in testosterone around here."

Between the amount of people, and the number of beer bottles, my gut was telling me this was the exact scenario that would set Kade off.

"I'm not sure..."

"Kade never comes here," she said. How she knew that was my problem was unclear, but I nodded. Missy dragged me over to a high-top table near one of the couches. "That's Bernie, Roger, Ted, Eddie, and..." She mumbled the last name.

"Huh?" I asked.

She leaned in. "I can't remember the other guy's name. He's just started coming around. Pretend I said it and smile."

I did what she suggested, giving the group a casual wave as I braced for the awkward questions to begin. What used to be normal small talk was now like dodging bullets. "Where are you from," "How did you end up here," and "How long you sticking around" were the most dreaded sentences I could hear.

An interception and a third down, combined with a lack of timeouts, trumped all interest for the minute and gave me some breathing room.

"Do they all work here?" I kept my voice down so I didn't take their attention off the screen. I'd seen some of the faces around, but others were definitely new.

"Some work at nearby ranches—everyone hangs out here for the games, since the bunkhouse has the best screen in town."

It really did. I'd never seen the projection screen on

before, but it was like watching the game in a theater. The thing had to be a hundred inches across.

Adam, one of the few not glued to the screen, walked over and held out a beer to me.

"I'm good, thanks." I was walking a fine line being here as it was. In fact, the line was about as thin as you could get. The last thing I needed to do was break a rule as big as drinking. I might've kidded that prison would've been better, but as I was settling in, this place wasn't turning out to be so bad, especially since I barely saw Kade.

"It's been a long week. You deserve a beer," Adam said.

"Really, I'm fine," I said.

"I'm going to put this right here. If you take a sip, no one is going to notice."

He put the beer right beside me on the table I was leaning against and then gave me one of those killer smiles, the kind that probably got him company any night he wanted.

"Can you go drool somewhere else? I left all the rags back at the barn," Missy said.

"Isn't it past your bedtime?" Adam replied.

"I'm staying up late while I wash the crabs you gave me out of the sheets." She followed that with the sweetest smile you'd ever seen. These two didn't play around, or at least not in the way they clearly had in the past.

It was a hard enough blow that Adam's face turned so red it was causing a rash all the way down his neck.

"Fuck you," he said, obviously out of original lines, as he walked away.

"I guess you two don't like each other much?" The

way she looked at him, I was glad there weren't any nearby knives.

"He's a real charmer until he realizes he's not going to get back in your pants because the first time wasn't worth a repeat."

"Ahh. Okay." The guy was so good-looking that he probably fell into that curse where he didn't think he had to do much—not that I ever intended to find out. But knowing what little I did about Missy already, there was clearly a lot more to the story than a bad go-around in bed.

"Hey, I've got to do a fence check tomorrow afternoon —you're welcome to come along if you want?" she said, shifting the conversation. "It might be a nice change. We'll take the ATVs and go around the different fence perimeters, make sure none of the wood posts are rotting or pieces are missing."

"You don't just walk it?" That could buy a lot more time away from the house, where Kade might be.

She was squinting as if I were nuts. "When you've got four thousand acres? No way. Heck, we won't even be hitting all the pastures, and it's still going to take most of the day."

"Four thousand acres?" Every time I looked around or found out something new about this place, I grew more impressed with what Kade had built. I shouldn't have been, but it was hard when I remembered the young guy working sunup to sundown to keep this place afloat. He'd worked himself to the bone to just pay the electric bill. To see him come this far was inspiring.

"Yeah. I mean between the horse and the cattle."

"There's cattle?"

"You can't train cutting horses if you don't have

cattle. You know, a horse can't cut cattle from a herd that doesn't exist. He's in the process of buying more acres, but the guy who owns the land to the north is being stubborn on price, even though he wants to sell. We'll get it, though. That'll put this place at over six thousand acres once it gets worked out."

How was Kade able to buy so much? Monroe had hinted that he had been pretty successful, but whenever Kade's name came up, I'd find a distraction or change of subject. Because when I did hear his name, all I thought of was a past that was too painful, a friendship lost, and a first crush that hadn't just been crushing but pulverizing.

I was on the verge of getting swallowed by that black hole of memories when the door to the bunkhouse swung open and the star of my nightmares strolled in.

There were greetings around the room, but I kept my attention trained on the game I'd been ignoring.

Sometimes I wondered if I'd ever known Kade at all. Other times, like now, I could sense his energy the second he entered the room and knew he was here for a fight before anyone else caught on. And what was sitting right beside me, giving him the perfect excuse? The beer.

The room went quiet, proving Kade didn't look happy as he walked over and stood in front of me.

"What are you doing?" he asked.

I finally met his stare. "It's the bunkhouse. As far as I'm aware, I'm allowed in here. I actually *have* to come here because my shed doesn't have a bathroom."

"You aren't allowed at parties," he said.

"It's not a party."

He reached beside me, going for that damned beer, as I prepared for battle.

He held it up in between us. "This yours?" he asked.

45

I wanted to tell him to go to hell but couldn't. The problem was, this *did* look bad.

"I didn't drink it. I didn't even ask for it." If I sounded slightly aggressive, it was his fault for being the one to ask. It wasn't as if he deserved any softness from me.

"Let's go. It's time to go to bed."

A few of the guys groaned. "Come on, Dad, let her stay out a little late tonight."

"We promise she'll be in bed by ten," another one said, followed by laughter.

Kade glanced their way and the room fell silent.

"It wasn't hers," Missy said. "Adam left it there. Look at it, it's full."

With my face burning red, and with the smallest scrap of pride I had left, I patted her arm. "Don't worry about it. I was ready to leave as soon as he showed up to the party." I was speaking directly to Missy but was loud enough that the room heard.

I got a couple mumbled laughs when I walked out the door, Kade on my heels as I walked the short distance to my shed.

I walked in, trying to shut the door after me, but I wasn't fast enough to keep him out.

"I don't care if you hate me," he said. "I signed a—"

"Yeah, yeah, yeah, I know. You signed a contract," I said, turning toward him.

"You want out of here? Just say the word. I'll gladly drive you to the prison myself."

"You want to drive me, I'll pack my bag tonight. Just give me the word." Even as the words came out, my chest tightened. He might call my bluff. I'd never been good at backing down from a fight, though, and if he kept throwing down the gauntlet, I'd damn well pick it up.

We stood, nearly toe to toe, while I waited to see what my fate would be. My heart felt like it was getting zapped as I saw the flicker of something remorseful in his eyes. Was it because he was going to tell me this wasn't working? Was it guilt I saw because of what he was about to do?

Then his eyes shifted to my lips, and for a second I could've sworn he was going to kiss me. I was so convinced that I parted my lips in response—from shock, of course.

He hated me. I hated him.

He backed up a step after a few seconds. "I don't smell beer on you. I'm sorry if I overreacted, but be aware you can't drink."

He walked out, and I swore it took me a few more moments before my lungs wanted to work. I walked to the bed and collapsed on it, absolutely drained and not even sure why.

CHAPTER 7

Kade

MY PHONE LIT UP WHERE IT SAT ON MY DESK BESIDE ME, "Monroe" flashing on the screen. Even when I was trying to think of anything but Leah, someone else yanked my mind right back to her.

"Hey, got a minute?" he asked when I answered.

"Sure. What's going on?" I leaned back in my chair, running a hand across a scruffy jaw. I'd been too tired and grumpy to shave today, or yesterday. I wasn't optimistic about tomorrow, either.

"Just wanted to see how Leah is holding up. I can't help but worry about her, even though she's with you." He sounded almost as worn down as me.

"She's okay. Bit of a transition, but she's fitting in well. The people around here all love her."

If he'd seen her at the bunkhouse with the guys, he might wonder if she was getting *too much* love. I'd caught a glimpse through the window before I walked in. The guys had been shooting her looks like she was filet mignon and they hadn't eaten in months. She'd come here in lieu of a prison sentence. This was not a dating service. Not to mention that she had a boyfriend, or at least appeared to in all the paparazzi photos. I remembered that but couldn't quite be sure if she did.

"What about you two?" Monroe asked, his normally smooth voice still sounding out of sorts. "I know you aren't getting along like you used to, but I hope it's been okay?"

Okay? Bringing her here was the worst mistake of my life, but there was no turning back. I'd almost kissed her last night. I hadn't even been aware of what I was doing as I walked toward her, my body taking control, bringing me to what I wanted, which was to the soft fullness of her lips, pulling her up against me, and...

I had to stop this craving that was becoming all consuming. I had to stop thinking of her. Of course, Monroe didn't need to know about any of this.

"It's fine. We're both so busy all day that we barely even see each other." Unless I was stalking her in the bunkhouse and scaring off the men while pretending to be a warden.

She had to own up to some of that mess last night. She'd been hanging out in the bunkhouse with a damned beer. What had she expected from me? It hadn't had anything to do with the men drooling all over her.

"I appreciate this more than you can imagine. If you hadn't reached out, I'm not sure what would've happened," Monroe said.

Those words hit like a hydrant in the face. If Leah ever found out my part in this? I'd lose any leverage she imagined I had. I'd be worse than a hog-tied calf.

"Except *I* didn't reach out, remember?" Thankfully, he wasn't on speaker. No one around here had any problems listening in, and I'd left the door cracked because it was unseasonably warm today.

"I know. Don't worry. I'm not saying a word. Just know I will find a way to repay you."

"All I want you to do is never mention it."

Missy poked her head in the open door. "Kade, do you have a minute?"

"I gotta go," I said to Monroe, and hung up. This was why I couldn't have him talking about that shit. "What's going on?" I said, waving her in. I leaned back in my chair, trying not to sigh. It was as much enthusiasm as I had in me. I had my limits, especially this morning after the lack of sleep.

"I have a bone to pick with you." Her tone was pricklier than I'd ever heard.

I leaned back farther in my chair, getting more comfortable, as I had a feeling this was going to be a long one. This was the price I paid for leaving the door open for some fresh air. But it was Missy, who up until recently had seemed to brace herself to not run whenever she saw me. I couldn't snap at her and tell her I wasn't in the mood for whatever it was she wanted to tell me, even if I did want to tell her to get the hell out.

She walked right up to the other side of my desk, crossing her arms and glaring down at me. "You were out of line last night. She didn't even want that beer. She told Adam that repeatedly. He put it there but she didn't even touch it."

I should let her get it off her chest so she'd leave faster, but that would imply guilt. I was *not* guilty.

"I realize that she might not have drunk, but she's not allowed to be at a party. That looked like a party to me."

I grabbed a file off my desk, flipping through some stats on the newest cutting horses making their way up the ranks. Perhaps she'd take the hint and leave.

"She came in to go to the bathroom and then we made her stay. What was she supposed to do? Pee in the bushes in the dark and not know if she's getting poison ivy or bitten by something?" She was leaning forward, her voice getting louder, as if my reading affected my hearing.

I threw the file down. "How was I supposed to know that? Look at it from my perspective. I walk in and she's hanging out at what looks like a party with a beer." This day was already bad, and it wasn't even noon.

"Maybe ask next time before you humiliate her like that."

"I didn't humiliate her. She was fine." It wasn't like she ran off crying or something. She pushed right back.

"Oh, so it's okay if you're mean because she can take it?" Her face was scrunched up as she threw her hands in the air.

"I'm not *mean*. I have responsibilities. I signed a legal document guaranteeing I'd hold to certain rules." Why was it that no one other than me could understand this?

"Rules? *Now* you're such a rule follower?" she scoffed. "What about when you—"

"I don't need a list of what I've done in my life." Or what I'd done just since Leah had come to the ranch. I wasn't the one who was doing a sentence. "Now if you're done, I've got things to do." My eyes shot to the door, making my meaning clear to anyone with half a brain.

Missy had a very competent mind, but it was

frequently overridden by a stubborn streak, like someone else I knew. This seemed to be another of those occasions.

"She's highly likable. Everyone likes her. You're just being a bully." She wasn't just insulting me now—she was pointing at me.

"You're calling *me* a bully?" I blinked several times.

"Yep, that's you. Bully boy Kade." She tilted her head back, trying to increase her height superiority.

"You don't know what the hell you're talking about," I said, about to get to my feet and reclaim the higher ground, if only physically.

"She's right," Chuck said as he walked in the open door and over to a stack of files on the side table. "You're being mighty mean."

"You're jumping on this bandwagon, too?" Of all people, Chuck was turning on me?

"There was a chat about it at breakfast. There was a vote on it," he said, flipping through papers as if their condemning my moral fabric was nothing.

"You took a vote?" What the hell was going on around here?

"Just an informal raise of hands. We didn't put it in writing, but man, you took a beating." He shuffled through another stack of papers. "Ah, here it is."

"You need to do better," Missy said.

"Can you get out so I can get some work done, please?"

She nodded, but then didn't walk out.

"What?" I snapped.

"I'm not in trouble for this, am I?" Missy asked, her voice growing softer now that she'd unloaded her grievances.

I gave her a hard stare, about done with the lecture. "No, as long as you get out now."

Chuck watched Missy leave and then stood there staring at me.

"I'm not talking about it," I said, knowing he wasn't going to be scared away as easily.

As if on cue, he said, "That little girl of yours is—"

"She's not mine."

"From the sounds of it, that's not the way you acted last night. She wasn't drinking. Missy said you knew because you picked up the full bottle. The guys all said you looked jealous. So what's the real problem?"

"How was I supposed to know that? It might've been her second beer."

"All I'm saying is that you seem a little unhinged around her, and you should probably think about that."

As if I didn't know that. As if that wasn't why I was trying to avoid her.

He held up his file. "Okay, I'm off to go grab the new trailer. See you in a bit," Chuck said, walking out as chipper as he walked in.

I got up and shut the door, locking it. I wasn't taking chances on suffering through any more impromptu chats.

The phone rang as soon as I sat, Alec's name flashing. He was one stubborn bastard when he wanted to get a hold of me. I either had to answer or turn my phone off.

"What's up?" I asked, zero warmth in my voice.

"You sound like shit. What's your problem?"

"Nothing. I have a long day. I need to get shit done, so tell me what you want or I have to go." I wasn't giving him an opening to dig into my situation.

"I heard about the vote." He started laughing hard.

"How the hell did you hear about the vote?"

"I have to protect my sources. Not like it's much of a secret anyway. You didn't fare well, though. From what I heard, it was unanimous. Man, you must've acted like a real ass for them to call a vote and for you to not get a single one. Usually someone will feel bad enough to just throw you a pity vote."

"I have work to do." I hung up.

Leah was stirring up my entire ranch against me—even Missy, who didn't used to want to catch my attention, was in here lecturing me. Now stories were leaking out to my brother, who didn't even reside in the state. How was I ever going to make it through a year of this?

CHAPTER 8

Leah

"YOU KNOW HOW TO RIDE ONE OF THESE?" MISSY ASKED AS WE walked into one of the smaller garages where some ATVs were parked.

"I might have moved to a big city, but I grew up here." Kade had taken me on my very first ATV ride on an old piece of junk he'd fixed up. He'd fixed quite a few things to help pay the bills, both here and over at my house.

Missy swung to face me. "You *did*?"

"Yeah. That's how I know Kade. My family lived in a house not far from here."

"Really? How long have you known him?" She leaned against the one ATV, watching me as if she couldn't get enough of this story.

"Long enough to have scraped knees together. Well, I was the one with the scraped knees. He's three years older and was usually trying to clean off my blood in the creek."

"Wow. I didn't know there was so much history. I wonder if that's... Never mind." She straightened and shook her head, grabbing some keys off a hook on the wall and tossing me a set.

"Wonder what?" I asked.

She let out a sigh. "I'm sorry. I'm just being nosy, and I'm trying to not blurt out everything in my head anymore. I haven't made much progress, though."

"It's all right. Blurt. I want to know." I shouldn't care what observations she'd made about Kade and me, but that wasn't working out so well.

She hesitated before she said, "Just that he seems quick to fight with you. He's so much more—*raw*. I don't want to say he's usually cold, but maybe not *that* emotional?" She was shaking her head and huffing, redoing her ponytail. "That doesn't sound any better. See? This is why I shouldn't speak so much."

"No, it's okay. I get it. You aren't trying to insult him. You just think I get under his skin."

She pointed at me. "Yes! Much nicer way to put it."

"After the other night? I don't care if you insult him. We were friends once, but we just don't get along that well now." The silence started to spread, and I patted the ATV near me. "Okay, so let's get these suckers revved up. Haven't been on one in forever."

"Yeah, let's get going. This will be good."

It was a beautiful afternoon, the nicest we could've wished for this time of year.

We rode slowly, stopping by posts that had any kind of issue. She'd call out a marker code and a certain length and I'd take notes. It wasn't quite as invigorating as the last time I'd been on an ATV, but it was a nice change and

I got to see a small portion of the ranch, which was staggering in size.

We made our way along the stream to where it narrowed, and the familiar terrain began to pull at memories I'd long ago buried.

We stopped just shy of where my old house sat across the width of the creek, and I wandered my way toward it. The paint was gray now instead a pale, chipping yellow. The yard was manicured and pristine, not overgrown with weeds and shrubs that hadn't been trimmed in years. It was nothing like the run-down little house of old, but the sounds of the creek, the rustling of wind through the trees, were like a distant lullaby from a life I'd once lived. I still wish we'd never left.

"Hey, what are you looking at?" Missy asked, stopping beside me and then following my line of vision.

"That's where I used to live a lifetime ago." I sank to the ground, still staring at the house.

"So you were neighbors with Kade?" she asked, and I could see all the questions forming again.

"Yeah, we were. I spent a lot of years crossing that creek. My brother, too. Monroe is in between Kade and Alec in age. Monroe stayed in touch with Kade all these years."

"But not you," she said, as if trying to piece it all together.

"No, not me," I said, the words coming out rougher than I'd intended.

"I'm sorry. I shouldn't have said that. Things always slip out that aren't my business," Missy said.

"No, it's okay." I patted her arm. "It's hard to explain it all, but he thinks I tried to hurt him."

"You wouldn't hurt anyone on purpose. That's not who you are," she said.

"Thanks," I said, and then took a deep breath, and another, surprised by how much hearing that from someone who barely knew me struck deep down.

"You two might still make up. It's not too late," she said, as if she were channeling Monroe.

"Maybe we could've, but that was before I moved here and he gave me a whole new list of things to be pissed off at," I said, then we both started laughing.

"Yeah, he's really been just awful lately. He's snapping at everyone, like he caught some sort of cranky disease."

"I'm sorry. I didn't want it to spill over onto other people. I was hoping he'd keep it contained."

"You're not the one being mean. He's the one who should apologize."

I got to my feet. "Okay, I don't want to mess up the whole day's schedule and set off Kade about something else."

I glanced back to the house one more time, remembering how I used to try to cook in that kitchen with Monroe, or tried to build a treehouse. It was hard to think about what life might have been like if we'd stayed.

"Do you miss that place?"

"I guess I do. It wasn't that nice when I lived there, but it was better in a way. Then my mother remarried."

"What happened to your dad?"

"He died suddenly when I was eight. It was a freak accident at work. He ran a small construction company. One of his guys was running a backhoe and didn't realize my dad was right there. He swung it around too fast, and it hit my father in the head. The crew had been working together for so many years that they'd gotten comfortable and sloppy."

"I'm sorry. That had to have been tough."

"Yeah, it was bad. My mother had always been a homemaker, and my father had worshipped the ground she walked on. Bought her everything she wanted, whether he should've or not. He'd handled *everything*. Once he was gone? Things got really messy."

"But then you moved to New York?"

"My mother found another man to take care of her when I was sixteen. He came from New York, so that's where we went. He called the shots and we jumped." I didn't want to sound bitter, but there was no way to discuss him and keep that tone out of my voice.

"You don't like him much, huh?"

"Nope, and even less now than I used to." I took another long, deep breath, this time so I didn't explode with the secrets I was so tired of keeping. "That's enough about me for the day. What about you? Your family from here?"

"Yeah, only about twenty miles or so from here, but I don't see them much."

Now she was the one looking off into the distance.

"You want to talk about it?" I asked.

"Not even a little," she said. "You?"

"I've already said more than I can stomach in one day."

"I'd say let's go grab a beer, but we know how that turns out, and we don't need to get Kade all hot and bothered again. He's already met his quota for the decade," Missy said. "I do have a piece of strawberry shortcake back at my room, and some kick-ass tea I'm willing to share."

"Considering I can't leave this ranch, I don't have any other plans I can think of, so I'd love to take you up on that."

CHAPTER 9

Leah

It was Sunday night. Kade knew tonight was the night I was supposed to make my calls. He was the one who'd just rattled it off from the list of rules and made me sit there and listen. Even convicts were allowed phone calls. He could've made it easier and come to me. Nope. He'd make it hard, of course. Well, fuck him. I was using the phone whether he liked it or not.

I walked over to the house, past the office that was dark and empty, and went to the front door.

"Kade!" I yelled as I knocked, peeking through the window.

When there wasn't an answer, I went from knocking to pounding.

"You're not ignoring me!" I hit the door hard enough that the glass rattled.

We were probably far enough away from the bunkhouse that no one else heard me yelling, at least not yet. If he didn't answer the door soon, I'd be screaming so loud the people in the next town over would hear.

I peered inside. The living room was dim but the fire was casting a glow and there was a light coming from farther back near a hallway.

I spun on my heel, checking for his truck, which was parked right where it always was. Then I noticed a small car behind it that hadn't been as obvious. It was some sort of little white coupe. When I got up on my tiptoes and angled myself, I could see a crystal hanging from the rearview mirror.

I was standing out here, getting colder by the minute, and he was getting laid. That was why I wasn't making my phone calls.

I was wondering where Missy had put those eggs from today when a flicker of movement drew my attention back inside the house. Kade was walking toward the door, barefoot, and more importantly, shirtless. His jeans were not even buttoned up and there didn't appear to be anything on underneath them.

Dammit, I hated this man. I'd told myself that he couldn't possibly look as good as he'd appeared in a t-shirt. Like, no one could look that good unless they worked out every day. I guessed the ranch was workout enough, because he looked even better than I'd feared. I'd seen personal trainers with more fat on them. When was the last time this man had seen a plate of pasta? Or even a single noodle?

I was staring so hard at his body that it took me a second to notice he was glaring at me as he approached.

Oh, he'd better not be looking for a fight. The way I was feeling right now, it would be like starting shit with a grizzly having a bad day.

He swung the door open. "What the fuck are you doing banging on my door on a Sunday night? I told you not to come here."

My cheeks were burning at the reminder I was too lowly to go to the house. The added reminder of my lowly situation only increased the rage.

"It's my call day. I'm supposed to get a half an hour. If you didn't want me to come here, you should've come to me instead of whatever else you were busy doing."

I could see the minute it hit him. He'd completely forgotten. It was probably easy to forget when you could make a call anytime you wanted. I was stuck with once a week. Thirty minutes every Sunday to reach out to the people I loved. That was it. That was all I got. Not so easy to slip the mind in my case.

"Yeah, okay." He dragged a hand through his hair, setting off rippling muscles everywhere. "I'll meet you at the office door."

No apology. No mea culpa. Just *meet me at the office*, which I could see the door to from where I stood with freezing wind blowing through my hair. He wouldn't let me set foot in the house, even now, after *his* mistake.

"Kade?" A sexy little brunette, wearing only Kade's t-shirt, was walking across the room toward him.

"Everything is okay, Melissa. Go back to bed. I'll be there soon."

She continued toward him anyway, scanning every inch of me with a calculation that seemed to take in that extra piece of toast I'd had this morning and the brand of my hair conditioner. Considering it was whatever I found in the bunkhouse bathroom, it wasn't working out so well.

She leaned into his side, her hand landing on one

beefy bicep as her big doe eyes continued to track me. She got up on her tiptoes, pressing her breast against him as she pretended to whisper, "Is this the convict?"

Well, didn't that say it all? Must be pretty interesting pillow talk now that I was around.

"Yes," I said, holding her stare. "I'd make sure to lock your door tonight. Never know what urges might come over me." I did a little shudder.

She stepped back, shifting behind Kade as if she needed his protection. I wasn't sure why, but that one little movement made me want to grab her by the hair and drag her out of the house.

"*Leah,*" Kade said.

Melissa smirked at me from behind where she clung to Kade's arm.

"I'm sorry. Just trying to live up to your expectations," I said with a big, fat, phony smile.

Kade rolled his eyes. "Go to the office." He shut the door on me before I could scare his girlfriend any more. After all, wouldn't want poor little Melissa rattled.

I took a step toward the office, but not before Melissa's voice carried through the door.

"Wow, she looked a little rough," she said. "You were so nice to take her in, but I don't know if you should've."

"I'll be back in a few," Kade replied, not responding to her comment.

Rough? See how she looked after going a week with no hair products and mucking out stalls. My nails had been perfect too, once upon a time.

I walked to the office door and waited. This wasn't anything more than I'd expected and one of the reasons prison would've been better. At least I wouldn't have little twits judging me for frizz and chipped polish. It wasn't as if I could go buy anything to fix my nails. I couldn't leave the ranch.

The wind was howling like a wounded wolf right now, and I leaned my shoulder against the doorframe, trying to avoid the worst of it. Whatever Kade was doing, he was taking his sweet-ass time. I didn't pound and rush him this time. I took the extra minutes to steel my spine against the recent blows.

He finally opened the door, having stopped to put on a t-shirt before letting me in out of the cold.

"What took so long? Had to calm your precious girl-friend over having a criminal in your house?"

"My private life is none of your concern," he said, watching me as I walked in.

He was staring at my arms, and I uncrossed them, refusing to show him any signs of weakness, even if it was from the cold. As far as he was concerned, nothing bothered me, ever.

"If you're going to get cold so easy, you should dress warmer," he said, giving me a once-over. "Don't you own a decent coat?"

"My clothing is none of your concern," I said, throwing his words back at him.

He didn't respond, just shook his head and pointed to the chair behind the desk, where the phone was.

I settled in as he fiddled with the thermostat by the door. I wasn't delusional enough to think he was increasing the heat for me. He only had a t-shirt on and was probably cold himself.

He walked over to perch on the corner of a filing cabi-net. "The speaker button is on the bottom."

I'd been mid-dial, but that completely stalled out my brain. "What do you mean, speaker?"

"I'm supposed to monitor your phone calls. It was in the contract you signed. What do you think that means?"

It took me a few seconds to register what he was saying. "Isn't hearing what I say enough?"

"No. I signed off that I would monitor your phone calls. I can't do that with a one-sided conversation. It's in the papers. I can pull them out, but it's coming off your time. I'm not wasting all night on this." He shrugged, as if he had no control.

"*You're* going to listen to my calls?" I made sure to glare, just in case he didn't hear the disgust dripping from every syllable.

"Do you really think I want to sit here and listen to whatever you have to say to Sally Mae and Susie Q about their hair or who blew who?" He pointed to the clock on the wall. "You've already wasted five minutes of your thirty, so I'd get dialing if I were you."

Every time I saw him, I wasn't sure how I'd make it a year. Another *week* seemed unsurmountable.

"What about the five minutes I waited for you to crawl out of bed with the little whore you're fucking?"

I hadn't had a conversation this mean with anyone since...maybe *ever*. It was like I couldn't be around him without my head exploding and the blood in my veins wanting to shoot out of my eyes. I was probably growing fangs and claws right now. As far as mistakes went, coming here was going to be top of my list.

Him? He was sitting calmly and looking at the clock. "Fine. I'll give you that. I'll reset your time to thirty, but start dialing, because I'm not giving a minute more." He tilted his head, motioning to the phone.

He might be acting calm, but I could see that vein in his neck starting to bulge. Did I waste another three minutes telling him what a bastard he was, or make my calls? He'd probably enjoy the fact that I was nearly frothing at the mouth. It was likely the only time his black, shriveled-up heart ever pumped with life.

Screw it. I couldn't waste any more time on him.

I dialed Cassie, my best friend—and also my only friend left. The one thing the bottom taught you was who was willing to visit the depths of hell to stay by your side. Turned out all my other friends would rather go visit the islands.

"Hello?" she answered.

"Hey, Cass, it's—"

"Holy shit, I've been answering every damn spam call waiting for you."

"I called as soon as I could. Just so you know—"

"How's the dickhead being?"

This was Cass. I either had to be aggressive in my warnings or this was going to happen. Kade *was* a dickhead, but I'd rather he didn't know we'd discussed him at all.

"The dickhead is just fine," he said.

There was a long stretch of silence before Cass said, "You're supposed to tell people when they're on speaker to avoid unfortunate situations such as these."

"I tried, but you kept talking." I would've felt worse about the awkward situation if I thought she really cared. I knew her better than that.

"Because my best friend, who I used to talk to every day, is basically in prison and I still can't figure out why."

No. Not this conversation now. Not in front of Kade. He might be grumpier than he used to be, but he still didn't miss a trick. That kind of thing didn't go away just because he'd turned into an asshole.

"I told you what happened. By the way, it's not even close to how I'd imagine prison. It's not that bad here. It's sort of calm, to be honest." If I had to compliment the place to get her off this line of questioning, I would. The strange part of it was how the truth of those words seemed to fit.

"You know what I remembered the other day? I think we were on the phone when you got that painting. I remembered—"

"Cass, I don't have that much time to—"

"You told me about some ugly painting at your apartment someone shipped to you by mistake, and you had to hang up and go make some calls. You stuck it right back in its crate, saying you couldn't bear to look at it because it depressed you."

Of all the things she had to dredge up, now, on speakerphone, with *him* here.

"That was a different painting."

"But that happened the day you got home. How many paintings did you get shipped?"

I tried not to look at Kade, but he was definitely looking at me. He was like a bloodhound when he caught a scent, had always been that way, and I was hoping he was so convinced that I was some sort of thief that he wouldn't believe anything she said. But I had to get this conversation shifted before he picked up the scent. From the feel of his burning attention on me, I wasn't sure it was possible to throw him off.

"Look, it's done. I screwed up. Now how's the wedding planning going?" Kade was still staring at me with an intensity that made me squirm in the seat.

"How's it going? Horrible. Everything is horrible. I'm getting married in less than a month and I lost my maid of honor! How could my planning be anything but a disaster?"

She talked about each detail going wrong. She continued for so long that I could only hope she'd bored Kade into a coma, erasing any of the previous details I'd prefer to bury.

I had to cut her off after a few more minutes to squeeze in the rest of my calls.

I called Monroe next, which was short and sweet, because all he cared about was that I had enough time to call our mother.

I dialed her next and quickly launched into a disclosure before she could humiliate me more, if that were possible. "Mom, Kade is in the room listening. It's part of the contract that he monitors my phone calls."

"Oh, Kade is there? Hello? Kade? Can you hear me?" She sounded like a groupie. When had he reached star level? Did she not realize that even though he was technically doing Monroe a favor for some unknown reason, he was my mortal enemy? Or had I forgotten to mention that to her?

I might not have told her that, now that I thought of it. It would've led to questions I hadn't wanted to answer.

"I'm here, Mrs. Loode. How are you?" Gone was his impatient tone, replaced by some fake pleasantry.

"I'm well. It's so wonderful to hear your voice. We haven't spoken in so long. I can't thank you enough for taking care of our little Leah. I know she did wrong. It's so generous that you stepped up in spite of what she did and welcomed her into your home."

"Of course, Mrs. Loode. It's not a problem."

Not a problem? That wasn't the song and dance I got.

Nice act. Next he'd be marching out the dancing penguins.

I let her gush another five minutes before I decided that Kade didn't need his ego inflated any more and I couldn't handle another second of hearing how he'd saved her daughter.

"Mom, I've got go. I have more calls I have to squeeze in, and I only get thirty minutes."

"Oh, but—"

"I can't debate this with you. I have to go. I'll try to call you next week." I hung up, immediately hating how sharp my tone had gotten.

It wasn't her fault I was here. I *knew* that. She didn't even know the truth, and yet I couldn't stop the rage from boiling up and spilling out onto her.

But the thing I couldn't quite get past was her bringing *that man* into our lives. If she hadn't, if she had been just a little more aware of things and not so blind...

It didn't matter. It was done and I'd get through this year.

"You done?" Kade asked, glaring at me like he hadn't in at least the past day. So what if he judged me a little more? Whatever.

"No. I have to make one last call."

"Then make it," he said, clearly looking to wrap this up.

If I'd had a modicum of privacy, this would've been the first call I made. But I hadn't, and now I was dreading it.

I dialed Greg's number. I'd told him I was going to call Sunday, that it was the only day I could call, but he wasn't answering.

I'd told him he wouldn't recognize the number. He should be answering all his calls today.

Kade raised an eyebrow. I hit end as soon as voicemail hit.

I redialed. Greg had probably just been in the bathroom or had his hands full.

It rang until the machine came on again, and I hung up. Maybe he'd had an emergency he needed to handle.

"I'm done."

"Not calling your boyfriend, or was that who didn't answer?"

"I'm done. That's all you need to know."

What I knew better than anything was that this next year was going to be a constant lesson in humiliation and helplessness.

CHAPTER 10

Kade

"That's not the way you should talk to your mother," I said as Leah was just about to walk out of the office.

I had Melissa in the other room waiting for me, and for some reason I couldn't explain, I felt more compelled to stay here and pick a fight with Leah. Why the hell was I bothering? It had nothing to do with me.

"My relationship with her is none of your business," she shot back.

She was right; it wasn't. And yet I still couldn't let it go. Couldn't leave this be. "If I have to sit and listen to you get fresh with a nice woman, it is."

She spun, her gaze as sharp as the spear she probably wanted to stab me with right now. "Unless I'm trying to smuggle drugs onto your ranch, my relationships with anyone are none of your concern."

Let her go. Let her leave.

I lost that mental battle and said, "Maybe you need to

work on who you've grown up to be. Maybe that's how you ended up here. You need to take some responsibility."

"You have no idea the kind of responsibility I've taken or what I've done for the people I love, so stay out of it."

And there it was, another glitch, a hint at something she was holding back.

"What's that supposed to mean? What great deeds have you done that justify what you did?"

She stood there, silent, not showing an iota of guilt. How was this the girl I'd known? Could she really have changed that much in the last ten years? Nothing added up anymore, and I couldn't let it go, ignore it, pretend it was lining up the way I used to.

"You're right. I'm a horrible person." She shrugged. "I'm going to go head back to my shed so I can think on all the wrongs I've done." She turned toward the door.

"Leah."

She kept walking.

"Leah!"

"What?" she snapped. She stopped but didn't turn around to look at me.

"Is there something I need to know?" If there was, I needed her to tell me on a visceral level I couldn't quite understand myself.

"No. I'm exactly the monster you think I am." She walked out, leaving the door hanging wide open.

I stood there, staring after her, replaying every word in my head. There were too many wrong beats, whispers of something deeper going on. Hints that maybe the Leah I'd known was still there, even if I was chasing her away every single day she was here.

· · ·

MELISSA WAS WAITING ON THE COUCH WITH A DRINK AND A pout. I'd wanted her to leave the moment she arrived, and now having to be around her at all was making me think about giving up my house and sleeping in the barn. And why? Because she didn't smell like strawberries and pineapple the way Leah did. Her hair wasn't silky and soft like Leah's. Her lips weren't as full and rosy as Leah's.

Even her voice as she said, "What took you so long?" sounded like a high-pitched squeal, as opposed to the soft sultriness of Leah's voice.

I put a hand up when she motioned me toward the couch. "I'm really sorry, but I got an emergency work call. It's something I have to go handle and it's probably going to take me all night."

"Oh no." She got to her feet, heading toward me. "Is it something I can help with?"

I dodged out of her way. "No, it's something I really need to focus on alone," I said as she gaped at me. "You can sleep in my room and I'll just grab my laptop and work in the guest bedroom."

I grabbed my phone and laptop, heading away from her before she could try to follow.

I settled onto the bed, on alert for footsteps heading my way. While waiting, I searched the internet for the complete story of what had happened with Leah and this painting.

There was something off about the way she had tried to cut off her friend Cassie on the phone. She'd stopped looking my way and been fidgeting in her chair. They'd had an investigation. She'd been convicted. What did she not want me to hear? Was she involved in something larger that no one knew about? Had she done it for that boyfriend of hers who hadn't bothered to answer the phone?

I scanned through all the articles I could find online.

Contractor discovers stolen painting while doing work in Upper East Side apartment

Mr. Alverdi was hired to hang a painting. He took a picture of the painting to send to his client while she was away, and later on that day, his wife saw and recognized the painting in the photo. Mr. Alverdi then reached out to his brother-in-law, who is an investigator with the NYPD.

Had I even thought about this for more than a second when I first read it? Whatever else someone might say about Leah, she wasn't stupid, and only an idiot would do something like this. I'd followed her career, not that I'd ever admit it to anyone. She'd been associated with the highest-tier companies. She hadn't risen to that level by making mistakes like this. Anyone with a brain wouldn't have a stolen painting in their apartment while they were away with contractors coming and going. Nothing added up.

I tossed my phone on the bed next to me, getting in the shower instead of fixating on what was going on in her head. Maybe she'd been in a weird headspace. People got careless. She'd gotten cocky, probably.

I needed to stop thinking about her.

I should tell Melissa I'd cleared up my issue, drag her into the shower with me, and fuck Leah out of my mind.

Except the thought of Melissa didn't even make my dick so much as twitch. She wasn't the one I wanted to press up against the wall and sink balls deep into. The one I wanted to fill my hands with.

I stepped out of the shower, the near-freezing water having done nothing at all for my emotional or physical state. I dropped down onto the bed and stared at the wall for all of two minutes before scrolling through my contacts to the one person I trusted to gather delicate information and be discreet. I had him listed as John, although that was an alias.

"Hey," he answered.

"I need you to look into something for me."

"Do you need to meet?"

If I'd called anyone else, they might've asked for specifics already. Not this guy. His phone had been bugged too many times for him to be throwing around details. Most of the people he worked with had a high likelihood of having their phone calls recorded as well.

"I don't want to wait that long, and this should be easy enough to handle." I wasn't willing to wait for a meeting. I wanted answers now. "You know that situation I just got involved with?"

"Your royalty issue?"

I guess I'd called Leah "princess" enough times to him that it had registered.

"Yes. I think there's something more going on, and I want to know what." *Had* to know what if I wanted to evict her from my head.

"Wouldn't surprise me in the least," he said. "I'll give you a discount to dig into this one, because it's actually piqued my interest."

Those words unnerved me to my core. He didn't even

know Leah but thought something was wrong with this situation, too. And if I trusted anyone's instincts, it was his.

"Keep your discount. Just get it done soon."

"The people I need to reach out to aren't going to come cheap, so you won't think you got a discount anyway. As far as the rush job, not a problem."

"Spend whatever you need."

Typically this would be where we'd hang up. Me and "John" didn't chat. We weren't friends, but business acquaintances. I'd be stunned if he had any friends at all.

So when John didn't hang up but asked, "So how's it going over there?" I nearly fell off the bed.

"You want to know how it's going?" I asked. "Is there something I should be aware of?"

"No, nothing like that. Just curious."

John, who both sounded and looked like he rolled people into the gutters on a weekly occurrence, was interested in my domestic situation? Why did that not feel comforting?

"It's fine," I said. I couldn't exactly tell him to butt out when I was asking him to dig around and I needed him. Little bit of a conflict there.

"So it's going smoothly?" he asked, again sounding as if he knew something.

"Where is this sudden interest in my situation coming from?"

"I just find it interesting, is all."

The only thing that had changed was Leah's being here. "You're referring to her presence?"

"Yeah, that."

I shouldn't ask. I should just hang up the phone now and not encourage this.

"Why?" I asked.

"I'm not sure. She seems interesting, spunky, kind of, and this whole 'you don't like her but you're helping her' situation has really caught my interest." He sounded truly invested.

"Okay, well, there's nothing interesting here to pay attention to." Hopefully that would nix any further interest.

"No reason to get all up in arms about this. Just making conversation."

John didn't *make* conversation.

"Is your curiosity appeased?"

"Not really, but I guess it'll have to be enough. Be in touch soon."

Leah was starting to throw every aspect of my life into chaos.

CHAPTER 11

Leah

MY NERVES WERE STILL FRAYED FROM THE CONFRONTATION WITH Kade a few nights ago, but it was getting easier every day I didn't see him, which was three at this point. Plus it was getting more comfortable here by the minute. It had been about a week and a half and it felt almost normal when I strolled into the bunkhouse.

Chuck was stirring something on the stove. He wasn't just the ranch foreman, but something like the ranch father.

"Smells amazing," I said, peeking into the huge pot.

"It's my famous chili. Was one of the missus's favorites," he said, referring to his late wife, who'd died ten years ago. Spending every minute with these people was putting all our relationships on fast forward.

"Can't wait to try it." I dropped my bag on the floor, taking a count of how many wet heads I saw. Being last on the list meant a lukewarm shower at best. No one tried to hog the hot water, but a forty-gallon tank couldn't work miracles. "Oh no, I'm last, aren't I?" I said, looking at Benny and Elijah, who appeared squeaky clean and were now laughing.

"I think Adam's in there now," Benny said, angling his head toward the bathroom and the sound of running water.

Missy had been offering to share her bathroom, but taking her clothes was enough. I couldn't accept anything else, even if I really wanted to. I'd been in her bathroom, with its little plants on the sill and candles on the cabinet. It was like an oasis, especially compared to the bunkhouse bathroom I was sharing with these guys.

I was about to settle onto the couch to wait my turn when Missy walked out of the bathroom.

"What were you doing in there?" I asked.

"My hot water heater blew," she said, and then looked at Elijah. "I need you to get on that."

He threw his hands up. "I told you I'd work on it tomorrow. I can't do anything until the plumbing house opens."

"And what about the broken lock?" she asked. "It's bad enough I have to shower here without feeling like I have to barricade the door."

I grabbed my bag, ignoring their bickering and heading for the shower. If Adam showed up, he'd try to jump the line. He had no scruples whatsoever. I was supposedly the felon, and yet he couldn't respect the basic universal law of first come, first served. Bastard was probably one of those last-in-line people who ran to the new register even before the cashier yelled, "Next in line."

I was stripping down a few minutes later when I heard Adam's loud mouth carrying on about something.

I'd only beaten him to the shower by minutes, which somehow made it all the sweeter. I was giggling to myself, and turning on the water, when the bathroom door swung open.

"Missy, use your own damned—"

Adam's voice drifted off as he stood there in front of wide-open door. I was completely naked. Not only was he there, but Benny and Elijah were standing across the room with a clear view.

I grabbed my towel from the bar as I yelled, "Shut the door, you animal."

My words seemed to jar Adam out of the spell that had frozen him. To give him credit, he shut the door immediately.

I wasn't exactly an exhibitionist, but I wasn't so modest I'd be dwelling on this. Still, someone really needed to fix that lock. I wasn't ready to give peep shows every day.

I CAME OUT OF THE BATHROOM AFTER MY SHOWER, AND SETTLED at the table, where everyone was already eating. Chuck, who sometimes ate while he cooked, was probably off doing the last run around the ranch that he liked to do before leaving.

I was already digging into the chili when Adam said, "Sorry for the, eh...situation."

The small smirk didn't ring of an authentic apology.

"Not a problem, but if you don't knock next time the door is closed, I'm going to kick you in the balls." My tough words didn't have the effect I'd hoped for, as he sat there still smirking to himself.

"Stop looking at her like you saw her naked," Benny said, glaring at Adam.

"It's hard because I have," Adam said, smiling at Benny, who was significantly smaller.

"You're so gross," Missy said, glaring at him too.

"Hey, let's not make this bigger than it is," Elijah said. He looked across the table at me, his cheeks getting a touch red. "Sorry if I accidentally caught a glance, too. Wasn't intended."

"Not a problem." At least his apology had a spark of truth.

"Why's it not a problem to flash him?" Adam asked, staring at me.

"Because he didn't stand there and drool, you loser," Missy said, answering for me. It was a pretty accurate call on her part.

"Shut the fuck up, you charity case," Adam said.

"Don't talk to her like that. Who do you think you are?" I said, his words finally igniting my temper.

"You're way out of line, Adam," Elijah said at the same time.

Missy got to her feet and leaned over the table, trying to poke Adam in the chest as she said, "You fucking bastard. You don't know a horse from an ass. You want to talk charity? Your paycheck might as well be a donation check to the needy."

Seeing as Missy clearly didn't need me to defend her, I grabbed her and the chili bowls and said, "I think we should go eat over at my place."

Elijah, who was physically blocking Missy with his body, nodded. "Yeah, that's a good idea."

Adam just stood there looking at her with a smile.

"Missy, come on," I said, bumping her with my arm, since my hands were full.

She hesitated for a few more seconds, while Elijah jerked his head toward the door, before she finally relented, following me.

"I hate that fucker," she said as she took her bowl from me and settled into my one chair.

I settled cross-legged on the bed. "He really is unpleasant."

She glanced around, the haze of rage she'd been in seeming to lift. "Why didn't we go back to my place?"

"Because I was trying to just get you out of there before you punched a guy who is twice your size and would probably punch you back."

She tilted her head. "Sometimes I get a little mad and seem to lose perspective of what I can do." She shrugged and then giggled.

"Yeah, I kind of noticed that," I said, laughing too.

She looked about the place again. "I don't want to hurt your feelings, but if you're going to be here a year, we should really do something to cheer this place up. Even if we get you a plant or two, maybe? Like, I don't want to be mean, but it's kind of a dump and depressing as hell."

"Yeah. I know. Strangely, it's sort of growing on me." Or maybe it was this whole place and the people, like her, and the guys, minus Adam. If I could just avoid Kade, I might even *like* being here for a year.

"Okay. Well, here's to shed life, then?"

"To shed life." I might be living in a shed, but I'd damn well make the most of it.

CHAPTER 12

Kade

"I don't know about you two, but I've never seen such good tits and ass. And did you see those nipples? They were the most perfect little nubs," Adam said. He was leaning on the fence of the horse pen, Elijah and Benny next to him, all watching one of the newer horses prance, all with their backs to me.

"You gotta shut up about it before you get us in trouble," Benny said.

"Just admit it. You know I'm right," Adam said.

"She was pretty top tier. I'll give you that," Benny said.

"E? Fess up. You wanna hit that, too," Adam said. "Admit it and I'll shut up."

"I've got a dick, so of course I do, but can we shut up about it now?" Elijah said.

They'd better not be talking about Leah. They couldn't

be. The way they were talking about her nipples—how the hell would they know that?

"Who you guys talking about?" I asked, strolling closer.

They all jerked, seeing me behind them. The guys all dropped their heads as I neared the pen. I'd seen less guilt on a mugger who was still holding a knife and a purse.

"They've got a new dancer down at Sinners Club," Adam said. "I dragged the guys there a few nights ago."

Not Leah. That was all that mattered.

"Elijah, check on the door on stall three in stables two when you get a chance. The lock felt loose."

"Got it."

"What's going on?" I asked as I stopped beside Chuck, who was littler farther down, kicking a fence post that looked like it might be getting some rot.

"Nothing much. Going pretty smooth today," he said, giving the post a little tug.

I turned back to watch as Benny said something to Elijah, who caught me watching and tried to causally nudge Benny in the ribs.

I turned back to Chuck. "When did the guys go down to Sinners with Adam?"

"They didn't, not that I've heard."

"Really? I heard them talking about a new dancer's tits and ass." And why was that bothering me so much? So what? I'd heard them talk about plenty of women.

Chuck tugged at another piece of wood. "Some of this needs to be replaced."

I didn't care about the fence. I cared that all my guys looked like they'd robbed a bank. "Chuck, what the fuck is going on with them?"

He finally stopped staring at the fence and took too

long a breath before he spoke. "It was an accident, but some of the guys might've seen more of Leah than maybe was decent."

I nodded, telling myself to let it go, to not go over and kill them all now. It was an accident. Why the hell did I care, anyway?

Let it go. Just walk away and let it go.

"Exactly how much more?" I asked in spite of myself.

"She was about to get in the shower and the lock to the bathroom is broken. They didn't know she was in there," Chuck said.

So in other words, *everything*.

I was not a jealous person. And I had no reason to be jealous, considering I didn't even like Leah. It was just leftover protectiveness. Old feelings that had been dug up by her presence.

But damned if it didn't feel like someone had hit my "go nuclear" button.

"Kade?" Chuck said. "Kade! Where the fuck you going?"

I stopped walking. "I'm not a psycho. I'm not beating anyone up over an accident."

If it happened again? Things might be different. But that was not going to happen again, and not because I was jealous. She was my responsibility. I couldn't have her in a position where people were walking in on her in the bathroom.

I barely slowed as I approached the guys and said, "Next person who doesn't knock when there's a closed bathroom door gets their nose broken. Is that understood?"

There was a flurry of nods before I kept walking to my target.

As luck would have it, she was walking across the field toward her cabin as I was making my way there.

"Come with me," I said.

"Why? What did I do now?" Leah stopped beside her door, hands on her hips.

"Either pack your shit or I'll pack it for you." I opened her door and walked in, looking for her suitcase.

"Pack me for where?" she asked, following me.

I knelt down, trying to see if she'd hid it under the bed. This place wasn't that big. It was here somewhere. Otherwise I'd toss all her shit on the comforter and move it. "I can't have you flashing every hand I have, so I'm not having you stay here."

There it was. I dragged the suitcase out from underneath her bed and unzipped it. I stood to go to her dresser and there she was.

"It wasn't my fault," she said.

There was a desperation in her voice that seemed to cut through my thoughts. I truly looked at her for the first time. She was pale and her hands were shaking. We'd fought before. Why was she so rattled this time? Never in her life had she ever been afraid of me, and to think she was made bile rise in my throat.

Then it hit me like a bat to the head.

"I'm moving you to the house." I straightened, really taking her in. "Did you think I was going to kick you out? Have you go to prison?" I asked, my voice softer.

"No, obviously not," she said, but with too much force. She'd really thought I was going to haul her off to prison, and it was like a sucker punch to my soul.

"Leah, I wasn't coming here to—"

"I know," she snapped. "I just don't want to go to the

house." She crossed her arms, as if that would stop me from seeing how unhinged she was.

"It's an upgrade. You want to stay here?" I said, struggling to regain my composure.

"I'm not moving to the house," she said, notching up her chin. "You said I couldn't even walk into that place. I swear, you are completely unhinged. I've never met a crazier man in my life." She might've been carrying on, but the color was coming back to her cheeks, even as I felt like I needed to sit.

"Look, I heard about the bathroom situation and I can't have that happen again, so I'm willing to make a compromise."

"What?" she asked, trying to cover up the obvious vulnerability we were both aware of. She was feeling so out of sorts that she wasn't paying attention to how rattled *I* was. I might've been more wrecked than she was right now. Lucky for me, she was oblivious.

"Since there are issues I wasn't aware of with the bunkhouse, I'd prefer it if you at least showered up at the house so I don't have to worry about any more incidents." I'd seen the bathroom at the bunkhouse. If she turned me down on this, she officially hated me so much that she'd do anything to stay away from me.

I was knotted up waiting for her to accept the offer. If she didn't, if she truly hated me? I wasn't sure I could handle that.

"How would that work? What if you're not home? Then what? I can't shower?"

The fact that she'd already gotten to the technicalities let me breathe again. She hadn't said no. She wasn't *that* revolted by me. "I don't lock the door to the house. Just go in when you want to shower."

"You said—"

"I know. I changed my mind." I remembered all the things I'd said, even when I didn't want to.

She shook her head and rolled her pretty blue eyes at me, as if that was supposed to annoy me. All it did was make me itch to pull her hair out of that ponytail and thread my hands through those beautiful locks. Even now, it was as if she were completely oblivious to how unbelievably sexy she was in just a pair of jeans and not an ounce of makeup.

"We have a deal?" I asked.

"Yes, I guess so if you're going to be crazy about it. It wasn't that big a—"

"I can't have that happen again," I said, for the sake of my sanity and the guys' health. "Come up when you're ready and I'll show you around."

She gave me a halfhearted nod.

I turned to leave but couldn't until I said it again and knew she'd really heard it. "Just for the record, I wouldn't just kick you out of here."

"Not that I care, but how am I supposed to know what's going to piss you off enough when just having a heartbeat seems to do it?"

"Because I wouldn't do that to you." I sounded harsh, but how could she even imagine I would let her get thrown in prison? Did she think I was so different from the man she'd known ten years ago? Whether either of us liked it, there was a history between us that was hard to walk away from, and I was finding it harder by the day.

CHAPTER 13

Leah

I STOOD ON THE THRESHOLD OF THE HOUSE, REGRETTING THAT I'd agreed to shower here, and I hadn't even done it a single time yet. Being here every night to shower was going to make it harder to avoid him, and that was penciled in at the top of my to-do list right now. For some reason, he came within fifty feet of me and all the calm composure I'd perfected in the last ten years melted away. I went from being carved out of granite to an unwrapped chocolate in a five-year-old's sweaty hand.

If he said one word out of line, I was going back to the bunkhouse bathroom, in spite of the fact that they never put the toilet seat down and the water was usually cold. And if I flashed every single one of them on a weekly basis? It was a small price to pay for my sanity. Why did Kade care about that anyway? It was my body. If I wanted to walk around topless, I could. As far as I remembered, there was no clause in the contract about nudity.

I was about to force myself to knock when he swung the door open and stepped out of the way for me to walk in.

I stayed on the porch. "I was thinking—"

"If you're going to shower here, you need to just come in."

My plan of staying on the porch was thwarted by his hand on my back, steering me inside. That gooey chocolate was now turning into a syrupy mess. I might've resisted with some distance, but when his hand touched me, something short-circuited inside, frying all my neurons until they no longer functioned. It felt like they were all stumbling around my brain like drunken sailors on a long weekend.

"You did tell me not to so much as even knock on this door," I said, trying to put enough edge in my voice that it would disguise how my body was butter in his hand.

"And now I'm telling you to do it."

If he didn't sound almost defensive, wasn't running his hand through his already tousled hair, I might've walked out. Instead, I stayed put, not backing up *or* walking in, my instincts battling it out and coming to a stalemate. It felt like there was some strange line I was crossing, and I couldn't figure out whether I should take that step or not.

"I'll show you to the bathroom you can use," he said, taking a few steps and then waiting to see if I'd follow.

I hesitated for another second and then forced myself to move another foot.

I'd caught glimpses of the inside, but standing in the living room, the heart of Kade's home, somehow felt different. It wasn't anything like how it used to look when we were kids, and it wasn't what I'd have expected from this man. Everything was well done but not to the point you were afraid to touch anything. The weathered leather of the couch lured you over to it, and the thick wool area rugs broke up the wide-planked wood floors, looking warm and inviting. Even the fireplace, currently burning through a stack of logs, filled the place with a lived-in scent. The most shocking thing about it was just how *warm* the place was, and not just in temperature. It was exactly how I would've imagined the old Kade might decorate his home and completely at odds with the man he'd become. I didn't know the man who stood before me anymore. And what I did know didn't mesh with this place.

"This place is really nice," I said, glancing around.

"Thanks. This is still the main room that was always here, but I gutted it and expanded. Same with the porch."

I'd already known that. I'd spent so many hours on that porch that I recognized every ding in the wood, even now. After my father had died, one of the things that comforted me most was sitting with Old Man Hawk on the porch. He'd make me hot cocoa and give me cookies. He'd tell me stories about the history of Montana and, most of all, just *be* there when so many others in my life seemed to be falling apart. When my mother wouldn't get out of bed all day and my brother was off trying to figure out how he was going to survive, he was here for me. That was before he'd gotten sick, though. Then I'd come here and slowly started to trail behind Kade, handing him tools as he fixed things, even though he wasn't much older than me.

"Come on, the guest bathroom is this way," Kade said.

His voice drew me back to the present. This was a

different time, a different person, and I couldn't forget that.

I didn't move. I'd felt like I could handle this compromise, but being anywhere close to Kade was a dangerous idea. I couldn't come here to his house and shower every day. No way. Not if I wanted to stay strong.

"Actually, I didn't come here to shower. I'm going to the bunkhouse. Elijah said he fixed the bathroom door, so it won't be an issue anymore." I backed up a couple steps.

"Then why'd you bring a bag?" Kade asked, watching me as if he didn't just read me like a book, but had read me so often that he could quote my opening lines.

"Elijah said he'd fix the problem, so I don't see the issue." I was gripping my bag as if he were going to try to take it hostage, even though he looked almost as lost in this space as I was.

Then he said, "Can you use it as a favor to me?" as if it were actually important.

I didn't know what to say. He sounded so much like the Kade I knew that I was nodding before I could stop myself.

I followed him down a hall and into a guest bedroom that had its own bathroom.

"You can have this one to yourself." He walked out of the bedroom, shutting the door to the suite.

I looked around at the comfortable room, with a queen bed and pristine white duvet. He'd had this empty bedroom available and put me in the shed to keep me away from him. I couldn't get soft just because he was having a *moment* for whatever reason.

I put my bag down and showered in what seemed like an endless supply of hot water.

I didn't dry my hair, but twisted it in a bun as I threw my stuff back in my bag to go.

When I walked out, Kade was in the kitchen cooking.

"Thanks," I said, walking toward the door. "I'll see you tomorrow."

"Hang on." He took a step in my direction and nodded toward the kitchen. "I made some extra steak if you're hungry?"

Again, he was trying to throw me off with glimpses of the man I knew. Or thought I'd known.

"No—I mean, thanks, but I'll grab something at the bunkhouse. Chuck is there cooking."

He nodded, looking disappointed, but I had to be imagining that. I couldn't forget who he was now.

CHAPTER 14

Kade

I WAS SITTING ON THE PORCH, SIPPING A BEER. THE SUN HAD SET an hour ago and every movement drew my eye in anticipation. The situation was becoming dire enough that I was calling the one person I shouldn't. Not because he was a bad guy, but because I'd pay a price for any help I'd get. Unfortunately, he was the only one I felt I could say this to.

I called my brother, who picked up right away.

"What's up?"

"I've got an issue." I took a long swig of my beer.

Alec's voice immediately dropped. "What's wrong?"

He might be a ball buster, but there was no one else I'd call in the middle of the night if I had a shovel in one hand and a bottle of bleach in the other.

"I'm going to tell you something I know I'll regret."

"You want to fuck her," he said.

I let out a soft groan. "Yes."

He laughed. "Sometimes you make things a little too easy."

Easy for him, maybe. I was being put through slow mental torture.

"I'm having an issue getting my brain off her. Can you not be an asshole for five minutes and tell me if you've ever had this issue and what you did?"

There was a pause, as if he were truly thinking it over. "Nope. I've never had this issue."

"Never?" I said.

"I'm good-looking, rich, and have charm for days. Someone starts to get under my skin, I fuck them like we were circus freaks for hours, days if needed, and exorcise them from my psyche before it can get out of hand. After that, I can move on and avoid any problems."

"What the hell do *I* do? I need an actual solution," I said.

"I don't see a way around this. There's only one way." He paused for a second before stating, "I hate to tell you this, but you're going to have to fuck her."

Why? Why had I called him? I'd known what I was going to get.

"That is not the correct answer. I'm not sure why I tell you things. I should know by now you'll tell me to go with the most morally bankrupt choice available."

"What's so bad about fucking her? Don't tell me you're turning into a prude. It's not like you've ever been a saint in that area."

"Even if there weren't a list of reasons why that was bad, I signed a *legal document* that I wasn't romantically involved with her, nor would I be. Not only would I be breaking my word, I'd be violating a court order if I slept with her." I wasn't going to tell him how I'd double-checked the paperwork again today, just to make sure there wasn't some wiggle room.

"You're acting like it's a problem, but I know that your *relationship* got this situation arranged in the first place. That judge won't do shit to you but slap you on the back."

He spoke like a person whose life always magically worked out. Even when we were kids, and I was working myself to death to keep the ranch, he'd walked away without a qualm to go work in tech. It had worked out well for him, like everything seemed to. Of course he didn't worry about what he said on an open phone line. The universe seemed to continuously protect him from fallout.

"That's not true," I said, not so sure I'd be included in his protection umbrella. I wasn't surprised that he'd figured out the connection with the judge, but did he have to call it out on the phone? I was going to have to slap him upside the head next time he was here and warn him to watch his mouth.

"Uh huh. Sure it's not."

"That wouldn't work anyway. One, she's got a boyfriend. Two, she hates me, so sleeping with her isn't a possibility." *Hate* might be a strong word, and yet it seemed to fit.

"One, who cares if she's got a boyfriend? Two, she only hates you because you hated her first, and for a stupid fucking reason if you ask me."

"She spoke out of turn and made me lose my loan. Not that it matters anymore. She hates me now, and she's not as fickle with her feelings as the hookers you bang." I'd met enough that they'd started to look like a carbon copies of each other.

"You dug in, didn't you? You couldn't just make the best of the situation. You had to be stubborn and make her know where you two stood." He was talking like someone who'd just laid down a full house.

"It's called setting boundaries, not that you'd know anything about that."

"Okay, well, how are all those boundaries working out for you now?"

"Like shit." There was no point in denying it at this point.

"So how bad did you piss her off since she's been there?"

I could hear him smiling at my misery on the other end of the phone. I should probably lie, but I was too desperate to care.

"Bad enough that fucking her isn't an option and I need to get her out of my head. Do you have any *real* suggestions?"

"You can't just fuck someone else?" he said, speaking like a man who had never been on the brink of getting pulled into the abyss.

"No. I seem to have no interest." I didn't bother telling him I'd already tried.

"Then you're going to have to fix things up and fuck her. It's the only way."

"What if that makes it worse?" For some reason, I was scared shitless that a one-time fuck might end up being not a one-time deal. I was beginning to fear this was a terminal sort of situation that wasn't going to heal.

There was a long pause before he said, "Nah. That shit can't happen to us. We fall when *we* choose. We aren't the kind of suckers that get hit with that lightning-bolt crap. Cupid can go fuck himself," he added, laughing. "Just hang tight. I'll be there in a few days and maybe I'll take her off your hands."

"Go fuck yourself," I said before hanging up on him.

My phone buzzed on the seat beside me two minutes later. I thought it was going to be a follow-up from Alec, but when I looked at the phone I saw a message from Melissa pop up.

MELISSA: ARE YOU FEELING ANY BETTER? I HAVEN'T HEARD *from you. Do you need me to come check on you?*

I SHOULD CALL HER, TELL HER I WAS FEELING BETTER. TELL HER to get her ass out here and then bang her until she couldn't walk straight and I stopped thinking of Leah.

Except not a single cell in my body wanted to see her, and the thought of her naked didn't make my dick even twitch. Yet I spotted Leah a hundred yards away bending over to fix her boot and I had to readjust myself.

ME: I'M ON THE MEND. BURIED UNDER WORK FOR THE NEXT *few weeks.*

HOPEFULLY SHE'D TAKE THE HINT AND I WOULDN'T HAVE TO spell it out.

My phone lit up again, Melissa calling now. I groaned for a second before I answered. Easier to hack off the dying limb than watch it go gangrenous.

"Hey," I answered, trying to sound cordial even as I dreaded this call. She would either get bitchy or sad, and I

105

didn't want to deal with either, but I had to. If I was lucky, she'd get bitchy. Sad always fucked me in the head.

"Hi. I wanted to see how work was going because I haven't heard from you."

Sad. Dammit.

"I'm sorry. Just been really snowed under," I said.

"Want me to bring you some dinner tonight? I make a really good meatloaf, and you have to eat."

I rubbed the back of my neck. She wasn't going to make this easy.

"Not sure that's a good idea. I'm going to be buried for a while. I've got a lot going on and I don't think I can spare time for distractions."

"Are you dumping me?" she said.

The edge in her voice was definitely harsher now, but things could always take a turn back to sad. I wasn't off the hook yet.

"*Dumping* is a harsh word, but I do think perhaps we should put anything romantic on the back burner for a while."

There was a pause, and I could almost envision her lips parted in shock.

"You *are* dumping me."

"I'm not dumping you. We weren't in a committed relationship. I told you I wasn't looking for anything serious."

"Do you realize how many men want me, and I wasted my time with you, some hick rancher?"

She'd taken the low road, making things so much easier. "Well, then you should probably give those men a chance. I wish nothing but the best for you."

"You're going to regret this, and when you call? I won't be answering the phone. I'll have moved on."

Nope, I wouldn't be calling. "Okay, I'm very sorry and I do wish the best for you."

"Actually, don't even try to call, because I'm going to block your number!" Her voice had gone shrill.

"It's what I deserve." I tried to sound somber. I waited to see what she'd fire off next, but then looked at my phone and saw she'd ended the call.

That had actually gone way better than I'd thought it would.

She'd probably make someone a good girlfriend or wife. Just not me, when I couldn't get my mind off Leah.

I leaned back, rocking on the porch swing and wondering if I should do exactly what Alec had said and just fuck Leah already. If I was sure it would help, I might, but I had a bad feeling that getting more involved was like playing Russian roulette with my soul.

CHAPTER 15

Leah

I WAS MUCKING OUT A STALL WHEN THERE WERE FOOTSTEPS stopping right behind me.

"Hey, little Leah," a deep voice called.

Of all the people in the world I dreaded seeing when I was dirty, dusty, and probably not smelling so fine, this was one of the few people I didn't worry about. There wasn't a judgmental bone in Alec Hawk's body. He was the absolute antithesis of his brother.

A ray of afternoon sunlight hit the same dark hair he shared with Kade. He leaned his shoulder against the stall door as he smirked. There'd always been a string of women trailing after the Hawk brothers, and for obvious reasons. The gene pool in this family was like rolling a hard eight over and over again. It just shouldn't *happen*.

"I never thought a chick could look so hot mucking out a stall, but here you are." He waved a hand at me.

Alec flirted like he breathed, all day long and effortlessly. Kade's intensity had always been my undoing, but that didn't mean I couldn't appreciate the work of art that was Alec.

"Alec Hawk. What the hell are you doing here?" I leaned my shovel on the wall, perching my gloves on top of it and dusting my hands off on the back of my old jeans. From his look, you would've thought I'd done a twirl in a thong bikini and stilettos.

"I'm related to the asshole who owns this place, remember?"

It was impossible to forget the owner of this place.

"And you've been running away from here ever since I've known you," I said. "I didn't think you even liked to visit." From what I'd heard, he'd made his final escape the day after their father's funeral.

He shrugged, his smile setting me up for whatever well-oiled line was to follow. "Once I found out you were here, I cleared my schedule." He waved me out of the stall. "Come on, let's go take a ride away from all the onlookers."

That sentence alone would get the onlookers chatting, and he hadn't tried to whisper it, either. If someone else was in the stalls, the chatter would start up fast.

I laughed. "You still love stirring up trouble."

As much as Alec might talk a big game, he'd never gotten close enough to blow one of my hairs out of place. We might appreciate each other's looks, but that's as far as it ever seemed to go. Maybe it was because I'd always been too busy staring at his brother and he'd been too busy with the always-waiting lineup of easy girls that didn't require any additional effort.

"Come on," he said.

It wasn't the work that was holding me back. I'd

already finished my assigned chores for the day and was just helping out. Problem was, as much as I wanted to take off for a little while, do some catching up, I didn't need more grief from Kade when I was actively avoiding him.

"I'm not sure I can do that. My boss is a bit of a dick."

"I'll handle the boss," Alec said, jerking his head for me to follow.

Screw it. Kade would find something to be pissed at me for no matter what I did. I left the stall and followed after Alec. We had the ATVs revved up and left the smaller garage a few minutes later. We drove them to the edge of the ranch property, and one of the highest peaks. This spot had always been part of Hawk land, and it was still as captivating as ever.

I got off the ATV and just sat there, staring at the mountains for a while without speaking, and Alec followed suit. That was one other thing the brothers had in common: they were okay with silence, not feeling the need to fill every moment with some useless chatter. They could just be.

Alec held out a flask to me a few minutes later, and I waved him off.

"No? If I can't get you drunk, how am I supposed to get any answers out of you?" he asked, then took a sip himself before pocketing it.

"Is that what this is? An interrogation? You know you're supposed to bring people to a cell or somewhere unpleasant for that sort of thing. Not a place that makes you relax." I wasn't quite relaxed, but I was about as close as possible under the current conditions.

"Yeah, well, I've never been one to encourage a

woman to talk. You'll just have to take pity on me for not knowing the correct protocol."

There was nothing shocking about *that* coming from him. Shellfish had a longer expiration date than the women he dated.

"Pity you? You're the last person I'd pity."

He smiled again. "Stop it with all the sweet talk or I might try to add you to my roster."

"Thanks, but I think I've got enough problems already."

"You sure? I get good reviews." He tilted his head with a devilish grin.

"Please. You don't stick around long enough to know your reviews." I dropped back onto my elbows, watching as the sky turned those beautiful colors of a spent day.

"That's okay." He laughed and bumped his arm into mine. "I wanted to keep my balls anyway."

"What's that supposed to mean?" I asked.

"Nothing. Just being silly." He shook his head. "What I really want is to know what happened with that painting. I'm not buying the story I'm reading in the news, and the one I'm hearing sounds just as stupid."

Gone was the flirt, who used his pick-up lines like armor, replaced by the man I knew was always right there underneath. The one who saw too much and always had.

If there was anything worse than going down for a crime I didn't commit, it was having to convince the people around me that I was a lowlife scumbag that would steal a painting from victims of the Holocaust. In that way, Kade was easier. He'd convicted me of all wrongdoing before I said a word. When I'd gotten here, he hadn't even asked me about it. And for some reason,

Kade's judgment hurt worse than anyone's, like our prior relationship gave him a pre-targeted kill shot right to my heart.

"Do I really need to convince you I committed a crime that a jury has already convicted me of?" Alec needed to take the bait, because defending this lie was getting old.

He made an exaggerated face, as if he were contemplating it, before he said, "Yes, I believe you do."

I laughed, the sound hollow even to my ears. "You should talk to your brother, then. I'm sure he could bend you to his way of thinking."

"Is he being the same hardass he's always been?"

"He's definitely giving it his all." The Kade I used to know had been the one I turned to when the rest of the world was beating me down. Now he was leading the charge.

"I won't press you on it, but for the record, I know it's bullshit. I just can't figure out what happened. You're too smart to get jammed up like this, which means only one thing—you're falling on your sword for someone." He was staring at me, watching for a reaction.

I sat up, letting my hair fall forward and do some of the heavy lifting instead of worrying about schooling my features. "I thought you weren't going to push me?"

"I had to try a little bit. The suspense is killing me."

"Then all I can say is I hope you have your affairs in order," I said.

He smiled but let it go.

We sat there for another few minutes as the light began to fade. As it was, we'd probably be driving part of the way back in darkness.

Right before I went to get on my ATV, Alec said, "I know Kade can be rough, but he's still the kid you knew.

Those feelings run deep, no matter what stupid shit he says."

"Deep as in fifty miles down? Because if you tell me he was born in hell, *that* I could believe."

He laughed again. "Okay, you two will have to work it out on your own. Let's get back, though. You want to see brimstone? Let him not be able to find you tonight."

I climbed onto my ATV. "Oh, I know. He spends all day waiting for me to screw up so he can make my life miserable."

Alec squinted but didn't refute what I said.

CHAPTER 16

Kade

I WAS STANDING ON THE FRONT PORCH, SEARCHING THE HORIZON for Leah, when the sheriff's car pulled up. It was in the contract that there would be periodic check-ins. I hadn't studied every line the way Leah insinuated, but I did know what was in it, mostly due to my lawyer's diligence.

Now here was Paul, on the one night that I had no fucking idea where Leah was. Luckily for everyone, mostly Leah, I'd had more than a few late nights with Paul before he joined the police force.

He got out of the car, leading with a friendly smile and nod.

"Hey, Paul, what can I do for you?"

"Sorry to bother you so late, but I have to do a check-in." He shrugged.

"Leah's still out working. Had a problem in the back pasture. I'd give her a call and tell her to head back, but she doesn't have a phone. She's quite a good worker. Won't quit until the job is done."

He nodded, as if that were all perfectly understandable. He also looked around as if he were at a loss for what to do now that his quick check-in wasn't working out so neatly.

"Can I get you a drink while you wait? I've got a really nice whiskey that just came in—a Macallan 1979."

Paul's eyes lit up like a true whiskey connoisseur's. Then his hands went to his hips as he looked about and back at his car, as if he weren't sure what to do with himself. "I'd love to, but I can't drink on the job."

He stared at me, as if I were the one who should tell him what to do.

"Hang on a second," I said, deciding I was going to help us both out of this little predicament.

I walked into the house and grabbed the bottle. I'd been trying to get my hands on one of these for months, thinking I'd crack it open for a special occasion or a rough day. Keeping Leah out of prison appeared to be that moment. This was going to hurt. The bottle had cost me twenty grand and I hadn't even taken a whiff of it.

I walked back to Paul, handing it over. "Here, take it for all the hard work you guys do. You can have a drink after your shift with the guys."

"You sure?" He took the bottle like it was a newborn baby.

"Not a problem. I've got another one." I waved it off like it was chump change, but it hurt like handing over my kidney.

I didn't actually have another one, but I would as soon as I could track one down. They weren't that easy to come by.

"How's the wife?" I asked.

He shrugged. "Let's just say I'm booking a lot of overtime," he said, and then laughed.

I'd known his wife for a while, too. Everyone knew what he'd been getting into, and more than one had tried to talk him out of it. Thinking about that woman made letting go of that whiskey slightly easier. If anyone needed it, it was him.

"You know, I'll just check off that I saw her," Paul said, still examining his bottle. "If you say it's all good, your word is enough for me."

I spotted two dots on the horizon riding toward the garages.

"No need. Looks like they're on their way back."

"Oh, well, that's great. Can check that box and won't have to even lie about it. I won't need to come by until next month" He coughed repeatedly, and it sounded like he said, "Last Tuesday of the month."

I nodded. "Appreciate that."

"Well, I can see her fine enough from here. See you around," Paul said, carrying his bottle back to his car and taking off like he thought I'd ask for it back.

His tires were still crunching the gravel when I headed toward the garage where the ATVs had just disappeared. Alec and Leah came strolling out before I closed the distance, smiling and laughing. Her hair was tousled like they'd been having a damned good time.

Alec rolled his eyes as soon as he saw me coming, as if he were going to have to listen to me. He'd be lucky if that was all he got.

"Where the fuck have you two been? I lied for your ass and you're out rolling in the bushes with my brother?"

Leah's eyes flashed with murder and heat, and the

fact that she'd just been fucking around with my brother did not do one thing to stop me from wanting to grab her and pin her beneath me. It might've made the urges worse—I wanted to fuck the memory of him out of her mind until not only could she not think straight, but couldn't walk straight either.

"Yeah, because I'm a whore, right?" she threw at me. "A felon, a whore, and a liar."

"You're out of line," Alec said, stepping forward.

"Stay out of this. You're causing enough issues," I said, pointing at him.

"You're being a bigger dick than I knew you could be," he said.

"I am? I'm the one who saved her ass from going to prison. I didn't see you stepping up to the plate," I said, closing the gap between us.

"Alec, I've got this." Leah stepped in between us, laying a hand on Alec's chest.

It was all I could do to not grab it and rip it off him.

Alec shook his head. "I—"

"Please, I can handle it," she said.

Alec threw up his hands and backed away toward the house. "Thank God someone can."

"What the hell is your issue?" she said, spinning back to me, ready to defend *Alec*.

As I looked at her, all I could think was, had he touched her? Had she enjoyed it? Did she want him now?

"My issue? While you were off with Alec, I was pretending to know where you were to the police who came by to do their check. You do realize I'm supposed to know where you are at all times, right?"

Her lips parted and her eyes flicked to the drive, where the car had just been. "That was..."

I could see her color fade. Her shoulders were rising and falling rapidly and there was a tiny tremble in her lower lip. She wrapped her arms around herself as she stared, as if terrified Paul would come back.

And damned if all I wanted to do was put her mind at ease.

"It was a deputy from the sheriff's office. It's fine. I handled it," I said. "But you don't get to go off with my brother and disappear whenever you want. I'm responsible for you. I need to know where you are every day for the next year. No exceptions. You can't take off and not let someone know."

She nodded, but her chin was up and her glare was hard. "I didn't mean to put you in a spot where you had to cover for me. For that, I'm sorry. But that's the only thing. Now I'm done speaking to you for tonight. I'm going to go take a shower *at Missy's*. If you feel some urge to yell some more, you'll have to wait until tomorrow."

She turned and walked off while I stood watching. I let her go. I had to because I was barely restraining myself, and if it went any further, I wasn't sure where it would lead.

I walked back to the house, wanting to be alone, but Alec was sitting on the couch, having a drink with his boots kicked up on my table.

His hands immediately went up. "I didn't fuck her. I didn't even *kiss* her. Not that you wouldn't have deserved it. You're acting like an unhinged lunatic."

That was the only thing he could've said that kept me from beating his ass. Of all Alec's flaws, he typically opted for the truth unless it would result in criminal charges or a divorce.

"Where the hell were you and what were you doing, then?"

"We went to the ridge. If I hadn't been fucking with you on purpose, I might be annoyed with you right now." He lifted his glass, toasting me.

"You did this on purpose?" How could I love him and hate him so much at the same time? "I had to lie to the deputy to save her ass."

He scoffed. "Please, we've both lied to Barney Fife more times than I can remember. We used to consider it a sport. Now you're saying that was a problem?"

Easy for him to blow it off as nothing. He wasn't the one who'd felt like he'd taken a throat punch when that car pulled up. There was a limit, even with Paul. "What if he caught her doing something?"

"He would've pretended not to and we both know it. You're only pissed because you couldn't find her and you think I banged her in the bushes. Which I *didn't*, because I *wouldn't* do that."

"Then what exactly were you doing?"

"Our conversation the other day got stuck in my head. I was trying to diagnose how bad you really have it. Unfortunately for you, I might've misjudged the situation." He took another sip and settled down a little farther into the couch. "I think you've taken a lethal shot from Cupid's bow, and I'm not confident you're going to make it."

"So you're swearing you didn't touch her at all?" Slowly, my heartbeat settled down. Still, I headed for the cabinet and pulled out a bottle of whiskey. I poured myself a generous glass and downed it in one go, feeling the burn settle deep in my chest.

"*That's* the part you heard?" he asked.

"It's the only part I'm willing to discuss," I said.

Alec watched me, swirling his own drink in leisurely manner.

"No McCallan?" he asked, lifting his brow. "Where you hiding that new bottle? If we're going to drink, where's that good stuff you said you bought?"

"Driving off with Barney." This might actually be the only salve to losing that bottle. Alec had wanted to try it more than I had.

His jaw dropped. "Please tell me you're kidding."

"Nope. I bought him off with good whiskey," I said as I walked over and took a seat on the couch.

Alec leaned forward, resting his elbows on his knees. "Man, that fucking sucks."

"Also, you have to stay in the small gray room. Leah uses the bathroom in the other bedroom now."

He gasped. "You're shitting me. You know I hate that bed."

"That's unfortunate for you." I shrugged.

"You better pour me some of that crap you didn't give away."

I topped off his glass and then leaned back.

He stared at me for a few seconds before he said, "In all seriousness, you've got to figure this shit out. If you keep acting like an ass, once this year's up, she's going to walk out of here and never look back."

I didn't respond at all. I couldn't. My chest felt too tight to speak.

CHAPTER 17

Leah

I WAS BRUSHING DOWN PRINCESS LATE THE NEXT DAY WHEN Missy walked over, giving the horse a rub on her head, and Princess leaned in.

She shot me one of those smiles. Missy was as transparent as cellophane. Her face told you so many details that words sometimes got in the way if she spoke.

"You heard." I was getting so used to my business being aired that I didn't even blush. After having a nickname like the Devious Debutante blasted throughout one of the largest cities in the world, a handful of people finding out about an embarrassing evening didn't have the same weight it used to. I just assumed someone would've heard our fight and then it would spread like fire through bunched-up newspaper.

"I swear no one was trying to pry, but it was hard not to know. First the deputy was here and then none of you were very quiet. Raised voices tend to carry around here.

After all that hoopla, it would be more shocking if we didn't know."

"Yeah, we had words. It's pretty much done now, though. Hopefully you won't have to hear us fighting again for at least a couple days." Our longest streak was three days, but that was only because we were avoiding each other on and off.

"I think you push his buttons like no one else can." Missy had a look on her face like she was holding back a secret.

"Don't get any crazy ideas. It's not like that." And it never would be. I was keeping Kade at arm's length. No way would I let that man close enough to hurt me again.

"Do you think he was jealous? It sort of seemed that way," she said, trying to sound naïve.

"I think he likes to fight. That's it." This girl was watching too many rom-coms. She'd be better off switching to murder mystery if she was going to label us, because I was about to bury Kade in an unmarked grave behind his ranch.

"I don't see him fighting with anyone else, though." She shrugged, keeping up the innocent act.

"Okay, he likes to fight with me. But that's all it is. There's nothing romantic between us. Trust me." Any illusion of caring on his part was just that. And me? I couldn't afford to care for him. This year was about survival and holding on to the last shreds of who I was. If I let Kade in, even an inch, he'd obliterate me.

That finally wiped that look from her face, but it shifted into furrowed lines. It was too much of a swing in the other direction. She glanced around before she stepped a little closer.

"So that thing Kade said about you and Alec, that wasn't true, was it?"

She looked like she was holding her breath while waiting for my answer. Oh no, this wasn't good. Of all the people to crush on, Alec was not the one. He'd been a playboy before he got out of his teens. He'd been born to it like a zebra was doomed to stripes.

"We're just friends. That's all," I said, not having the strength to break her heart—not that *he* wouldn't if given the chance.

The breath visibly left her as she put a hand on Princess's neck and leaned in to the mare.

"I wouldn't care. It's just I think Kade might be upset —at least, that's how it seemed last night," she said.

"The fact that I exist upsets Kade."

She giggled.

"So are you interested in Alec?" I asked.

"No," she said, shooting that out a little too fast and hard as her cheeks pinked. "I mean, he's hot and all, but I don't like him like *that*. I know what he is. He's visited before, and I've heard the talk about town."

"That's good, because even though he's an amazing friend, he likes to live a little fast."

Her lips turned down as she shifted her toe in the hay. "Yeah, I know. But he is awfully nice. Maybe it wouldn't be the worst thing ever to get used by him, you know? As opposed to being used by someone like Adam." She shrugged, as if this were just another casual musing that she hadn't been playing out in her head.

"If you can deal with the casual situation." Some women might be able to enjoy the night and move on, but Missy seemed already half smitten with him from the few breadcrumbs she was giving me.

"Hey, don't you have to go make your calls?"

"Yeah, maybe later." If I could force myself to see Kade. "Would you mind if I borrowed your shower again?"

"I don't know why you keep asking when I keep telling you to come use it."

I followed her out of the stable. I'd figure out if I had the energy for calls later.

CHAPTER 18

Leah

THE SUN HAD SET TWO HOURS AGO, BUT GOING ANYWHERE NEAR the house felt like inviting disaster. But if I didn't make my calls, my mother, my boyfriend Greg, my brother, and Cassie might spiral into a panic. They might think I'd gone on the lam, running across the country like a loser.

As bad as that might be, if I did go make the calls, I'd have to see *him*. Seeing *him* was to be avoided at all costs.

Screw it. If they got nervous, they all had Kade's number and none of them were bashful. They'd call him up and he'd have to figure out what to say about why I hadn't called. It wasn't as if I felt like listening to my mother talk about her drapes or the latest event she'd attended while I was dead on my feet after mucking out stalls all day. I hadn't cared before, and my tolerance had been way higher then.

My tolerance for *everything* she did was higher before I ended up here. For the thousandth time, I reminded myself it wasn't her fault I was here. She hadn't realized who the man she married was. I couldn't let my rage for him spill onto her. And if I just kept reminding myself of that, maybe it would work one day.

This wasn't the day, though. I thought about my life and where I'd ended up because of that man. I'd known better. I'd kept my distance from him for a reason, and still, look what had happened.

I settled onto my little bed, turned on the light, and picked up the book Missy had lent me. Not much else to do, since I wasn't allowed to be in the bunkhouse socializing in any kind of way, I didn't have a phone or Wi-Fi, and there was no TV in here.

I pulled my blanket up over the fuzzy sweatpants, also thanks to Missy, and tugged up the extra throw from an unknown donor that I'd found on my bed. It was thick and felt like wool. I'd have to find out who'd dropped it off. With the lousy heat in my shed, it was a lifesaver.

There was a knock on my door.

"Come in." I looked up from my book to see Kade walking over the threshold. "I take it back. Get out." I went back to looking at my book, feigning reading.

"You didn't come up to the office to make your calls or shower."

"I showered at Missy's and I didn't have anything pressing to say. Now get out."

He didn't move, and I was in my pajamas in the only place I could go for privacy, or was before he came.

"You get to make calls once a week and you have no one you want to call?"

"No. And I believe, according to the agreement, the one you've obviously studied intensively, I'm under no obligation to *make* any calls. So I'll say it again: get out."

Not only did he not leave, he walked a couple of steps and leaned a hip on my dresser. He shoved up his shirt sleeves and crossed his arms.

He might be a different man, but he still smelled like the Kade I'd always known. When I was a kid, in his arms had felt like the only safe place in the world. His smell had been the scent of my happy place. I'd bury my face in the crook of his neck, and for a few minutes, nothing could hurt me because he wouldn't let it.

Now he was the one inflicting the pain. Had all of my memories been skewed by a childish adoration that the adult couldn't ignore?

I tried to pretend he wasn't there and read the book. It didn't work. When he was around, he stole all my focus. Even if I couldn't ignore him, I wasn't letting him know that I couldn't.

"You're going to be here a year. You can't give me the silent treatment for another fifty weeks because we had some words."

That's what *he* thought. I'd never been the passive-aggressive sort, but I'd lost my ability to just be straight-up aggressive and punch him in the face. So, passive was the lane I'd have to take. After all, if he could cause a scene and act like he had last night, my ignoring him was the least he deserved.

The way he was staring at me, I was clearly getting to him.

"Really? You're going to lie there and ignore me like a child?" he said.

Problem was I didn't have any practice at the passive form of aggression. It was tougher than people realized.

"Child? Really? You think that's what I am for not talking to a person who acted the way you did?" *Dammit.*

This passive stuff was going to need a lot of practice. Well, I did have almost a year left to perfect it.

"You disappeared and I had the *deputy* on my *porch*."

"And I told you I was sorry, for *that* part." Even hearing about it again chilled me.

His jaw shifted. "They're leaving messages for you. You don't want to take your time and make your calls? So be it."

Dammit. They were calling. I did want to speak with Cassie at least, and Monroe might feel bad if I didn't check in.

"Fine. I'm coming." I shoved my feet in my boots and threw on my jacket, trudging up to the office in my pajamas.

He held the office door open for me and took his usual spot as I settled behind the desk, neither of us saying anything, as if we'd been doing this for years.

First I called my mother, bracing myself for what was to come. "Hey, Mom. How's it going?"

She let out a long, dramatic groan. "I didn't get an invitation to Brook's opening gala. I didn't really expect it after Lucy didn't invite me to her luncheon for up-and-coming cellists."

"Mom, I told you I'm very sorry for any spillover," I said, like I'd said fifty times before.

"It's all right. I'm not upset with you."

And yet she mentioned every slight, more than once. She'd be telling me about Lucy and Brook snubbing her another ten times before that was put to bed. If she only knew the person truly responsible for her dip in popularity was the man she slept beside every night.

"So how was your week?" she asked.

"It wasn't bad." That was as flattering as I'd get with

Kade listening in, even though I'd started to not quite hate living here. "There's a pregnant horse that—"

"Kade's horse? Is Kade on the phone, too? Kade, are you there?"

"Hello, Mrs. Loode. I'm here. How are you?"

"Wonderful," she said, lighting up as if he were the one she'd given birth to. "I read about your horses on the computer. So interesting what you're doing there."

She was talking as if she knew all about cutting horses, the woman who hadn't wanted me to get a dog because a stray hair might land on her outfit. Had she been studying all week in the hopes of luring him into a conversation? Sure seemed like it.

She'd hit the right topic to get him talking, though. I'd never seen him as excited about something in my life, or not in a long time, as he launched into details about his horses.

He used to get this way talking about his plans for the ranch when we were kids. Seemed that same fire was still there if he was talking to someone other than me.

I pretended to look at my nails while they kept on talking. Although that might've been a godsend. What had happened to my well-manicured fingers? The least I could do was get rid of the last of the color clinging for dear life. I'd have to see if Missy had some nail-polish remover I could use.

The speaker clicked as Kade hung up the phone and I checked the clock. Eighteen minutes.

"That was on your time. Not mine," I said.

He nodded, not even arguing.

Next, I called my brother, who had never been overly wordy. After a rudimentary check that I still had a pulse, he was done. I then called Cassie, who was in the middle of trying to calm her mother over losing the tulips because of some global shortage. Cassie's mother was almost as bad about this wedding as Cassie herself.

I hung up knowing there was one last call that had to be made. I hadn't spoken to Greg in two weeks. I hadn't missed him. In truth, I didn't even think of him that much. Didn't that say it all? If there was one silver lining in this mess, it was really showing me which relationships truly mattered to me. It might've been time to really break it off, let him move on and not wait out a year, but it was hard to break up with an audience.

But was it fair to judge a relationship under this kind of duress? Everything had been so up-in-the-air crazy that I'd barely had time to think about anything beyond getting through the next moment.

I dialed.

"Hello?" the familiar voice answered. I'd warned him I wouldn't have my own phone, so he'd probably answered at least five spam calls by now.

"Hi, it's me." I tried to sound upbeat and as much like my pre-conviction self as possible, while avoiding looking in Kade's direction. He was surely judging this too.

"Hey," Greg said.

That was it—one word and I knew something was wrong. All I could hear in his voice was dread. Had he been getting the spillover of my conviction too? He'd always said he wasn't getting fallout, but I'd suspected he was lying to protect me. There was no way my mother had and he'd gotten off scot-free.

"Is everything okay? Did something happen with your business?" It wasn't like I was available to call and stay informed anymore.

"No, everything is okay with *that*."

With *that*. So what was the problem? I looked over at Kade, who was too busy pretending to watch something outside to give me a glimpse of his judgment in action.

"There's something we need to talk about," Greg said, sounding graver with each word. I could picture him now in his crisp shirt, looking out his apartment window as he shuffled from foot to foot.

He was never good at spitting things out, and what I was going to say next wouldn't help him out. "Just so you know, you're on speaker and we have company."

"Company?"

"Kade, the guy that owns the ranch. I told you about him." Hopefully he had enough sense to not launch into any details about what I'd added onto that description, the way Cassie had.

There was a pause before he audibly sighed. It was one of those long, drawn-out types that always meant something was wrong.

"You should take me off speaker," he said.

I didn't bother looking at Kade. He wouldn't do me any favors. "Yeah, I can't do that because of the terms of my deal with the court."

"Oh." Another sigh, this one louder than the last. "Look, I didn't really want to have this conversation with other people listening, but it has to be had."

I had a sinking feeling I knew what was coming next, and I didn't want an audience. Greg was going to break up with me, and if it were any other time, any other way, I wasn't sure I would've cared. I'd given him an out before I came here.

But now? I wasn't capable of having another round of public humiliation just yet, but that wasn't going to matter. Kade wasn't looking at me, but I could see his profile and he was listening intently.

"What needs to be said that wasn't said before?"

For the past month, he'd told me over and over again how he didn't want to break up. But no, he had to do it now, with Kade listening to every detail.

Or maybe not?

Without a glance in my direction, Kade straightened and walked out of the office. He shut the door behind him. It didn't look that thick that he couldn't still hear, but it was more grace than I'd imagined he'd give me.

I tried to prepare myself for what Greg was about to say.

"Well? What is it?" If he was breaking up with me, I needed him to spit it out now.

"I've been thinking about it, and a year is a long time to be apart from someone."

"I believe I said that to you two weeks ago, when you were assuring me that I was the love of your life. What was it you said? Oh, I remember. That you couldn't live without me, couldn't imagine breathing without me, and that you would wait an eternity for me to come back to you."

If my doubts had been merely niggling before, now they were punching me square in the face. Greg had always been the guy that looked perfect on paper. So perfect that I'd ignored the occasional twitch from my gut that said no one was *that* good. I was paying for it in pure humiliation now. This was so bad that even Kade didn't want to witness it.

"I do love you," Greg said. "That's the problem. I'm finding the whole situation too painful."

"*You're* finding this situation too painful?" How had I

dated this guy for so long? How could I have been this stupid?

"Please, don't make this harder than it needs to be. I really want us to part as friends."

Yes, *of course* he did.

"It's fine, Greg. I wouldn't want to cause you any *undue pain*."

He sighed *again*. "I sense sarcasm."

"Trust me when I tell you that I agree and think this is for the best." It would've been even better if he'd agreed when I mentioned it repeatedly before getting here. "I'll let you go. I'm sure you have a lot to do." And if I had to keep talking to him, I was either going to scream or cry.

"I'm glad you see the situation the way I do."

"Oh yes. Bye, Greg." I hung up on him before he could offer any more brilliant comments or insights.

I sat still for a moment as the impact of getting dumped hit me. Had I truly loved Greg? I hadn't been sure before if I'd been going through the motions or what, but it didn't matter anymore. He'd joined the rest of the people who'd decided it was too hard to have me in their lives.

Kade walked back into the office as I was putting the phone on the cradle, confirming my suspicions on the thickness of the door. It would be a miracle if I made it through this year with a shred of pride left.

I glanced over briefly, having a hard time meeting his eye. I got up and headed toward the door.

"You're done?" he asked, motioning to the clock. "You've got ten minutes left."

"I don't need them." My privacy, my career, most of my friends were gone, and now my relationship. I'd been ready to end it, and yet it was just *one more thing*. Everything was over for the foreseeable future and I had to wait a year to try to rebuild. If I hadn't saved so much of the money I'd made, I wouldn't have been able to pay the mortgage and taxes on my apartment.

I was just about out the door when Kade was there beside it.

"You okay?" he asked, somehow managing to sound sincere.

"I'm fine," I said.

I went to open the door, and he blocked it. "You're clearly not fine."

I paused for a second, wishing I could go back to that girl who didn't know any better and could fall into his arms. Would it hurt to just pretend for a minute? Take some comfort wherever I could find it?

The way he was staring at me right now, with that intense look, the way he used to…

"Move," I said, sounding weaker than I wanted.

His eyes shifted to my lips, as if he wanted to kiss me. He was standing so close that I expected him to hug me at any moment.

My gaze dropped to the floor, and I felt his arms wrap around me. I let him. I didn't hug him back, but I rested my head on his chest, not pulling away.

"I don't want to fight with you," he said.

I nodded, wishing the same, even if I couldn't find the words right now.

"I just need to know why you cost me that loan years ago. Was it a mistake?"

I froze, and then put my hands on his chest to push away.

"What are you talking about? I didn't ruin your loan. I had nothing to do with that loan," I said, regretting I'd softened for even a second. Was *that* the grudge he'd been holding against me? A loan from a decade ago?

"You repeated what I said to you to Jerry, who was giving me the loan. Why would you tell him I didn't know how I was ever going to pay? It could've cost me this ranch. You knew what that meant."

"I never repeated anything you said to me in confidence."

"Stop lying. He knew what I'd said to you verbatim."

There was only one place that I'd ever repeated anything Kade said to me, and that was in my diary. My asshole stepfather had read it.

How did I even explain that? Kade would probably think it was a lie anyway. He didn't trust anything I said.

It wouldn't convince him of anything. He'd gotten his chunk of soul for the day. Now I wanted to go curl up in a ball and lick my wounds.

"Let's not pretend we're friends when you've repeatedly made our situation clear. Now just get out of my way."

He dropped his arms and stepped back.

I left, reminding myself again that he wasn't a safe place, not now, and he probably never had been.

CHAPTER 19

Kade

THE SECOND I HEARD THAT MAN'S VOICE LAST NIGHT, MY muscles had immediately reacted. They'd tensed like they knew Greg needed a beating before my consciousness had caught up. I hadn't meant to overhear, but once I'd caught some of it, I hadn't been able to stop listening. My instincts had been right. It was the next morning and my hands were still fisted.

Chuck walked into the office as he often did. He'd probably seen Leah twenty times today. I leaned back, giving up the pretense of reading through my file. "Hey, how's everything going?"

Chuck stopped and turned, tilting his head like he was trying to figure out what I was really asking. If there'd been any kind of problem, he would've already told me, and we both knew it.

"Good?" he said slowly.

"What's everyone up to? Everything going smoothly?" I asked, tilting my head in the vague direction of the stables.

"She's a little quieter, maybe, but otherwise fine, if that's what you're trying to ask me," he said.

Quieter. That wasn't good. "I wasn't asking about her specifically, but it's funny you'd single her out. So she's quiet? How quiet? Is she speaking at all?"

He leaned on the table, devoting all his attention to me. "If you're worried about Leah, you could try talking to her."

"She doesn't talk to me," I said. "And I'm not worried. It was a question based on what you said."

"If she won't talk to you, it's because you don't talk to her. You growl at her." He was looking at me, brows raised in what was beginning to feel like judgment.

I rubbed a hand across the back of my neck. "I don't *growl* at her."

"Yes, you do. She's not the first person to have a hard time. She'll be fine. She's a tough one. She's in the stables right now, not that you'd want to go talk to her"—he waved his hands in the air—"but in case you wanted to check on the horses."

Chuck turned and walked out, leaving me alone in the office.

If I did go check the horses, it was my ranch. If I happened upon her in the stables, they were my stables. I was allowed to go there.

My phone buzzed beside me, but I ignored it, until it went on, and on, and on. I finally grabbed it, seeing Monroe's name.

"What's up?"

"Hey, I have to talk to Leah," he said. "It's sort of a

sensitive matter. Something happened today that can't wait."

"Everything okay?"

There was a pause, and I could imagine his sitting there deciding whether he should tell me. If I knew Monroe as well as I thought, he wouldn't need much of a push.

"I don't want to pry, but if it's bad, maybe I can help," I added.

His fidgeting could be heard through the phone. "I probably shouldn't tell you this first, but you'll find out anyway. What does it even matter?"

"What is it?" This wasn't anything to do with me, and I was already getting to my feet, tensing, and I didn't even know why. If he was going to tell me, he needed to spit it out already.

"Leah's mortgage company is pulling the loan on her apartment in New York."

I paced the length of the office as I waited for that to sink in. *Not now.* She didn't need this on top of everything else. "Are you kidding me? Has she been making the payments?"

"Everything is up to date. It's nothing financial. They're using some morality clause or something. I don't know exactly how they can do this, but my lawyer is saying it's legal."

"That doesn't make any sense. As long as she's paying the loan, they don't typically pay attention to anything else. Someone has to be stepping in and making a fuss for this to happen." This situation stank worse than a bucket of rotting fish.

"Maybe, but they won't tell me. I've been on the phone for hours, getting the runaround from about ten different people, and no one can give me a straight answer or tell me how I can stop this. They're all just saying she'll have to pay the balance due or lose her apartment. If I could pay it off for her I would, but even if I had that kind of cash lying around, it's not just my finances, but my wife's. I can't ask her to do that."

I knew where Leah lived. I had an idea what kind of money it would take. There weren't many people who could bail her out.

"No, I understand. It's a tough spot to be in. Look, it'll work out somehow. I'll tell her to call you and I'm sure something will get figured out."

It would have to be, one way or another. I wasn't sure I could watch her lose her home, no matter how much I wanted to strangle her at times.

Monroe groaned. "I don't know, Kade. This is going to be bad."

"I might know a banker or two that can help out. I'll check around and call you tomorrow with some names."

He was silent for a few seconds. "I'm already neck deep into favors with you, but I can't turn this one down. But..."

He didn't say anything else.

"What?" I asked.

"Maybe it's best not to mention this to Leah. I'm not sure she'd accept that kind of help from you. She's got a lot of pride."

"I completely agree."

I WALKED INTO THE STABLE, SLOWING AS I APPROACHED THE stall. Some people might've called it sneaking up, but it was my damned ranch. When I owned the place, I was allowed to walk any way I wanted, as slowly and silently as I chose.

There was a soft singing coming from a stall as I neared.

As I peered inside, Leah had one arm around the mare's neck, gently rubbing Princess as she softly sang what sounded like a lullaby.

She turned, as if she'd felt my eyes on her. Neither of us spoke for a minute, but Princess whinnied, as if she could sense Leah's sudden unease.

Leah moved her hand along Princess's neck. "It's all right. It's all good." The pregnant mare seemed to calm under Leah's attention.

She finally glanced over at me. "She was seeming out of sorts again. I'll stop visiting her so much if it bothers you."

How bad had our relationship crumbled if she thought I wouldn't want her to touch my horse?

"No. Not at all. Visit with her as much as you want. She likes it."

Leah looked at me and nodded, not saying anything.

She continued to comfort Princess while I stalled, knowing I was going to be delivering yet another blow.

She kept glancing over at me, as if she sensed something was out of sorts.

"I did come find you for a reason. Your brother needs you to call him," I said.

Her hands stopped moving. "It's not Sunday."

"It's a legal matter that has to be handled." I cleared my throat, those words feeling like they were choking me.

"Do you know what's wrong?" she said, turning toward me.

"No. Just go up to the ranch office. Door is open. I've

got something else I have to do, so I'll meet you there in a few minutes."

"You're not coming?" she asked, her antenna way up now.

"My truck engine light came on and I want to check it out before it gets dark." Hopefully she forgot that I not only had a garage, but floodlights I could turn on.

CHAPTER 20

Leah

I SAT IN THE OFFICE, MY HANDS SHAKING SO BADLY THAT IT TOOK me two tries to dial my brother. There was no way it was good news, not when even Kade appeared to be pitying me. He said he didn't know, but at the very least, he too expected something bad.

"Hey," Monroe answered.

"What's wrong? Kade said I needed to call you." I was gripping the receiver hard enough to crack the thing.

"Leah, I'm really sorry, but they're pulling your mortgage for your apartment."

The room nearly swirled around me as I felt like I'd taken a hit in the head. It took a second to get my bearings before I said, "That has to be wrong. I'm up to date on all my payments. I know because there hasn't been enough time to have missed one."

"It's not the payments. It's some morality clause."

Monroe was speaking to me like he was a doctor with a patient who was getting a bad diagnosis.

"I didn't sign a morality clause in my mortgage." There was a mistake, or someone had been screwing with him.

"Leah, I had a lawyer look it over, and I've been on the phone with people all day trying to get it fixed. It's something in the fine print because of the conviction. The lawyer said that we could try to fight it but that odds were the bank would find something to hang their hat on and you'd still be screwed. You'd only end up racking up legal fees."

I dropped my head into my hand. "How long did they give me to come up with the balance?"

"You've got ninety days to pay the mortgage in full or they'll take the property and sell it at auction."

They weren't just taking my home, they were going to obliterate any equity I had. "They'll never get what it's worth at auction. By the time they discount it, take what I owe and whatever fees they can screw me out of, I'll get nothing."

He didn't say anything for a few seconds because he knew I was right. There was no silver lining in this storm cloud.

"Leah, I'm trying to find a solution. I'm going to see if Dad—"

"No. Don't say a word of this to him or Mom. And he's not my dad." Hearing my brother call him that was like a thousand nails on a chalkboard.

"Maybe he can help, though," Monroe said, almost pleadingly.

Damned if I'd let that man into my life even an inch after what he'd done to me.

"He can't, and it'll stress Mom out. You know she can't handle stress, or did you conveniently forget our childhood?"

There was another long pause while I stared at the door, expecting Kade to stroll in and get another front-row seat, this time for *The Devious Debutante's Downfall Part Three*.

"Maybe Tiffany's—"

"No. I won't have you go to your wife and her family. That's too much. You can't do that." My life might be in the shredder, but I wouldn't have his marriage be part of the collateral damage. It wasn't like I had a small mortgage. My financials would strain the sturdiest of foundations.

"I might have a few leads on different lenders that could step in. It's not a done deal yet."

"Okay," I said, struggling to get more words out without my voice cracking.

"I'll call as soon as I know anything else. Kade obviously understands this is different and can't wait until Sunday. Just hang in there and—"

"Does Kade know? What did you tell him when you called?"

The long pause said it all. This time it wasn't due to a lack of what to say. This was straight-up fear about what he'd already said.

"Dammit, Monroe! You told Kade, didn't you?"

"He was going to find out anyway."

I leaned back, squeezing my eyes shut, refusing to sit in Kade's office and bawl. Monroe was right. Kade would've found out anyway. Everyone would once it went up on the auction block.

"Leah?"

I took a deep breath, forcing myself to hold it together for a few more minutes. "It's okay. Just keep me posted." I hung up, trying to come to terms with the fact that I was losing my home.

It was only a place. It wasn't something I couldn't build back from. I'd built up a life before, and I'd build it again. I could do this, even if it didn't feel like it was possible right now.

————

KADE

THE SECOND LEAH WALKED INTO THE OFFICE, I PULLED OUT MY phone.

John answered on the second ring. "Yeah," he said.

"There's a new development with the princess situation," I said. "Her loan got called in early and I need to know who's behind it."

"Oh no, that's horrible." He groaned like he was some little old grandmother hearing bad news. "How's she holding up?"

This new version of John was really throwing me off my game. "Just find out the situation, okay?"

I was having a hard enough time holding the reins on my own emotions. There was no bandwidth left to help the reformed knee breaker with the sudden conscience from melting down.

"Trust me, I'll find out who screwed her," he said, sounding a little more normal.

"Good. Let me know as soon as you do."

"You're going to fix this, though, right?" he asked.

"Huh?"

"You're sitting on some funds. You can't let her get screwed like this when you can fix it for her."

There were so many issues with this situation. First, how did he know what was in my bank account, and second and more importantly, why the hell did he care so much?

"John, I'm starting to become concerned with your level of empathy toward this particular person and case. I expect a certain amount of detachment from you."

"I know. I'm working on it with my life coach. There's just something about her that makes me want to take care of her."

"You haven't ever met her, have you?" I was beginning to worry about what he'd do, or had done. They'd both been in New York, after all.

"No, but I feel as if I know her. Like she could've been my daughter. Strange, right?"

"Very. You need to work on that."

At least he'd said *daughter*. That was a plus. I hung up on him before he started getting more emotional. It was like my entire life was flipping upside down, and all the people I knew with it.

I called my accountant next. "I might need you to free up some assets. I'll send you information on a loan I might need to buy out."

"I swear you juggle more shit than the clowns at the circus. What are we doing now? How messy is this one? I just finished moving the other funds around to fix your other issue, which wasn't cheap."

Being "friends" with a judge never was.

"You do get paid to do this. I swear if I hadn't known you from grammar school, I'd fire your ass."

"You can't fire me because you don't trust anyone else to see your holdings or what you *do* with them."

He was one thousand percent correct. "Just shut the fuck up and handle it."

I pocketed my phone and popped the hood of my truck and then pretended to tinker while I waited for Leah to walk out of the office.

Alec walked over. "What's up with your truck?"

"Just checking some levels."

He looked at the engine compartment. "Nothing's open, though."

"I *just* popped the hood," I said, watching the house.

Alec watched me watch the door. "I saw Leah going into the office. What's going on? She trying to get switched to prison because you're a lunatic?"

"Nothing is going on."

"Then why are you watching the office door like there's a bank robbery in progress?"

"Alec, do you ever take a hint?"

"I prefer not to. It's really not my thing."

"Go find something else to—"

Leah walked out of the office, her step quick. She wasn't actively crying, but she didn't look good by any stretch.

"Whoa, what's wrong with her?" Alec said.

"I have no idea."

"Well, that's clearly bullshit, or you wouldn't be out here with your truck hood open and not even a cap undone. Is it something you did? That would be my guess," he said, then had the nerve to laugh.

"No. I didn't do anything." Although I might punch him if he didn't shut up and leave me alone right now. It almost felt like I'd lost the ranch, watching her.

"You sure?" He raised his brows as he stared hard. "I *heard* about the vote."

"You people and that vote can all fuck off."

He shrugged. "I guess someone who was voted unanimously against might have that attitude about it."

I ignored him as I watched Leah walking away, debating whether to follow her or leave her be. *I'd* want to be left alone, but not following her didn't feel right either.

"Well, you'll have to fix this one on your own. I have to leave. Hopefully you won't screw things up too bad while you're left to your own devices."

"Don't worry about rushing back," I said, squinting as I tried to track where Leah was heading.

CHAPTER 21

Leah

I'D TURNED THE HEAT UP IN THE SHED BEFORE MY SHOWER. Typically my heater was a bit like the Little Engine That Could—it might take a little longer to get going, but this place would eventually be nice and toasty—but this time it didn't feel like it was doing anything.

I'd lost my freedom. I was losing my home. It was only fitting that now I was losing my heat as well. What was life without the perfect trifecta of disasters?

I pulled the bed covers higher, my wet hair feeling it like it was forming icicles. In hindsight, blow-drying might've been a better option. Ponytails had been my daily go-to because the horses and chickens didn't really care how smooth my locks were.

After another solid fifteen minutes, I forced myself out from under the blankets and put a hand to the baseboard. It felt colder than the room did. *Dammit. Dammit. Dammit.*

I pulled the comforter up around my head and shoulders, slipped on my boots, and trudged over to the bunkhouse. Luckily, Elijah was still up. He was the one who fixed all the broken things around this place—well, except me, but it was hard to expect miracles.

"Hey, what's wrong?" he asked, looking away from the big screen, where he'd been flicking through channels.

I wasn't sure if it was my showing up late with my hair drenched, or the comforter cape that was putting off desperado vibes. Either way, I'd obviously nailed it.

"I know it's late, but could you come check my heat? It won't come on."

"Yeah, sure." He stretched as he got up, clearly having been winding down for the night. Working a ranch wasn't for the weak of heart. A full day here felt like forty-eight hours. When you hit the bed, you were ready to sleep. Except when you were shivering like I was.

Twenty minutes later, Elijah was kneeling at the heater and shaking his head.

"I'm not sure if it's the element or the limit switch that isn't working."

"What does that mean?" He might as well have been teaching rocket science.

"It means I need to swap out some parts." He poked around and looked at different things as he explained. "It's so old, it might not even be worth fixing. You might need a whole new system."

"So you're saying I'm not getting heat?" I asked.

Elijah finally stopped fiddling and looked over at me like he wasn't sure what had happened to my brain. "Yes. That's pretty much what 'it's not working' means." He stood up, brushing his hands off on his jeans. "You should either come stay at the bunkhouse, or I'll go talk to Kade. I'm sure he'd be fine with you staying up there at the house."

I couldn't have shaken my head any harder. "No, no. I think I'll be fine here. I'll just burrow under the covers."

He looked around the place, as if trying to figure out what I was so attached to that I was willing to sleep in what amounted to an icebox. "We're getting a cold snap. It's dropping below freezing tonight."

"If it gets too cold, I'll head over. I'm not worried."

He nodded but then stood there. Clearly he had a different opinion on what I should do but wasn't quite sure if he was in a place to argue with me.

"I'll be good. Trust me. Now it's getting late. I don't want to keep you up. I'll see you tomorrow unless I get cold, and then I'll be over." I got up, as if I were going to walk him to the door. It was a little odd, since the door was only three feet away. That was shed life for you.

He kept glancing back at me but finally left.

I went through my things that I'd finally put into the dresser and dug out a wool sweater and the thickest socks I could find. I mummified myself in the comforter and settled onto the bed.

There was a knock at the door ten minutes later. I'd been expecting someone to show up ever since Elijah left looking like he was the unwitting driver of a getaway car. There was no way he hadn't run to someone, most likely Kade or Chuck. The fact that they'd knocked meant it probably wasn't Kade and safe to answer.

"Come in."

Chuck took a step inside. "Whoa, it's like the damned Artic in here." He gave a mock shiver.

"It's fine. Elijah said he needed some things in order

to fix the heater, but I'm good." He was going to be a little harder to run off than Elijah but I was confident in my abilities.

"Yeah, he told me. You sure you want to stay here tonight? You can come stay at my place. It's just a little bit down the road." He pointed in a vague direction. "I'm not sure you should be staying here."

"Chuck, I'm good. I swear. Plus, I'm not legally allowed to leave the ranch."

He rubbed his jaw and grimaced. "Oh, yeah. I forgot about that little issue."

It was amazing how little my felon status seemed to occur to any of them. "If I get too cold, I can go to the bunkhouse. It's not like I have nowhere to go."

He took a second to think about it but then shrugged. "Don't be stubborn about it," he said in his gruff way.

"I won't."

"Okay. I'll see you in the morning, then. I'll be making my famous pancakes."

"Sounds amazing. Thanks." The best thing about this conversation was that he was going to leave this be. "Chuck? Can you do me a favor? Can we not mention this issue to anyone else?"

"*I* won't. Can't count on the rest of the blabber-mouths around here, though." He smiled as he walked out.

True to his prediction, Missy showed up five minutes later.

"Damn, it's cold in here. You need to come to my place."

"No, really, I'm fine. It doesn't feel that bad under all these blankets."

Plus, I couldn't risk having company tonight. The

cracks in my emotional foundation were already starting to show. I could feel a magnitude-ten quake about to hit, and I wouldn't have any witnesses when it all came crashing down. As it was, I could feel each conversation starting to unravel me a little more, and for no reason. If I had to pretend to be okay for even another few minutes, I might really crack.

"Are you crying?" Missy asked. I'd seen less horror on a five-year-old's face when watching *The Shining*.

I ran an arm across my face, not realizing I'd already started falling apart. Guess my prediction had been off. But when you were trying to hold the water behind a cracked Hoover Dam with a small bucket of cement, who noticed a couple drops here and there?

"I'm good." I smiled and sniffled. "I'm getting allergies or something. Promise. I'm just really tired and ready to sleep."

She nodded but was staring very intently. "Okay, but you'll come by if you get too cold? I don't lock the door. Just walk in any time."

"I'm good." I faked a yawn and nodded, pretending I was about to drop dead of exhaustion. And it *was* a type of exhaustion I felt, just an emotional one. I was spent, utterly and completely, and wasn't sure how I was going to even wake up in the morning and keep going.

But I *would*. The way forward just wasn't really clear right now.

She nodded as she left, but not without looking back at me fifty more times before she made it to the door.

I held it mostly together all of five minutes after she left before I cracked wide open.

CHAPTER 22

Kade

My phone buzzed in my pocket.

John: I've got something. Call me.

I shut both of the office doors and called him immediately.

"Hey," he answered.

"What do you have?" I went to sit and found I couldn't stay that still. If there was something off, if she turned out to be innocent...

"I didn't get any leads on what happened with the painting yet, but as I poked around, some other information came to light you might want to know. At least, *I* would."

"Just spit it out already." I was glad he wasn't here because I might've shaken him.

"You know her stepfather has a lot of connections in the art world?"

"Yes. He's an art dealer. It would stand to reason he's well connected."

"Well, he might be connected in a way that isn't public knowledge. He's definitely doing some shady transactions, or at least that's what some of my connections implied. There are also two different sources who know him personally, and are on the darker side of the art world, who insinuated that he had some sort of weird obsession with Leah. I wasn't even asking about that. They offered it up, and that happened twice without any prompting. Whatever was going on there had to be pretty pronounced."

My skin suddenly felt too tight for my body, my lungs too big for my ribcage, and like my body had just discovered how to produce adrenaline.

"What exactly did they say?" I could barely get the words out because my jaw was clenched too tight.

"One source said he'd met Leah, with Edwin, her stepfather. My guy said Edwin stared at her in a way that made this guy want to punch him in the face. Apparently Leah was only sixteen at the time, and my guy has a daughter her age. He said there was just something dirty about it, considering it was her stepfather."

"And the other?"

"He mentioned that Edwin had said something along the lines of, 'Can you imagine what it would be like to be balls deep in that?' when one of the guys asked about his stepdaughter."

I couldn't speak. I felt like someone had just punched

me in the throat, reached down, and grabbed my stomach, and was trying to rip it out. I couldn't form words
because I couldn't breathe. I felt like I was going to
combust and take out everything around me.

"Kade?"

I swallowed hard, trying to get a handle on the
pending explosion within. If I let this ignite, I'd be on a
plane and beating the shit out of Edwin in a matter of
hours, and the only proof I had was a couple of criminals
possibly running their mouths. Nothing was confirmed,
and although utterly disgusting, it didn't mean anything
had actually happened.

"Hey, you still there?" John asked.

"Yeah. Keep digging. I want to know everything you
can find out about their relationship. Spend whatever you
have to. I want answers."

"Already on it. Be in touch soon."

I threw my phone on the desk, the past luring me
back a decade in time.

*She was sitting near the stream, low on the bank. If her
blonde ponytail hadn't been sticking out, I never would've
seen her. She'd be gone soon and I shouldn't care. I had too
much to do here. I couldn't handle anything or anyone else,
especially someone who pulled at me so strongly. It was a daily
struggle keeping this ranch afloat as it was.*

*Still, I couldn't walk past her. I never could. I dropped
onto the bank right beside her.*

*"I'm leaving in a week," she said as if she were getting
pulled under by the weight of those words and a future
looming like a storm on the horizon.*

It wasn't new information. We'd known she was leaving

for months, but each day she seemed to lose a little more of the light in her eyes as the fear crept in.

"It's change. You hate change, but it'll be great." And it would be better for her. Everyone in town knew her mother had barely functioned since the death of Leah's father.

"Yeah, I guess you're right. I mean, my mother sure does love him."

"He's a good guy. He wants the best for her and you."

There was a flicker in her eyes, like the storm gathering steam.

"What is it?" I asked.

"Nothing. It's probably just the change, like you said. I hate change."

That was the answer I'd been hoping for, the one that let me go on and do what I had to in order to survive.

HAD I MISSED SOMETHING? OR MORE ACCURATELY, HAD I *wanted* to miss something? I'd been so buried in work at the time, it had felt like I hit my bed at midnight and barely slept before starting all over again. Alec had washed his hands of the ranch in favor of a future in tech, refusing to "waste his life," as he'd put it. My father had been nearly bedridden.

Thinking about those moments before she left were like poking at an arm that was turning black with gangrene.

I needed to leave it alone. Wait and see what John came back with. I couldn't let a few shady criminals make me get on a plane and commit murder.

Missy appeared at the door. "Hey, Kade? You got a second?"

"Not a great time. Can it wait? I've got a list of things

to get through tonight before I can sleep." I would've said I had a kidney stone if it would get her to leave. I couldn't handle one more thing tonight.

"Not really. We've got a problem." She was twisting her fingers and her feet weren't budging, like she was standing in cement.

I let out a sigh so that I didn't snap and tell her to get out anyway. Anyone else, I would've let loose. It had taken Missy months to be confident enough to say no to me, and I didn't want to smash that flare of confidence that'd just started to burn, even if I did feel like I was in emotional hell at the moment.

"What's the problem?" I asked, breathing deeply to keep my tone calm.

"Leah."

I ran a hand through my hair as I leaned back. This was going to take more than deep breathing. This was going to take monk-like meditation skills to stay calm.

"What's the problem?"

"I think she's broken." She crossed and uncrossed her arms.

"What do you mean?" I came around the desk, heading to the door. "Did she fall? She knows better than to ride at night." I didn't see Leah out in the field.

"No. Her body is okay. I think it's more of a mind thing."

I swung back from the door I'd been about to run out of. "What do you mean?"

"I was talking to her and tears were running down her cheeks. She said she was fine, maybe even good. I can't remember exactly, because all I could think was that she didn't seem like the crying type, and yet they just kept coming."

"Are you sure she was crying?" Leah didn't cry. I'd seen her break her leg when she was twelve and she hadn't cried.

"Yeah, they were just running out of her eyes like she didn't have any control of them."

"Where is she?"

"In her cabin."

I didn't wait for more information before I took off in that direction.

CHAPTER 23

Leah

I WAS LYING IN BED, TRYING TO FIGURE OUT HOW TO STOP THE current meltdown that was occurring. Once the tears had started, they seemed impossible to stop. Not only that, they were coming faster and harder.

Of course that was when another knock would come. This one didn't wait for a greeting before the door flew open.

Kade's eyes landed on me. "What are you doing?" he asked, his voice soft.

For the first time since I'd known him, he sounded more unsettled than I was.

"I'm crying!" No matter how hard I tried, I couldn't stop. He'd have to point that out.

If he thought I was crying now and it threw him, he better hang on, because a fresh wave hit me, hard, shaking my whole body. I didn't care anymore. I was going to cry all night if I wanted, or even if I didn't want.

"Leah." He said my name like he was in physical pain.

Missy appeared as a blur through my tears.

"See? She's broken. You probably broke her. She's my friend, so you better fix her," Missy said, nearly screaming.

Kade jerked at the sound of her voice, as if he hadn't realized she'd entered. "I *didn't* break her. She's tough and she's not broken," he said.

"Look at her. She's *broken*," Missy said, pointing at me.

"Well, she's definitely not right," Elijah said, also walking into my shed. "I'm willing to give the benefit of the doubt that it wasn't you, but you definitely didn't help things."

Missy was heading toward me, but Kade cut her off. "You can both go. I'll handle this."

Missy looked over his shoulder at me. For some reason the concern in her eyes lit off an even harsher round of sobs.

"Out," Kade yelled.

"You better fix her!" Missy glared at him before she turned and left.

"Yeah, this isn't good," Elijah said, sounding as if he were lecturing Kade before walking out behind Missy.

"Just get out," Kade said, then shut and locked the door after them before drawing the shade on the window.

He turned to me. "Did something happen? I mean more than what I know about?"

Wasn't that enough? "Just get out!" I managed to say in between sobs.

He stood there as if trying to determine his next

move. I continued to crumble and couldn't seem to stop it.

Kade took a look around and then settled his eyes on me. "It's freezing. You can't stay here."

"Just *leave*."

"No." It was surprising he could get a word out with the way his body seemed to be locking up.

I readjusted the comforter around me, wishing I could throw it over my head and hide from the entire world. My nerves had been frayed since this whole ordeal started, and his presence here right now felt like the final blow that cracked my shell wide open. I'd always been raw around him, but now it was hard to breathe and I was too shattered after hearing about losing my home to keep it together any longer.

He looked around the room and muttered something about this place being a problem, as if he was just discovering it.

"You're moving to the house. You can't stay here anymore," he said.

"Moving? What do you mean, moving?" That word sounded a lot more definitive than staying a night. I inched back onto my cot. "I'm not moving to the house." What if this meltdown situation was going to be a new thing of mine? Where would I go hide and cry then? Clearly my body was becoming unpredictable.

"Why? You're showering there anyway. What's the difference? It'll be easier than bringing a bag up."

There? In his lair? Every night? Just the two of us under the same roof? Or worse, the three of us when he decided to have company? No way. Absolutely *no way* was I putting myself through that.

"I shower at Missy's now, and I'm not moving to the

house." It was hard to sound assertive with all these damn tears still flowing and hiccups accenting my sentences.

"This isn't open for debate. You can't sleep here. It's freezing, and..." He was watching me fall apart as he said, "You just can't."

"I'll move into the bunkhouse until the heat is fixed."

He locked eyes with me. "The bunkhouse is already tight."

Had he always been this highhanded and bossy? Had none of my memories of him been accurate? "I'll sleep on the couch. I don't even need a bunk. I won't be putting anyone out."

He didn't budge from his spot. I wasn't sure how I'd get him out of here, especially in my current state of hysteria.

"What is your issue with staying at the house?" he said.

"You made it very clear I wasn't supposed to ever set foot in your home. Why would I want to *live* there?" He couldn't be this dense, could he? Sometimes it felt like we were living in alternate universes and only meeting for these rare conversations where none of our experiences seemed to match up.

He shook his head. "It's freezing in here. You can't stay in this place, but you never change. You are as stubborn as you always were. You'll keep digging even when it's your own grave."

"Don't act like you know me or care about me." How dare he tell me what I did or didn't do?

"Except I do, and you can't stay here."

"I'm not going to the house." I got to my feet, getting

ready to go toe to toe with him, but I tripped on the corner of my comforter and went sprawling.

But I didn't hit the ground, as he lifted me off my feet.

"Don't you dare bring me up there."

He didn't so much as pause as he walked out the door and started heading to the house. I was torn between screaming or trying to keep my head buried in the blanket. As it was, I was all tangled up in the comforter.

He made it over to the main house in record time, the heat hitting me as we walked in. He walked across the room and dropped me onto the couch.

I would've gotten to my feet immediately, but I had some detangling to do first as I got to my feet.

He blocked my view. "Don't even think about it. In no world am I letting you freeze to death out of stubbornness," he said.

We were only inches apart. Sometimes I forgot how tall and muscular he was until we were right next to each other. He was still as fit as ever, maybe even more so. I used to love finding every excuse I could to be in those arms. They'd been my safe place. When I was with him, it felt like nothing could ever touch me.

Now he was the one rubbing me raw. Being this close to him made me want to run fast and hard, because he was the most dangerous thing in my world. Nothing could hurt me the way he did.

I sat, just to avoid more touching. At least the crying seemed to be easing up.

"You can take the bedroom attached to the bathroom you use."

I watched as he walked into the kitchen and eyed the door. There was no way he wouldn't follow me out, and where was I going to go? I couldn't leave this ranch anyway.

A few minutes later he put a cup of tea in my hands. There was no milk and just a touch of honey. He remembered how I took my tea. It wasn't a big deal. He had a good memory, was all. He always had.

"Now I want to know what your problem is with staying here?" he said as he took a seat on the opposite end of the couch. "Forget what I said before about your coming in the house. I didn't mean it. I *want* you to stay here."

My problem wasn't just that he'd insulted me. His demanding I stay here now sort of eased that hurt, but there were other issues. There was no way around it. He wasn't going to let me leave unless I made my objections clear, no matter how uncomfortable this situation was going to be.

"Everyone is going to talk. They'll think something is going on between us if I stay here."

"The heat is broken and everyone knows that. What about that situation is going to make anyone think that we're doing anything?"

"At first it'll be fine, but that will change if I stay here too long." People always talked. That was life, and I had too much on the line for that kind of talk to happen.

"If things get weird we can discuss it then. Does that fix that?"

I didn't say anything. Not because I didn't want to, but this next problem was too embarrassing to just spit out. It shouldn't have been, but it was.

"What? Just say it." He laid an arm along the back of the couch and angled his body toward me, waiting for answers.

"What about the next time Melissa visits? You'll need your privacy, and the whole situation will be too awkward." It was bad enough having to hear her last time. I couldn't imagine being stuck under the same roof with her for more than a few minutes.

"Melissa won't be coming back."

"You say that now."

"She's *not* coming back. It wasn't working out for us."

For them or for *him*? I'd seen her grabbing on to him like a lifeboat in a stormy sea. No way she'd willingly jumped off that boat. So what had happened? Had he realized how horribly bitchy she was, or was that just a quality that came out for my sake? Either way, it didn't bode well for his taste in women.

"Melissa might be gone, but what about the next one? And the one after that?"

"I won't bring them here."

There was no way that he'd be able to hold to that agreement. No. Way. Why would he possibly do that for me?

My stare must've said it all, because his next words were, "Can we at least call a truce for tonight? I'm tired of us hurting each other, especially when you're already... not good."

I looked down at my hands. "I'm not bad. I was just having a moment." One that I hoped didn't come back, because it had been horrific. There was no sugarcoating the meltdown I'd just had.

He didn't argue with me, but he reached forward, dragging me into his side and then tucking my head under his chin. He wrapped his arms around me, and damned if I didn't let him.

"For tonight, let's just pretend we don't hate each other, okay?"

"Fine, but don't start accusing me of blowing up your loan, and you aren't allowed to use this against me tomorrow," I said.

"I won't. I promise. I swear on everything I hold dear."

That promise was the final blow to my wall. I stopped resisting and leaned into him the way I used to when we were both younger and nicer.

CHAPTER 24

Kade

LEAH HAD FALLEN ASLEEP AGAINST ME ON THE COUCH. NOW I could barely sleep knowing she was down the hall, already rethinking this idea. I'd fought too hard for her to stay to make some other arrangement now. It was done, for better or worse. When she wasn't here I still thought about her, so what was the difference?

It was just before six and it didn't seem there'd be any more sleep on the horizon. I got up and headed into the main living area, where the smell of coffee hit me like a siren's song.

It wasn't even dawn, but Leah had always been an early riser, probably made worse by staying here on the ranch.

I grabbed a coffee and my attention was drawn to motion on the front porch. She was on the swing in the soft light of predawn.

I was drawn out the door by her presence and moved

to stand in front of the swing. I looked at the empty side of the seat, and she tilted her head in invitation. I settled onto it and she tucked up her toes under the blanket. I took over rocking as if this were something we'd been doing for years. I definitely needed to watch getting too at ease. It was strange how quickly a habit could form, and that could lead places I couldn't go, or at least shouldn't go.

"I'm glad you kept this swing," she said.

"I'm surprised you recognized it." It had been sanded down and repainted since she'd sat on the porch of the old ranch.

"How could I not?" She ran a finger over a knot that marred the third board.

She had always paid attention to every little detail. Every little change in someone's mood. It had always amazed me how she took in every single thing around her. I'd never been surprised that she'd been successful in life after she left here.

Which was why it was so confusing that she'd taken that painting. She hadn't needed it. She'd been a rock star in her field. All the biggest brands had been trying to hire her. Nothing about this situation made any sense.

She glanced over at me, and I tried to wipe the thought from my mind, afraid I'd give away some detail of where my mind had gone.

"You always such an early riser?" I asked.

"You already know the answer to that."

"I just figured that living in a big city might've changed you."

"You mean like I'd be up all night partying and sleeping all day?"

"Isn't that what you city folk do?" I asked, smiling.

"The only time I stayed up late was to work." She pulled a knee up to her chest, wrapping her arms around it. "About yesterday, I didn't... I don't know what that was exactly, but—"

"Nothing happened yesterday but your heat breaking."

She didn't move for a second and then gave me the slightest nod. She dropped her head, running a hand over the arm of the swing. "This is very belated, but I'm sorry I missed your father's funeral."

I jerked my head so fast in her direction that I could've given myself whiplash. It was the last thing I'd expected to hear from her. If my shock showed, she didn't seem to notice.

"I didn't expect you to come." Her eyes flickered and her mouth turned down a little. By the time my father passed, we'd stopped talking. "You were in New York," I added, trying to soften my slip.

Everyone had liked him. He was that kind of guy. Maybe a bit rough in looks and manners, but gold where it counted. I still ached when I thought of him, even now, and probably always would.

"He was a kind man. I *wanted* to be there for him. To say goodbye." She gripped her coffee mug tight in her hands.

There was something about the way she said *wanted* that made me wonder exactly what had stopped her. It sounded a little like it hadn't just been geography. But we were once again in a place of peace, and I desperately didn't want to fight with her right now. It was wearing me down, exhausting me and keeping me awake at night. It felt like being at odds with her was ripping apart my very being.

"You were good to him in life. He knew you cared for him. That matters more than anything else you could've done after he passed away," I said.

When my father had started getting really bad at the end and had a hard time getting around, she used to bake baskets of muffins for him and bring them by at least once a week. When he got so bad he'd had a hard time even getting out of bed, she'd bring him a chessboard or cards and play with him for hours.

I'd been working the ranch from dawn to dusk a lot of those days, trying to keep the bills paid, and that help had meant the world to me.

And then one comment from the banker that had echoed what I'd said to her, and I'd turned on her without any real proof. The longer the situation sat with me, the more it felt like I was sitting on a bed of nails.

What if it had all been a plant from an ill-intentioned asshole of a stepfather? What if she had repeated my words in passing to Monroe, and her stepfather Edwin had heard them? Should I really have crucified her? I'd dwelled for so long on the bad, held on to that part of her for so long, that these buried good memories were like little shocks to the system as they fought their way to the surface.

"I'm sorry. I didn't mean to bring up a sensitive topic in an effort to make myself feel better." She stared at me, reading the concern, if not the actual cause.

"It's not you. I think of him every day whether he's mentioned or not, especially on mornings like this. He loved sitting here and watching the sunrise."

"I remember." She was still trailing her fingers over the wood of the armrest and gazing out at the sky.

There had been mornings I'd be getting up to work

and she'd already be out on the porch with my father. Sometimes she was here so much that it seemed like she'd moved in. I used to wonder what it had been like over at her house that she was always coming here, as if sitting with one dying man and one overworked kid had been preferable. There were so many memories now that I let myself think on them. I was starting to feel like I'd had self-inflicted amnesia.

The silence settled in again.

I let it drag out a few more minutes before I said, "I was thinking about inviting your parents and brother here for a weekend. Monroe has been worried about you. I'm sure it would make your mother feel better if you all got together."

The hand that had been absently rubbing the wood stopped, and her eyes shifted to me and then away, as if she were trying to hide whatever emotion lay behind them.

"Why would you do that?" she asked. "It seems like a lot of trouble for you."

"I was just thinking it might be nice for your mother to come out. It's got to be hard for her, and I still care for the woman. Of course, I'm sure you'll want to see both of them, and it'll be easier on your mother to have your stepfather to travel with."

She stiffened when I mentioned her stepfather, and I had to sit calmly, forcing my hands not to curl into fists.

She shook her head. "That's not a good idea. She hates flying and she'd feel compelled to say yes if you ask. I really wouldn't do that."

"I'll just put out a soft invite, no pressure," I said.

It wasn't her mother I was trying to pressure, after all. Feeling like I was in the dark, that there might be so much more going on with her situation than I knew, was becoming intolerable.

"No." She got to her feet. "I don't think it's a good idea. She'll feel compelled to come if you offer."

"I think—"

She spun. "It's my family. It should be my call, and I'm saying no."

She turned and walked back into the house.

So much for keeping the peace. I felt like the asshole everyone else thought I was for pushing her for a reaction.

I didn't follow her right away, mostly because I was barely keeping myself calm. She hadn't seemed to notice. She was too riled to see that I was right at the edge with her. What had happened with her stepfather? How could the world think so highly of him, and yet he was involved in this dark underbelly no one knew of? What else did no one know?

It was becoming clearer that Leah might know, though. I wanted to ask her, wanted to grab her and force her to tell me everything, but she wouldn't. She'd trusted me once, but that was so many years ago, and so much had gone on between then and now that it might as well have never been. I'd obliterated any residue of trust since she got here.

Please, don't let me have misjudged her. If I found out I'd piled on when she needed me...

A few more minutes passed before I followed her inside. By then she was sitting on the couch, tugging on her boots, her hands looking steadier, the emotions in her eyes shuttered and locked away.

"I don't care if you're mad. I'm not changing my mind, and it's my call," she said.

Okay, maybe she had been reading my temperature. She was simply wrong about what had triggered it. I had to calm down. The last thing I'd meant to do was get her upset. I probably shouldn't have pushed at all. But this was Leah, and I'd never been able to leave things alone when it came to her. Never.

"It's your choice. I'll let it go. I'm just distracted about some other business. One of the suppliers is trying to overcharge me. Has nothing to do with you."

She nodded, her spine relaxing, and I could visibly see the pressure that had built being released from her shoulders.

All I wanted to do was hug her, ask her what had happened, but I couldn't.

She glanced my way a few times as she got to her feet. "It's getting late. I need to go get changed and start work," she said, before turning as if to leave.

"Your stuff was moved into the closets in the bedroom you slept in last night. I moved it while you were sleeping."

Her lips parted, and it looked as if she were going to say something. Then she nodded and turned to walk down the hall instead.

My phone buzzed on the counter.

ACCOUNTANT: IT'S DONE. NO IDEA WHY YOU WOULD WANT TO *do this, but it's your money to throw away.*

I'D JUST FINISHED READING THAT MESSAGE WHEN I GOT ANOTHER one.

• • •

Monroe: One of your contacts came through. I can't believe that they're willing to take on the loan for no percentage. They said they make something, but I don't understand how. Either way, thank you. I can't wait to tell Leah.

Nope, I'd be making nothing, but I was glad my man hadn't told him that.

"Before you start work, you need to call Monroe. He said he's got news," I said to Leah as she walked back into the living room.

She looked up, her eyes widening. Her chest began to rise and fall faster.

"I think it's good," I said.

She turned and headed into the office. She didn't shut the door behind her, probably figuring I'd follow. I didn't. I already knew what the conversation would be.

CHAPTER 25

Leah

I sat down to call Monroe, running through the worst-case scenario in my mind. This was about the fiftieth time since he'd initially told me I was probably going to lose my home. One more mental go-around wouldn't hurt if it kept me from having an epic meltdown like yesterday.

I still wasn't sure how I'd meet anyone's eye today. I didn't cry, and now I'd be known as the ranch crybaby. Not only was I a felon, I was a bawling one. That thought alone might've set off another wave, except I didn't have a tear left in me. I was probably dehydrated after yesterday.

I dialed Monroe's number before I chickened out, like literally went to tend the chickens and let them out in a last-ditch excuse to not hear the bad news.

"Hey! I've got—"

I cut him off immediately. "Look, before you say anything, I want you to know that I appreciate everything you did to try to save my apartment. I know if you could've, you would've. I'm okay with it."

"Leah—"

"I just want you to know that. It's okay. I'll rebuild and I'll get another one."

"*Leah*, you're not losing your apartment."

I sat still for a second. "I'm not? How is that possible?"

"Tiffany had a few connections—"

"Oh no, Monroe." I groaned. This had been the last thing I wanted. "I told you I didn't want you to do that. I don't want you to ever put your marriage in a strained situation for me. My mortgage is too much to ask that of her." I covered my face with my hand, wondering how many lives this situation was going to wreck.

"It's not strained because I didn't ask. It was offered by a distant relation. It's not a gift. We're going to pay it back and they'll make something on it. It's a win for them too."

"Who is it?" I asked, trying not to sound too skeptical in the light of his happy tone.

"Tiffany's third cousin."

"Who? Have I ever met them?" I didn't think Tiffany even had a third cousin she was close to.

"No. But they do deals like this all the time. It's already done. I signed the paperwork last night. It was our best and only option, so I leapt at the opportunity."

It was so strange to have given up my power of attorney and be informed after the fact that I had a new mortgage, especially when something didn't feel right. Was I getting charged loan shark numbers?

"Did you read the paperwork over before you signed? Made sure there was nothing weird?" My brother had never been great with numbers, but he would've known better than to sign for some crazy interest rate. I hoped, anyway.

"Yes, and it's all good. I didn't sign over your second born, only your first."

He laughed while I was still trying to figure out the catch.

"I'm glad you have a sense of humor about this, since mine is circling the drain."

"I have no problem picking up the slack for my incarcerated sister."

"What's the interest rate?" I asked. There was a problem here somewhere. I knew it.

"Uhm..."

"You don't know the interest?" I said. That should've been the first number he had in his head.

"I think it was five percent."

"Five?" No way. That was too low for someone in my predicament. How was that possible? "Are you sure?"

"I'll double-check, but I think so."

"Where is the paperwork? Can you look now?" New York hours were later, but he still must've just signed it. He'd probably done an electronic signature. My guess was that he only needed to open an email.

"I can't. I've got an appointment. I'll get around to it later."

"Monroe, this is—"

"Leah, love you, but I gotta go."

He hung up and I stared at the phone for a few minutes. This definitely fell into the good news category, so why did it feel like something was oh-so off?

Was I becoming too screwed up to be happy? I used to be able to be happy. I *needed* to just be happy.

I strolled back into the main living area, still trying to muddle through the fog of emotions.

Kade was leaned on the counter, watching me. "Everything okay?"

"Yeah. Thanks for letting me use your phone," I said. "Monroe seems to have figured out a way to fix my loan problem. I know he mentioned the issue I was having."

"I'm glad." He motioned to the table. "Sit."

I walked farther in to see there was food out on the table.

"Thank you, but I'm not hungry."

"You haven't been eating enough. You're losing weight." His gaze swept me from head to toe.

If I was losing weight, it wasn't from lack of food being available. It was because the stress seemed to be filling up my belly more than an eight-course meal.

"Really, I'm not hungry."

My stomach growled so loud that the sound filled the room. Yesterday my body had decided to cry all over the place and now it was broadcasting hunger. It was like it had decided that it didn't take orders from me anymore.

His eyes called me all sorts of names, but mostly Pinocchio.

"Fine, I'll have a quick bite, but I don't want to be late," I said.

I sat, and that was when I saw the stack of bacon on a slice of toast, covered in melted cheese. I hadn't eaten that in years, technically not since I'd been *here*. No way had he remembered that was my favorite. First the tea, and now this, like he'd kept notes or something. It had to have been an accident. Maybe he ate this every morning. Whatever the deal was, I couldn't build it into some mythical act of kindness.

Whatever it might've been, it was too hard to resist. I took a bite, and he filled my mug with coffee as I did.

"So when you get done tonight, you'll come here," he said. "There's nowhere else on the ranch for you to live, especially since I told the guys to bulldoze the shed this morning. After looking it over, I think it was a fire hazard."

I stopped eating and just stared. He was bulldozing my shed? What happened if I had another breakdown? I didn't even have a cold shed now. Shed life as I'd known it was officially over, and that alone was sending me into a bit of a panic.

I was going to eat and leave. I couldn't risk another breakdown, and my body was untrustworthy at the moment. It didn't help that Kade seemed to be more intent on watching me than eating his breakfast.

"Leah, I want you to know if there's something wrong, something more than what I'm seeing with your current situation, you can tell me. I'll help you any way I can."

He was staring at me with a straight face, as if he believed what he was saying wholeheartedly.

It was like a gift from the fates, exactly what I needed to shore that wall back up nice and strong.

The last time I had really been looking for someone, anyone to help me, I hadn't been able to get more than a few words out before he shut me down.

"I can always call you?" I said. "If I remember correctly, that's what you had said to me before I left here ten years ago, and I remember how that went. I think I'll pass on the offer. It's easier than counting on you." The hurt of that day still ran deeper than I could handle thinking about at this moment. No matter how many times I'd tried to forget, tried to get past it, I'd never been able to. His cutting me off, his words short and cold. It had been like getting freezer burn on my heart, and it had left one hell of a scar.

"When did you ever call me for help that I turned you down?" He froze, his face contorting as if he were trying to piece together what I was talking about.

He didn't even remember.

It dragged me back into reality, the one where Kade didn't even care enough to remember crushing me.

I shouldn't have even brought it up. What was the point? Clearly it hadn't been a blip on his radar.

"Forget it. I never called you. My mistake." I tossed down my napkin, getting up from the table.

"Leah, when?" His voice was soft, almost like the way he used to talk to me, back when I thought he'd cared.

"Leah?" Missy's voice rang out as she appeared at the door, breaking the moment before it could swallow me whole.

"I have to go. I have things to do." If he couldn't remember, I wasn't going to tell him. This had been reminder enough for me why I couldn't trust him.

CHAPTER 26

Kade

I SHOULDN'T HAVE LET LEAH WALK AWAY WITHOUT ANSWERING this morning. Now all I could think of was that conversation. She'd reached out to me for help and felt rejected? I never in a million years would've done that to her. Not her. Not if she'd needed me. But the pain I saw in her eyes had been as real as anything I'd ever seen. She wasn't making this up as a taunt.

When she walked in tonight, she'd barely looked at me. So much for the truce.

My phone buzzed where it was sitting on the kitchen counter, John's name flashing. The sound of the shower was still going, but there was no way I'd risk taking this call with her in the house. I grabbed it and headed outside. I grabbed a beer, too. Considering what I might hear, I had to be prepared.

I popped the beer and took a gulp before I called him back, walking out toward my truck.

"What do you have?" I asked.

He let out a sigh. "I heard something concerning."

"What?" I asked. I took another gulp, waiting for details that seemed slow to come. I didn't typically have to pull information out of John. He wasn't this dramatic.

"I'm hearing some rumblings and just want to check in that you aren't being mean to the princess."

I checked the name on the phone again. Had he really asked me that?

"Huh?" It was the best response I could muster.

"I heard you're not being nice to her," he said, his normally gruff tone sounding way off.

"Not that it's any of your business, but I'm not being mean to her. Where did you hear otherwise?" Did no one mind their own business anymore? They didn't know our past or what was really going on.

"You told me to dig around. Stuff gets leaked. Occupational hazard that there might be some gossip flowing. I *have* to let people talk."

"I'm not being mean to her. There were certain situations that had to be taken care of, but at no point was I out of line." Everything I'd done had been warranted, and fuck anyone who said differently.

"Don't take this the wrong way, but you're sounding a little defensive. Perhaps there's a thread of truth in those rumors?" His voice was creeping higher, almost into lecture territory.

Who the hell was this man becoming? "Don't you break legs for a living?" Someone needed to remind him, because he'd clearly forgotten what he was.

"I'm only suggesting that you might be too hard on her and you should think about your actions."

"Did you have any actual updates, or did you call to annoy the fuck out of me?"

"Her dog died a few months ago," he continued. "He was a senior no one wanted that she adopted from the same shelter she volunteers at."

Obviously I didn't know that, not that it surprised me. It was such a Leah thing to do, or at least the Leah I'd known. She'd been constantly tending to some old or hurt furry thing she found.

"Anything beyond dogs?" I asked.

"I think she had a really rough time after she left Montana."

"Why do you say that?" She'd moved from a house that was falling down around them to New York with a well-off stepfather. There might be rumblings of his being a bastard, but nothing was confirmed yet.

"No one who has a happy home life is excited to go to a boarding school, especially when it's states away and hard to visit your family."

"Boarding school?" I leaned on the back of my truck. "Why do you say she was excited to go there?" I hadn't even known she'd gone to boarding school after she left here.

"I accessed the reports, internal and external. Hang on a second." There was the sound of shuffling papers. "It says here, 'We find her transition to be one of the smoothest we've seen. Although she doesn't seem to have made any real friendships yet, she seems very content.' That was from one report."

"Obviously they're going to say that to her parents," I said.

"Listen to this one from internal notes. 'Quiet and reserved, but seeming less jumpy and more relaxed as each day goes by.' That was from one of her first teachers there."

Less jumpy? Leah wasn't one of those jumpy people. Never had been. If I wasn't sure that John knew his shit, there was no way I'd believe we were talking about the same person. Although up until a couple of days ago, I hadn't seen her cry either.

When I didn't speak for a minute, he continued. "I'm just saying, I think she had a tough time, and I'd feel really bad if you were mean."

Fuck. When did I become the villain in this story?

"Look, I'll try to make sure I'm more sensitive." I'd already been doing more than that, but I wasn't telling him. "I want a copy of all the information you've gotten so far. I want to read all those reports."

"Already being sent over."

"Is there anything else?" I took another long swallow of beer.

"Yeah. I'm following up a lead on a warehouse the stepfather owns under a fake corporation. The setup smells to high heaven. My gut is saying this is all going to come back to him, but I don't have anything concrete yet. I'll be in touch soon, though."

Dammit.

I hung up, went back into the house, and poured a whiskey. A beer wasn't going to cut it today. I headed back out onto the porch, too afraid of what I'd say to Leah if I saw her right now.

Chuck, who had been heading over to his truck, detoured my way.

He glanced at my glass. "You're drinking a lot lately. I've never seen you drink this much, and I've known you for a long time."

"Well, this is my moment." I raised my glass to him, not caring if he thought I was becoming an alcoholic. Tonight, I needed to drink.

"You want to talk about it?" he asked, fixing his hat.

"Not really."

"We all screw up."

"Who says I screwed up?" For someone who was complaining about my drinking, he was sure pushing me in the direction of another shot.

He leaned a shoulder against the porch post. "If you did screw up, it's easier to apologize."

"If I *did* screw up, it's too big for an apology." How could I fix turning my back on someone that needed me and then piling on when the world was beating them down?

"I don't think so. She's got a soft spot for you a mile wide. I think you can fix it."

"Chuck, if I fucked up, this was a really bad one." And that soft spot he imagined didn't exist. That woman had a cement wall up between us that was at least a mile thick.

"First thing you need to do is stop digging," he said. He nodded at me as he headed off.

He had no idea how deep this hole already was.

I WAS LYING IN BED, REPLAYING EVERYTHING IN MY HEAD, FROM John's call to the last time I'd spoken to Leah, and that was when it hit me. I'd been so wrapped up in my situation, I hadn't even realized why she'd called.

I'd been walking out of the bank, the ninth one I'd tried, and finally secured enough financing to get by at an interest rate that was almost as high as my age at the time. I hadn't had a choice, though. It had been just enough to keep everything going, and I'd been stressed to the gills. Then she'd called, her name flashing on my phone.

She'd barely said hello, her voice shaky and uneven, when I cut her off, telling her I was too busy to be bothered with whatever frivolous thing she wanted to complain about. At the time, I'd thought it had been nervous guilt over screwing me, but she hadn't even known.

At that moment, I'd locked her out of my heart. I couldn't handle having her in my thoughts anymore, and I'd cut her off mentally at that moment.

My chest felt tight, as if someone had a stranglehold on my throat. The craziest part of it was that all I wanted in the world right now was for her to open up to me. But she wouldn't, and I couldn't make her.

It was ten years too late to make that moment right, and yet I didn't think I could go a day longer. It was only ten. She'd still be awake. If she wasn't, she was just barely sleeping, and that didn't count.

I got up and walked over to her room, determined to get an answer. I should leave Leah be, and yet I couldn't.

I didn't knock because she'd only get up and lock the door if I did, not that I blamed her at the moment.

She was in bed but wide awake, and looking as happy to see me as she had been earlier.

"We need to talk," I said.

"I'm not talking. I'm sleeping and you need to learn to knock." She rolled over, giving me her back.

"Leah," I said, one last time, hoping she'd give me a minute.

"What?" she said, sounding exhausted as she rolled back so she could face me.

"I'm sorry. I shouldn't have shut you down like that."

There was a flitter of shock in her expression before she shuttered her emotions away again. She gave me a quick nod and then shrugged.

"It's fine. It was a long time ago." She rolled over again, making it clear she wanted me to leave.

It wasn't much, but it was something. It was a start.

CHAPTER 27

Leah

IT WAS SUNDAY. AFTER SUCCESSFULLY AVOIDING KADE AS MUCH as possible for days, there was no way around it tonight. I had to make calls or Cassie might kill me, and I couldn't trust my mother not to reach out to Kade and get herself an invite here.

Kade was in the kitchen, leaning on the counter, when I walked into the house, his dark hair gleaming and his skin glowing as the place was filled with the scent of him. It was bad before, but now he was being *nice*.

"I'm going to go hop in the shower really quick before I make my calls, okay?" I said.

"Sure. Are you hungry? I've got some steaks I can throw on."

He pointed to the fridge, the muscles on his arms flexing even with that small movement. It was like life was just trying to screw with me now.

"I grabbed something at the bunkhouse already, but

195

thanks." I'd been eating there every night before trying to sneak back in here and avoid eating with Kade. Why? Because this nice Kade was even more dangerous than asshole Kade.

He nodded, still watching me. We'd barely seen each other in days, said only a handful of words, and yet there was this strange shift in our energy that was impossible to ignore. If someone asked me what it was, there wasn't any clear way to describe it. It was almost like we'd stumbled upon a well-worn pathway into a forest but only taken a step or two on the trail, not sure what lay within those woods.

I came out a half an hour later to a mug sitting on the counter, while he sipped his own.

"I made you some tea," he said.

"Oh, thanks." Did I mention it was like we were both wearing ill-fitting shoes as we took those first couple steps? Like mine were two sizes too big and his were pinching his feet.

I took the peace offering, or whatever it was. In no universe was this just a bag of leaves steeped in hot water.

I took a step toward the office. He nodded, following me.

My first call was to my mother; I figured I'd get the worst over with. I was handed a small miracle when she said she was at a function and couldn't talk.

Monroe was the second call, and short and sweet. He couldn't get off the phone fast enough, dodging my questions about the new loan. As long as he managed to hold on to the place, I'd worry about the details after this whole ordeal was over. If it came down to selling a kidney, I'd deal with it then.

The door to the office was open, but Kade had been drifting in and out, instead of hovering the way he normally did.

I dialed Cassie as he walked out again.

"I don't have a venue," she answered, immediately launching into utter panic. "Not only do I not have my maid of honor, I don't have a place to get married!"

"What happened to the venue in Aruba?" At least, I thought that was what she had said. I couldn't remember all the rambling bits of information anymore.

"There was a storm, or a tsunami, or some crazy shit. I don't know what the hell happened, but the whole place was flooded out and now my life is ruined!" Her voice was quickly escalating into a screech.

"Have your wedding here," Kade said, having snuck back into the office when I was distracted by Cassie melting down worse than an overcooked s'more.

"What's your place look like?" Cassie asked before I could get my wits about me. "Never mind, I'm looking it up," she said. The sound of typing proved she was already busy doing just that.

"This is not a wedding venue," I said, not liking where this was going.

"Not currently, but I've held some events in the past." Kade leaned against one of his cabinets and shrugged.

"I don't think that's a good idea," I said.

"How much to use your property, Kade?" Cassie asked.

This was spinning out of control way too fast. "Wait, I don't—"

"Free," he answered.

"Sold!" Cassie squealed. "You know what this means, Leah? You are officially back as my maid of honor!"

Oh no, this was not happening. *No.* Absolutely not.

"Cassie, how are we going to have a wedding here in less than a week? It's freezing and there's no place indoors large enough to hold it." There, that should quash this nonsense. What were these crazy people thinking?

"We can set up a large tent and heat it," Kade offered, his voice smooth and even. "I've done it before."

"I love it!" Cassie let out a little scream. "We could have a mountain backdrop from what I'm looking at! It sounds like the most beautiful thing ever!"

I felt like a tidal wave was sweeping me up along with them in this crazy plan.

No. No, no, no. This was *not* happening. "But we're out here in Montana. All your guests are in New York."

"It was a destination wedding anyway. It's a different destination now. We just have to change the flights," Cassie said, as if that were the most ridiculous objection yet. "I have to go. So many things to work out. Oh wait— Kade, I'll have to call you as I work out details. I'll need your cell phone so we can arrange things."

Kade looked like he'd just gotten shot in the gut with a round of rubber bullets. Finally someone else was looking as shell-shocked as me.

"Yeah, just text me and I'll have Leah call you back, and you two can handle it when you need things."

Oh, yeah, wonderful. He offers and then dumps it back on me again.

"That's great. We can handle it. I'll call you back, Leah. I've got lots of arrangements to work out fast."

"Cassie?" There was no reply. "Cassie!"

She'd already hung up. She was probably calling her mother, calling *everyone*, and then they'd all be showing up here, to see the felon in her natural habitat. My chest was starting to tighten up, the way it had before the last meltdown, and I didn't even have a shed to go hide in.

"I can't believe you did that," I said to Kade, shaking my head as I made my way to the door.

"What are you talking about? She needed a place and I was trying to help."

"Any chance to humiliate me and you take it."

"What are you talking about?" He reached for me, and I pulled my arm away before he could touch me.

"Just leave me alone," I said, running out the door.

"Leah, I really—"

"I need a minute. Please."

I THREW A ROCK INTO THE STREAM AN HOUR LATER, NOT looking up to where Kade appeared on the bank.

"How'd you find me?" It was dark out. I'd thought it would be a little harder.

"The barn was empty."

I used to hide in the old barn every time I was upset. It seemed I was as predictable as the sun rising. I wish I could say the same for him. If anyone tried to set their watch by him, the world would spin into chaos. One second he was trying to banish me to the dark ages, exiling me to shed life, with no plumbing and sketchy heat, and now he was insisting I live in the bedroom near his and hosting my best friend's wedding.

The wedding offer had seemed like a way to parade me around in humiliation, but he might've been trying to be nice. Why, I didn't know, but we were dealing with *Nice Kade* now. It was also the worst favor he could've done me, which suited pretty well, considering it was him.

He walked closer and took a seat just out of arm's length. He must've known I'd try to shove him in the freezing water and drowned him if I could've reached.

He took off his jacket and held it out to me. I'd been too busy running out of there to bother with something as silly as a coat.

"I'm fine," I said.

He kept his arm out.

"Fine," I said, throwing it over my shoulders.

"Are you upset with me?" he asked.

"What tipped you off? My running out of the office or my hiding by a stream in order to avoid you at the ranch?"

"Hiding? You did come to a spot that *you* knew *I* knew."

"I did not. If I'd thought you'd find me here, I would've gone somewhere else."

He tossed a stone into the creek. "Ten years ago, a couple weeks before you moved away, we sat in this very spot together."

How had he remembered that? Even I hadn't remembered, and I'd logged every moment we had together in some secret notebook in my mind.

"Thanks for the heads-up. I'll never make that mistake again," I said, but the heat was sucked out of my voice, and it wasn't just from the cold.

"Should've known better. Now you're stuck with me," he said. "You know, you used to like talking to me when you were upset."

"I can't imagine what changed that."

He didn't reply, and we fell into silence for a few minutes.

I tried to ignore his presence but couldn't stop my gaze from darting to him. I'd force it away, only to have the same battle a few seconds later.

I saw his head dip for a second before he looked back toward the ranch, as if he were battling whether he should give me space.

"Whatever you might think of me, I really didn't do this in an effort to embarrass you," he said. His tone was gruffer than normal, like it hurt to get the words out. As if vomiting razors would've been less painful.

I might've thought it was his intention to torture me when he first said it, but no one could fake this level of unease, which probably meant he was being sincere. That made it so much worse, since now the only person I could rage at was innocent of the crime. If we hadn't had such a rocky second start, if it had been *anyone* else offering to host the wedding, I'd have assumed it was with the best intentions from the get-go. But nothing between us was simple.

"Why do you still look pissed? Do you not believe me?" he asked.

I let out a long, pitiful sigh that would've made Eeyore jealous. "I do believe you. That's the problem. I'd been daydreaming how I'd go all scorched earth on you, how I'd ruin your life, and now I can't. It's hard when your dreams die." I laughed softly at the ridiculousness of what I'd said.

"Don't get too sad about it. I'm sure I'll do something horrific tomorrow. You can hate me for that instead and renew your plotting." He laughed.

"That is true. You are pretty good at being an asshole, so I really shouldn't give up *all* hope."

We were both laughing now.

"I mean, hell, you'll probably sleep with my best friend the night before her wedding and split the couple up." I found myself forcing the laughter to my own joke, as that one tasted a little too bitter. The easier he laughed, the worse it tasted.

"Actually, I could be a real asshole and rescind the invitation," he said, this time not laughing at all. "I'll tell Cassie that I forgot for a minute that I was an utter dick and I don't make those kinds of offers."

I turned to stare at him, gauging how serious he was. It might not seem like that big of an offer, but I knew Kade, or at least some version of him. He didn't like to take back his word once it was given.

"Really," he said. "I'll say I messed up and she can't do it here. I'll figure out some excuse."

"Thank you, but no. She's too happy. I can't take that from her." Even if I wanted to for my sake, as I thought of all the people who would show up here just to see my fall from grace.

The silence stretched out again, and this time instead of animosity, we were in this weird place, like we'd taken another step onto that well-worn path but were watching for signs of monsters about to jump out of the trees.

"If you want to do one thing for me, all I want is to have a truce of a sort, at least for the wedding. I can't handle..." The mass humiliation? The spectacle of it all? "It's just a lot to do and also be fighting with you."

"I thought you enjoyed fighting with me?" he teased.

He leaned back on his elbows, not an inch of fat to be

found on his stomach. Why did he have to be so damned attractive?

"Only on my off hours. So truce until after the wedding?"

"Deal." He smiled at me in a way that created something warm in my stomach.

"You sure you can manage that? I don't want to stretch your goodwill out so far that you sprain something."

"O ye of little faith. I'm a fast healer. I'll bounce back to my asshole ways fast enough."

He was still watching me, smiling, as if I'd agreed to something beyond a truce, and it was scaring the hell out of me.

CHAPTER 28

Leah

K<small>ADE WASN'T AWAKE YET, BUT THEN AGAIN, I'D EVEN BEATEN</small> the roosters up this morning. I walked into the kitchen and put on a pot of coffee. I might not have wanted to be at the main ranch, but there was no getting past the joy of having plumbing without putting on my boots.

I poured myself a cup before it was finished brewing and grabbed a throw blanket off the couch, then settled onto the swing on the front porch.

The sun hadn't made its way over the horizon but the sky was beginning to lighten, showing off the mountains in the distance. If nothing else, this was a beautiful place to get stuck.

I sipped my coffee, swinging back and forth with a single toe on the ground.

A few minutes later, the front door opened and Kade stepped out onto to the porch.

"Good coffee," he said, and then sipped from his mug. He looked at the swing. "Are you going to scream bloody murder if I sit there, or are we still firmly in truce mode?" he asked, his voice light and playful.

"I guess I can share."

"Technically, I'm the one who's sharing, since this is my usual morning spot." He sat down beside me and took over the rocking of the swing. I tucked my chilly toes under the blanket.

I didn't mean to stare, but as he sat there, sipping coffee in his worn-out jeans, there was something about the dark lock of hair falling forward and his deep-set eyes that made it hard *not* to stare at him.

"The view never gets old," he said, as the sun began to creep its way over the horizon.

I forced myself to focus on the mountains instead of him. "It's beautiful. Reminds me of one of those made-for-TV movies where everything wraps up in a perfect bow and ends with a grand gesture."

He gave me the side-eye and then scoffed.

"What? *You're* not into grand gestures? Who would've thought it?" I laughed softly.

"If a man did something lousy enough to need a grand gesture, it's time to cut bait and run," he said with confidence.

"Why do you say men?" I'd known plenty of women that could stand to use a few grand gestures.

"Because that's how ninety-nine percent of those movies end up. It's always the guy who screwed up and is begging for forgiveness."

I thought of the last ten I'd seen, and he did have a point, not that I'd give it to him. He was already too cynical.

206

"You don't have a romantic bone in your body. I can't imagine why Melissa stayed with you," I said.

He shook his head. "I think you're overselling what our situation was, which makes sense, considering you obviously like those mushy movies that are all sappy." He smirked as he drank his coffee, teasing me the way he used to.

"Well, I guess now I know why it was so easy to kick her out of your house for the foreseeable future. Did Melissa know that you weren't really together?"

"Of course. *I'm* not a liar."

Unlike me, at least according to everyone that read the news, and probably according to Kade as well.

I sipped my coffee, losing my interest in our conversation and trying to pay attention to anything but him, which was difficult when I could feel him staring at me.

"Don't do that," he said, his voice almost as soft as the early morning sky.

"I'm not doing anything," I said, trying to keep my tone as normal as possible.

"I wasn't implying that you were a liar," he said, his voice not only soft but husky in a way that made my toes curl.

"I didn't say you did. We're in truce mode, right?"

"Yes, truce mode, and there will be consequences for whoever breaks it first."

"I don't remember agreeing to that," I said.

"It was implied." The mischievous smirk on his face told me to avoid this conversation at all costs.

Nope, not going there. I needed to focus on how he obviously used and discarded women without a thought.

"She seemed nice enough," I said, grasping on anything I could find to kill the mood forming between us. And it was a major grasp. Nothing about that woman had seemed nice.

"Now you're really laying it on thick. No one thinks Melissa is nice, not even her mother."

At least he hadn't been blinded by the sex. That was something. "Why did you date her, then?"

He laughed. "Dating is a very nice term for what we did."

Yep, it was all about the sex.

"So I guess there'll be no grand gestures in that future?"

"No grand gestures." He stared ahead, as if pondering this question deeply. "If I believe in anything at all, it's the little things that happen day to day that mean everything. You do the right things, you don't need a grand gesture."

I watched the sunrise as his opinion settled in. He had a point.

The sound of crunching gravel drew our attention to a truck coming down the drive.

"You expecting something?" I asked.

"Not that I know of," he said.

The driver jumped down from the cabin and called out. "Hawk Ranch, right?"

"Yeah," Kade called back.

The guy went to the back of the truck and opened up a trailer packed to the gills.

"This a good place to unload?" the driver asked.

"Sure," Kade said. "How much of that is ours?"

"All of it," the driver yelled back.

"What the hell is this?" Kade mumbled, looking stumped.

"*This* is Cassie."

"Really?" he asked.

"You offered," I said, trying not to laugh.

IT HADN'T EVEN BEEN A FULL DAY SINCE KADE HAD OFFERED Cassie the ranch and everything was already in a complete upheaval. She'd had so many boxes delivered with wedding items that there wasn't even enough room to store them. Last I'd seen Kade, he was cursing as he tried to get them all moved into the tents he'd gotten brought over.

Along with wedding supplies were boxes filled with dresses from my mother, as if she imagined I'd wear a potato sack to the wedding if she didn't help me. Or help *her* was more accurate, as she was probably much more concerned about how she'd appear if I were a mess.

"You were looking for me?" Missy asked, poking her head in the open bedroom door.

"Yes. Come in and look at some of these dresses. My mother sent me a pile of them along with Cassie's wedding stuff. See if there's anything you want."

She froze where she was, eyeballing the pile like it was a snake pit. "I'm not sure I need a new dress."

"You don't want one for the wedding?"

She shook her head as she took a step back. "I'm not sure I'm going."

"To the wedding? I thought Kade told everyone they were invited? He said he was going to make sure you all knew this morning. Everyone who works on the ranch can come. Plus I'm the maid of honor, which means I've got some pull, and I *want* you to come. You've become one of my best friends."

"But your New York friends are really fancy, right?"

She was chewing on her lower lip like she hadn't eaten lunch.

"Most of them are a bunch of assholes. Don't worry about them." I started pulling some of the dresses from the pile, separating them out.

"I don't know, Leah. I'd be so out of place."

"You, out of place? *I* don't fit in. I'm a convicted felon. Everyone will *love* you. Plus I need you there with me." I studied her figure, thinking which dress might suit her the best. "Look, I've got these amazing dresses and they're all going to go to waste. Cassie said she was sending me something special, so I won't be wearing a single one, and I won't be going to any other affairs anytime soon."

She came a little closer, and then leaned in to look at a price tag. "Oh, I can't take one of these dresses from you. They cost a fortune!"

"You have to. It's crazy to let them all go to waste. I think this one would look amazing on you." I grabbed a deep green, holding it up to her. It made her hair glow.

"Leah, I just don't think..."

"Please, just try one or two on for me? It'll be fun." I shoved the green one into her hands and then piled a few more onto her arm, then pushed her toward the bathroom while she was still trying to figure out how to stop me.

I closed the bathroom door before she got her words back.

"Leah, I don't know if—"

"Just try them on! And I want to see each one after you do." I took a seat on the bed, waiting for her to walk out and give me a fashion show. After too much time had passed I called, "Missy?"

"I feel stupid."

"You've seen me covered in horse manure. You can't pull that card."

"*Fine.*"

She walked out in the green, and I was literally speechless. I'd known she had a good figure, but what she did for this dress? She looked so beautiful that I got goosebumps.

"I'm not going to make you try on any other dresses," I said.

She sagged in relief. "Thank you, because this is so not my thing. I'm so awkward in this it's painful." She patted the dress with her hands. "I'm afraid I'm ruining it just standing here in it."

I got to my feet. "Oh no. I'm not making you try on any of the others because you're wearing *that* one. You look *insane*. We just need to pick out shoes. I've got a box of those too." I began moving boxes, trying to find where those had gotten buried.

"Leah, come on! I feel like an idiot. I'm going to break out in hives!" She was following me around the room.

"But you look like a bombshell, and that's what counts. As far as the hives, we'll get you an antihistamine." I moved another box, finding the shoes.

"I just don't know."

I straightened and looked at her big eyes. Hopefully the universe would forgive me for what I said next. "You know, Alec will be coming."

Or he would be after I called him tonight.

"He will?"

"Yep."

"Well, what shoes do you think would look right?"

"I saw something just perfect." I tried not to smile like

a crazy cartoon character. Even if her crush worried me, I couldn't help wanting him to see her like this. I wanted the world to see her because she deserved to be seen.

CHAPTER 29

Kade

I walked into the kitchen and Leah was up on her tiptoes, stretching to reach for a glass. Her pajamas were one of those silky shorts and tank top combos that smoothed over her figure effortlessly.

I walked behind her, grabbing the glass and handing it to her, my body flush with hers for a second longer than was good for my mental wellbeing. Even the way she smelled nearly undid me, reminding me of cotton candy. I moved to a safe distance.

"Thanks," she said. "Did I wake you?"

"No. Not at all."

"Actually, I'm glad you're up. I need a favor."

"Sure." She was asking me for something? Had we finally turned a corner? I went to get a glass for myself so she couldn't see me smiling.

"Could you ask Alec to come to the wedding?"

Not the favor I was hoping she'd ask for. Did she have a thing for him? She had to. Why else? Was he holding out on me? I was going to punch him in the face when I saw him if he was.

"Kade? Is that okay?"

"Huh, yeah. I'm not sure if he'll come, but I'll ask. Does Cassie know him?"

"No. I just thought it might make Missy feel more comfortable."

I spun, going from a boiling rage to suspicion.

"They don't have a thing, do they? I'm not sure that's a good match."

"No, I don't either, but..." She threw her hands up. "I don't want to get into the details, but can you see what you can do?"

"Yeah, sure."

"Thank you. See you in the morning."

This was the first thing Leah had asked me for since she'd been here, and I'd be damned if Alec wasn't getting his ass here. I grabbed my phone as soon as I went back into the bedroom.

"You up?"

"Would it matter if I wasn't?" he asked. He sounded like he was wide awake.

"I need you to come out here for a wedding." It wouldn't hurt to have another set of eyes on Leah's stepfather.

"Will there be available women there?"

"It's a wedding. What do you think?"

"Okay, I guess I can make it. Text me the date and I'll add it to my schedule."

"Can you do me a favor, though, and not bang your way through the entire guest list?"

"Now you want two favors?" He groaned. "I won't touch the bride or Leah. It's the most I can promise."

"Fine. Just get here."

"Alec? What are you doing? I'm getting cold all alone," a female voice said in the background.

"I gotta go," he said, and hung up.

I tossed my phone to the side and remembered the last time Leah had looked up at me and asked for a favor.

Ten years ago

Leah was sitting up in the barn loft, waiting for me.

"You know that wood is half rotted," I said.

I walked until I was standing right below her and raised my arms. Sometimes I had a feeling she hung up there just to have me catch her.

She scooted off, dropping into my hold.

Normally I'd step back away from her, but she wrapped her arms around my neck, squeezing me tightly, as if she wanted to hold on to me like this forever.

"I'm leaving tomorrow," she whispered.

"It'll be better than you think. It's just different, is all." She'd been dreading this move more by the day, but she'd be okay. She had her mother and brother, and now a stepfather who seemed like a stand-up guy. She'd be okay.

I felt her nod, the movement barely perceptible, as if she were trying to convince herself more than me.

"You can always call me if you need me. I'll come. No matter what it is or where you are, I'll come."

"Kade? Can I ask you for one thing before I go?"

"You know you can."

I waited, but she didn't say anything right away. Her fingers twisted in the fabric of my shirt, like she were trying to gather the courage to speak.

"What is it? You can say anything to me. You know that."

She tilted her head back, staring at me with that strange intensity she had. "Will you kiss me?"

I tensed, but not because I didn't want to. I'd wanted to kiss her too much—that was the problem. But she was only sixteen. There might not be that many years between us, but there were more life experiences than I could explain. Nineteen to sixteen seemed like a lifetime at the moment.

She pulled away stiffly. "I'm sorry. I shouldn't have asked. I didn't mean to make you uncomfortable. I just wanted my first kiss to be from you. I didn't think it was that big of a deal for you since, well, it's not like it would be your *first or anything."*

I'd suspected she'd caught me fooling around in this very barn with Becky a couple of months ago. Now I was sure of it. I hoped that was the only one she'd caught me with.

"You aren't like other girls, and you're only sixteen." How the hell was I supposed to explain to her that I didn't want to just have sex with her?

"I just thought that, I don't know, the way you called me pretty... I thought you might want to," she said, her voice growing even softer.

She was killing me. My arms tensed around her, pulling her closer again.

"You're not just pretty. You're gorgeous."

She looked up at me, eyes so big and blue that it felt like I was holding spring in my arms. I couldn't look at her and not get lost in them, or the way they looked back at me. I'd tried to deny wanting her, but I wanted to be her first kiss more than she'd ever know. I wanted to be her first and last everything, but that wasn't meant to be. I was a nineteen-old nobody who was holding on to the family ranch by pure grit and force of will, and it probably wouldn't be enough. I had no future and she deserved a castle on a hill.

But one kiss wouldn't be the end of the world, would it?

I leaned my head down toward her and she licked her lips, instinctively understanding that I was taking her invitation. I pulled her snugger against me, and onto her tiptoes, until her body fit into mine from thigh to chest.

"Just a kiss," I said, my voice growing rough with strain as I reminded myself that that was all I'd take from her.

Her lips were soft as I grazed them. Her whole body was as she arched against me. The taste of her was so sweet, and her breath hitched as I pulled her even closer. The way she responded made it hard to keep it just *a kiss.*

She let out a small, helpless sound against my mouth, and I pulled back before this took on a life of its own and spiraled into something that wasn't so harmless.

She looked up at me, mouth parted and breathless, her fingers still threaded through my hair. Pulling away from her might end up being the hardest thing I'd ever do in my life. There was an ache that settled in my chest, making me fight to not kiss her again.

"I already miss you and I haven't even left," she whispered, dropping her head to my chest.

"Me too," I said.

"We're leaving in the morning, so I guess this is goodbye."

"Goodbye, Leah," I said as she pulled away from me. She walked out of the barn and I knew I'd never see her again.

. . .

AFTER THAT DAY, I'D MADE A DETERMINED EFFORT TO FORCE her out of my mind and my heart. I'd thought it had worked, at least somewhat. What a fool I'd been. She wasn't the type of woman you forgot about. She was the type who could take down an empire with a look.

CHAPTER 30

Leah

THE BLACK GARMENT BAG WAS HANGING OFF THE MANTEL IN THE living room while I plotted how it could accidentally catch fire. The grate was closed, and the logs weren't burning, but that wasn't a high hurdle. Just a few careless moments, and it would be gone.

Unfortunately, so would the small fortune Cassie had probably spent on it. I'd also have to be cautious not to burn down the ranch, which was possible, since I was new to arson.

Although there *was* a handy-dandy little fire extinguisher just a few steps away in the kitchen.

But no. It would be wrong. Very, very wrong.

Kade walked in the door and glanced at my face, then the bag.

"You planning on burying me in that bag or something? Because that look is usually reserved for me."

I jerked my attention to him. "No. That bag isn't big

219

enough for you. They sent the wrong one. You're off the hook."

"Ah, that's why you're mad."

He was staring at me with that flirty smirk of his, like we were in on something together.

"Don't look at me like that or I'll cut you up and squeeze you in somehow," I said, reminding myself that I couldn't let myself get pulled into his little flirtations. He was unreliable at the best and a real bastard when he was in a mood. I needed to stop joking around with him like this. It made our relationship feel too good.

"So what's in the bag that you're so angry at?"

There wasn't any point in not telling him. It wasn't like it would be a secret. He'd see it when I wore it. "If you must know, it's a dress from Cassie."

"The dreaded bridesmaid dress? Is it a confectioner's dream come true? All whipped frills and lace? Too many ruffles? Weird neck that chokes you?"

"No. It's none of those things. I mean, it's nice enough. It's just... It's, it's—*nice*." He kept staring at me, waiting for more details. "We really don't need to talk about this."

"Have to. I'm invested now."

"You're *invested*? In my dress?" I said, raising my eyebrows.

"Yes." Kade kept eyeing the bag, like he was hoping for x-ray vision.

"If you have to know, it's just a lot. She knows Greg is coming and so she wanted me to stand out in the most obvious ways."

"For *Greg*? She wants you to lure that asshole back in?"

"Why do you care if Greg is coming?" He was really

taking this truce, this fake-friend act, to the limits now. He was even getting more color in his face, as if truly insulted by the notion.

"*I* don't. But I'm stuck here, while he's off living life, and Cassie wanted me to look my best to stick it to him. The gesture and thought is appreciated, but I think this dress might be a little too much *sticking it to him* for me. What I care about is everyone on the ranch thinking I'm a hussy."

He walked over to the bag and unzipped it before I could stop him.

There it was. The Jessica Rabbit dress. Only difference was it was black instead of red.

"It's pretty," he said, like a man not used to looking at or caring about fashion. He ran a hand over the slightly shimmering fabric. "And shiny."

"Oh, it's shiny, all right. Wait until you see it on. I look like a desperado. I'm trying to figure out how to return it without pissing off the only friend I have left. It's not like I can spare any at this point. Being a criminal tends to alienate the more upstanding individuals in your circle." I walked over to the bag, zipping it back up.

"You're very likeable."

"I might've been, but not anymore. Do you realize what painting I got caught with? It was a historic master-piece stolen during World War II from a prominent Jewish family. That's not something you can bounce back from. It sort of sticks with you for life."

"How did you manage to get your hands on such an old and valuable painting like that?"

I stiffened for a split second before catching myself and falling into calm movements again. "It just fell into my lap."

It was one of the first times I'd openly discussed the painting with him, and his focus narrowed in. Kade's antenna went up way too fast and accurately. I felt like I'd just stepped out on a frozen lake on a sunny spring day.

"Come on, you have to give me more than that. It's not like you can get tried again."

"I'm sure you'll understand if I don't want to discuss it when I've got bigger issues coming, like looking like a hussy at this wedding."

"No one is going to think you're a hussy." He brushed a loose hair away from my cheek, tucking it behind my ear.

"What was that?" I asked.

"What?" he asked, shrugging. "You had hair about to go in your eye."

I wasn't going to fall for this man, not again. Last time I'd caught feelings for him he'd crushed them under his heel like a dirty cigarette butt.

"You don't have to lay the act on quite so thick," I said.

"What act?" There was pure innocence in his eyes.

"The nice act. I can't take it anymore. I'd rather you just be an asshole. It's easier."

"What if I don't want to be?" he asked, smirking.

"You'll get the urge again." I grabbed the tin of cookies that had come with the dress off the mantel. This was a day that definitely called for cookies.

"What do you have?" He tilted his head back, as if the butter in the shortbread cookies was luring him like a candy-crazed bloodhound.

"They're mine," I said.

"But what are they?"

"You know what they are. They're cookies from

Cassie, and I'm not sharing," I said, hugging the tin to my chest.

"You know how I feel about shortbread cookies. You're really going to eat that entire container yourself?"

"Yes."

"Give me a cookie."

"No. The note explicitly said not to share with you."

"Cassie wrote a note telling you not to share with me?"

"Technically the note said 'eat the whole tin yourself,' but that means the same thing."

I put the lid on the tin, keeping it close.

"We're supposed to have a truce. *This* is not truce-like behavior. I told you there would be consequences if you broke the truce."

"You are not getting my cookies," I said, backing up.

"Then you suffer the consequences."

I took off around the couch, but he lunged over it. He grabbed me around the waist, bringing me to the floor with him as he straddled me and started tickling me.

"Stop," I said in between laughing. "I'll give you cookies."

"Nope, now I want more." His body was flush on top of mine, one cookie still in my grasp. He grabbed my wrist and brought the fisted cookie to his mouth.

His gaze was on my lips. He was going to kiss me and I wanted him to, whether it was sane or not. I *needed* him to.

His head dipped lower, his mouth feathering over mine as our lips touched. It morphed from something soft and light to a desperate need in less than a second. His hands threaded into my hair as I arched against him.

"Kade?" Elijah called as he walked into the living room.

We jumped apart from where we'd been entangled on the floor on the other side of the couch.

Elijah immediately turned around. "Oh shit. I'm sorry. I didn't see anything. I promise. Nothing at all." The door closed a second later.

Kade rolled back and then stiffened when he looked at me. "Are you all right?"

Elijah had seen us kissing. Nothing was all right.

I shook my head, afraid to speak because I knew my voice would crack.

"I'll go buy you more cookies. I'll buy you as many cookies as you want. Just don't cry." He sounded like he were terrified a tear might hit my cheek.

"I'm not crying," I said, even though my voice was shaking.

"What's wrong?" His hand shifted to cup my face. "Why are you upset?"

"What if he talks?" I said.

"Elijah isn't like that, but I'll go talk to him and make sure he understands." Kade's face lost all its softness.

He got up, pulling me up with him before taking off after Elijah.

How could I have been so foolish? This was my life at stake, prison. And for what? To kiss a man who'd already turned his back on me once? I couldn't be this foolish.

CHAPTER 31

Kade

I'D KISSED LEAH YESTERDAY, AND EVEN THOUGH WE'D ACTED AS if nothing had happened since, my brain couldn't move past it—or how to make it happen again. Would it be the smartest choice I'd ever made? No. Did I care? Didn't seem to.

Alec walked into the office, where I was sitting thinking.

"Do you know what's going on out there?" he said, hooking a thumb toward the chaos right outside the door.

Even if I couldn't see it, the noise was impossible to ignore. I hadn't quite been ready for what Cassie had planned, which was nothing short of erecting the Taj Mahal in a few days. There were fountains, ice sculptures, and I'd heard talk of swans this morning.

"Unfortunately, yes. How was your flight?"

"Total shit. There was so much turbulence it felt like

I'd gotten tossed into a bouncy house with a bunch of cracked-out five-year-olds." He took the seat opposite me and kicked his boots up onto my desk, running a hand through tousled hair. "Why am I here? You never did tell me why I had to come to this wedding. I have to say, the angel wing archways? It doesn't look like it's going to be my scene."

"Leah wanted you here. I didn't really give a shit."

"Oh, did she now?" He smiled at me in a way that was going to get him knocked off his seat.

"Not like that. She wanted more people she was comfortable around." I wasn't mentioning a word about Missy. No need to direct attention that way.

"When did you start caring about what she wanted? Wait, let me correct that. When did you start *admitting* to caring about what she wanted?"

Leah was out near the stables, but just in case, I got up and shut the connecting door to the main living area.

"That's not the only reason I asked you to come out. There's something not right about this situation," I said.

"I've been saying that for weeks."

"Maybe you might've been hinting at an issue, but I needed to be sure myself."

"Hinting at?" He straightened, getting to his feet as he scanned my office. "I've been screaming it for weeks."

"Fine," I said, holding up a hand. "You've been screaming it. Point is, there's something off."

"What has brought you to this great epiphany? Enlighten me." He leaned on a filing cabinet and crossed his arms, waiting for the lowdown. Knowing him, he'd only stay still for another five minutes.

"There's some stuff that my guy has dug up on her stepfather that looks off."

He tilted his head slightly, studying me. "You finally got your head out of your ass and got John to working on this. Good for you. And now you think her stepfather has something to do with tossing Leah in a shitload of trouble?"

I nodded, shoving my hands into my pockets. "He's got an art collection. He's dabbled in trading, as far as we know, and I've got a hunch he's behind this somehow—whether he put her up to it or forced her, I don't know, but it's something. He's got his hands in this."

"Did you try to ask her?" His tone softened as he unfolded his arms.

"She shuts it down immediately. She's never been an open book, but this is like it's locked in a vault."

"You should still ask her about it. Just put it out there that you know something is going on."

"And what? Tell her I called in a quasi-PI? No way." I fidgeted with a folder in front of me just to have something to do with my hands.

"You think that's overstepping?" He laughed. "After the stories I've heard, that's the least overstepping you've done in weeks."

"Sometimes I'm not sure why I tell you things."

"Because if you held any more in, you might explode."

He had a point.

The door to the office swung open, Missy storming in with more fire than she should be able to carry in her little frame.

"You need to stop being mean to her," she said.

Alec cleared his throat from where he was leaning in the corner.

She looked over, spotting him. "Oh, sorry. I didn't realize you had company. Hi, Alec."

"Hey, kiddo." Alec straightened. "He's all yours. I'm going to go unpack and get a shower."

He reached out and ruffled her head like she was a kid before he walked out.

Missy stared at his back as he walked out of the office, and then continued to stare at the door. And Alec called *me* blind.

"Missy," I said, drawing her attention, "I can guarantee I have not done anything mean to Leah in the last week." Actually, I'd done some pretty nice things for her, but I wouldn't be sharing those.

"Then why is she so sad today?" she asked.

I scowled but couldn't stop myself. "Did she say she was sad?"

That was one thing Leah never did, period. She held her emotions in tighter than a homeless man holding the Hope Diamond. I'd seen her break down one time, recently, and even sobbing, she had still fought admitting being upset.

"She doesn't have to. I could tell she was out of sorts, and you're the only one around here who makes her sad, so *obviously* you did something."

"I didn't, or at least not intentionally." She'd been weird at lunch. I just figured it was because things had been awkward since the kiss. What had upset her to the point that she was sad?

"Where are you going?" Missy asked as I walked past her and toward the stables.

"Missy, you're pushing it."

"*You're* pushing it, mister."

If it had been anyone else, I would've told them to go fuck themselves, but I didn't have the heart to quash the progress she was making.

"Actually, take a walk with me." I got up and walked to the door, holding it open for her to follow me.

She nodded, falling into step with me. We weaved in between the many workmen setting up around the place.

"Am I getting fired?" she shot out.

"Should you be?"

"No. I work damned hard around here, even if I do yell at you sometimes."

"I know, which is why I'm not firing you. This talk has nothing to do with you at all, really."

Missy was as solid as they came. Her only issue was a touch of paranoia, which occasionally worked to my benefit around the ranch, as she was continuously looking for things that were about to go wrong. The yelling was getting a little old, but I'd put up with it. Hopefully it was just a phase.

"Then what do you want?" She might be a valuable hand, but she definitely lacked a certain finesse. As long as she wasn't planning to go into politics, she'd probably be fine.

"You and Leah have gotten pretty tight."

"She's good people. I don't care what they say she did. I don't buy it."

"She ever talk to you about that?"

"No, it's just a hunch, but my hunches are usually right," she said, almost as if she were on the fringe of betraying a confidence.

"I'm not asking you to tell me her secrets. I'd never do that." Mostly because she'd never tell me, but I wasn't above using whatever I could to find out what was going on. "You just sound very convinced of her innocence."

"Yeah, I don't know what happened, but I'd bet she had nothing to do with that painting."

"I've known her since she was a child, and I've never known her to steal anything."

"I wouldn't be surprised if it's something to do with that stepfather of hers. He is in the art field. Have you noticed how weird she gets when he's brought up?"

How had this slip of a girl, barely a woman, figured this out while I'd been completely blind? Willfully blind was more like it. I'd met Leah's stepfather, and I'd swallowed the good ol' boy act the same way it seemed most did.

"Yeah, that's interesting," I said, not having much more to add. I couldn't. Leah had never brought him up in front of me. "I'll talk to you later, but thanks for sharing."

"Where you heading?"

"Where do you think?"

She just nodded and smiled.

CHAPTER 32

Leah

THEY'D ALL START PILING IN FOR THE WEDDING IN A FEW DAYS. All my old friends, the ones who'd cut me off quicker than they could run off a rat-infested boat in the middle of a surge of plague.

There were footsteps and then a pair of broad shoulders filled the doorway of the old barn, the moon shining behind him. Didn't matter if I couldn't see his face. I'd recognize him anywhere, in spite of wanting to forget.

Kade walked over, stopping right below me. "What are you doing up there?"

"Just checking out the old place."

"Can you come down? The wood up there hasn't been checked in ages. This whole building is rotting and about to collapse."

"Yeah, I noticed. Surprised you haven't torn it down."

"Haven't gotten around to it."

That seemed almost unfathomable when I looked

around and everything else had been redone around it. Maybe it was like that old swing on the porch he'd saved. Some things seemed to hold a soul of their own and it wasn't so easy to toss them away.

"Come on, come down." He was holding his hands up to me the way he used to. How many times had I climbed up here just so he could catch me? I was glad it was dark and he couldn't see me well up, or the heat infusing my cheeks at the memory of how much I used to want him. Actually, I couldn't really think of it as "used to" after the way I'd reacted when he kissed me yesterday.

"I'm fine. I swear." I leaned, and a piece of wood groaned.

"I'm not leaving you up there."

I shifted and another round of creaking wasn't helping my argument. He might have a point about this place.

"I'll climb down." I got up and the wood creaked again, like an old man gasping his last breath. There'd been some rotting boards I'd stepped around, but it was getting hard to see where they were now that the sun had set.

I tested a step and realized I'd found at least one of the rotted spots.

"Jump. I'll catch you. There's too much rotten wood up there."

"You can't catch me," I said. This hadn't been one of my better ideas for sure.

"Why? I've done it a million times before."

This was like one of those exercises where you fell backward and hoped whoever was behind you would catch you, except worse. Ten years ago, I would've fallen blindly.

"Leah? You can't walk around up there," he said.

Was I really afraid of his dropping me, or was I scared of his catching me?

"You're too old to be doing this." It was a bit ridiculous, since he was probably stronger than he'd been at nineteen, or at least his arms were thicker, like he'd been toting logs around on his back for these past ten years.

"I think I can manage," he said, with some earned arrogance.

Dammit. But I did want to get down sometime tonight. "Fine. But if you break your back, don't blame me."

"Leah, shut up and jump already. I swear I just heard more creaking."

I shimmied to the edge. "I'm jumping," I said.

"Any day now."

I pushed off the side and he caught me, just like he used to. But he didn't put me down right away like he used to.

"What are you doing?" I asked, my voice already growing raspier at the contact.

"Is it the wedding?" he asked.

"It's not the wedding." My voice had come out so harsh that I might as well have written a confession. "Or it's not *just* the wedding."

"I wouldn't have offered if I'd known you didn't want it."

The nicer he was, the worse this situation grew. The physical attraction had never gone away, but I'd been able to cling to his being an asshole. If he was going to take that away, what shield was I left with now?

I chewed on my lower lip as his gaze narrowed in on

my mouth in a way that made it feel like my ribcage had been shrink-wrapped around my lungs. "Don't do that."

"Do what?" he asked.

"You know."

"Fine. Maybe I do, but I can't seem to help it. I want you."

I'd craved those words for so long. I'd wished on stars, blown out candles, and tossed coins into wells. Now, when my world was on its ear and the cost could be the small amount of freedom I had left, he'd said them. It was the definition of bittersweet.

"We can't do this. We both signed contracts saying we wouldn't." In spite of my words, I hadn't made so much as the simplest attempt to get out of his arms. Why now? Why did he have to do this *now*?

"We could be discreet," he said.

"I'm a thief, remember?" I said, trying to get the dick in him to wake up again.

"You are the most beautiful woman I've ever known. I want you and I don't think I can shut it off."

"But I'm a thief and spoiled and a princess," I said, reminding him of all the things I'd been called lately, some of which he'd cosigned.

"*Spoiled* and *princess* are redundant. That's really just one, not two." He smirked. "If we tallied it up, I think you dislike more things about me than I dislike about you, and yet I don't care about any of them."

"If someone finds out, they'll send me to prison."

"No, they won't. No one is taking you off this ranch and throwing you in prison. No one." His arms tightened around me, as if he were fighting off some invisible threat already.

"We both know there's a risk."

He held me in silence for another moment before his arms loosened. I slid down his body, fighting my own urge to wrap myself around him.

He took a step back, as if giving us both the buffer we needed to *not* take this to the next step.

"We should head back to the main house," he said.

I took a few steps, waiting for him to come. He was standing there, watching me.

"Aren't you coming?"

"I'll follow in a few," he said.

I nodded, leaving him in the barn and walking back alone, letting my mind once again wonder what things might've been like if I'd never left this place.

CHAPTER 33

Leah

"Where is she?" I heard my mother calling from all the way in my bedroom.

I walked into the living room, prepared to see my mother, somehow imaging she'd be alone, only to find Edwin as well, standing beside Kade.

"I hope you're doing the right thing," Edwin said.

"Don't I always?" I replied, daring him to say differently. My mother didn't chime in, as she took her lead from Edwin, always. If he didn't make a thing of it, she didn't. If he did, I'd hear about it for days. As much as I loved her, I never wanted to be like her.

Kade was watching Edwin like an eagle who'd spotted a rat in a field.

"Edwin, let's give them time to go get ready. There's lots to be done still. Where's your dress before we leave? Where's your room? Let me see it."

She followed me out and into the bedroom that had become mine.

"This is quite cute," she said, looking around.

Thankfully, she hadn't come when I was still living the shed life. I might never have heard the end of it.

"Yes, it's quite comfortable."

"It's probably a good thing Cassie didn't have a rehearsal dinner. I'm not sure I could handle being back here for a minute longer—no offense to Kade, but Montana was never my thing."

I pulled the garment bag out of my closet. "Well, I have to start getting ready. Cassie should be here soon too, and I want to be out of the shower before she comes."

My goal of getting her moving backfired, as she took a seat on the bed.

"You still love Kade, don't you?"

I was too busy making sure the door was all the way shut to bother responding.

"I don't know why I thought that would go away," she said. "You're my daughter. I should've known that you'd fall for him again the second you saw him—if you ever really got over him, that is. Although I can't really fault you for it. He's still as hot as ever." She nodded, waving her hand at her face.

"Mom, I don't love him." And I did not want to talk about this with her.

"You were a kid, though. I thought it was just a crush, but I should've known," she continued, as if I hadn't denied it.

"Mom. I'm *not in love with him*, and can you please keep your voice down?"

"Maybe you should try to make it work? Before, when he didn't have two cents to rub together, it was much more concerning, but he looks like he's doing well now." She glanced around the room, as if tallying up price tags on all the furnishings.

"Are you not listening to me? I don't love Kade."

"Honey, when you love, you *love* with every single fiber in your body and soul. This is it. He's it. You should try to make it work."

Now that he had money, that was. I wasn't going to bother hashing this out with her because it was not a discussion I was willing to encourage.

"I'm here on a work parole. There's legal documents." This at least might sink in and shut this down. "Now, I really need to get ready."

She continued, completely ignoring the hint. "You sure don't take after me. When you jump, it's not just a few feet in. You launch yourself into the abyss. Your dad was that way too. He loved with everything he had, and unfortunately you got that rancid gene too. Kade's it. He's the one your heart wants, and so help him God, he better deserve the gift you're giving him, because no one deserves that kind of love."

"You're saying you didn't love Dad?"

"Oh, I did love him. But there's different types of love. I love. You *love*." She waved her hands around in an exaggerated motion, all emo-like.

"We need to stop talking about this. People are arriving."

She leaned back on one arm. "He loves you too. I can see it in the way he looks at you."

"You don't know that."

"I might not love the way you do, but I know love when I see it. He loves you." She got up and kissed my cheek. "Okay, go take a shower. I'll see you in a little bit."

Just when she'd landed on a subject I wanted to hear about, she decided to leave. She had a knack for giving what I wasn't looking for and too little of what I needed to hear. It was the story of our relationship.

I didn't bother asking any more. She'd finished what she had to say and was done. I didn't have time for this anyway.

I hopped in the shower and was barely out when Cassie and her "crew" arrived. She had hair, makeup, everything you could imagine.

"Leah," she said, folding me into a hug. "You did not tell me how hot he was," she whispered.

"I didn't want to dwell on it," I said.

"And I thought that dress was for Greg." She smiled. "By the way, he left. He saw us heading in and gave up his bedroom suite. He said he'd get ready down the street at Chuck's."

"That sounds about right," I said. He'd never wanted to deal with a lot of fuss.

"Hey, guys, you can go start setting up and I'll be there in a few."

They all smiled and filed out.

She pulled me over to the bed to sit with her. "Now how are you really doing? This is the first time I've gotten to really talk to you."

I spilled all the details, feeling like I could unload for the first time in weeks.

"So do you want Kade or not? I'm confused."

"Yeah, so am I. That's the problem."

There was a soft knock on the door. "Cassie, we need to get going if we're going to make you both fabulous," one of her people called.

"Both?" I asked.

"You don't think I wouldn't share, do you? Come now, we must be fabulous. There are men that need to be wowed into submission."

She pulled me along with her before I could refuse.

"Hey, do you think there's enough fabulousness to squeeze in one more?" I asked.

"Of course. You know I always come prepared."

I TRACKED DOWN MISSY IN THE BUNKHOUSE, DRINKING A BEER on the old couch, never looking more down and out than she did right now. "What are you doing?"

"I was just thirsty and taking a break."

"Come on. Cassie brought a glam squad with her, and we're getting your hair and makeup done."

"No, I don't need all that fuss. I'll catch up after you're done."

I planted myself on the couch next to her. "Then I'll wait for you."

"You're really going to do this to me?"

"Yes."

She eyed me over her bottle as she sipped. I could see the wheels turning, whether or not to try to hold out.

She finally let out a little huff.

"How'd you know I was going to try to bail?" she asked.

"Because if I wasn't in the wedding, I'd have done the same."

"So because you have to go, you're dragging me down with you?"

"Misery does love company, and my current misery knows no ends." I tilted my head down as my eyebrows rose. "At least you don't have an ex visiting the place you are an indentured servant at."

"You're right. I don't have a leg to stand on."

She sucked in a breath through her teeth before she stood up, then held out her hand to help me up, and I let her.

"Good to know my shitty circumstances could help you out," I said. "They should help someone, right?"

CHAPTER 34

Kade

THERE WAS A SOFT KNOCK ON MY OFFICE DOOR AND PRISCILLA was standing there, smiling through the window. I'd thought I'd be able to hide here until the wedding started, but it didn't appear to be working out.

I returned her smile, mine taking a lot more work. I liked the woman, but seeing her and her husband when they arrived had set my teeth on edge. I didn't have time for whatever she wanted, and my mood didn't have an inch left to give. If it got any fouler, someone might try to bury me in the field, thinking I was rotting away.

"I just wanted to stop by and thank you again for everything you're doing for Leah." She was near beaming as she came over and patted my arm. She oozed gratitude from every glance, every touch of her hand.

Damn this woman knew how to make me feel like a dick.

"Of course. Your family has always meant a lot to me."

"You've always had a piece of my heart as well." She was looking about, appearing distracted, as she said, "Leah will be here quite a while. I know that's a lot to take on." She spoke like it was a statement, but the way she was studying me out of the corner of her eye seemed to hold more of a question.

"She's actually very helpful," I said, wondering if Priscilla was looking to alleviate some burden. I'd probably say just about anything to get her moving along so I could get back to work and not get buried in guilt. I had too much to catch up on after having everyone here for the wedding.

"You know, Leah seems tough, but she's also very vulnerable, especially around certain people." She nodded, watching me like a hawk.

I perched a hip on my desk, finding this conversation a little more interesting than I had thought it would be. "Certain people?"

She pursed her lips, playing coy. "It's just that *certain* people have always been able to get under her skin—you know, unravel her a bit."

Why was it that her mother knowing I unsettled Leah made me want to push out my chest? This was getting a little ridiculous. Who was I becoming?

"And this is a bad thing?"

She shook her head vigorously. "Oh, no, not like that. In a *good* way. You know, she doesn't let that many people in. Even if it unsettles her a little, I think it's better for her. I thought her and Greg might get engaged, and yet she never seemed to be thrown off by anything *he* did."

My chest just inflated another inch while I waited, hoping she'd feed me another tidbit.

"That said, anyone she lets in to her inner sanctum is luckier than they can imagine. It might seem like she gives in inches, but once she does give? It's for eternity and without reservation."

Alec walked in. "Here you are. Didn't mean to interrupt."

"No interruption," Priscilla said, walking over to him. "It's so nice to see you boys again."

"You too."

"Well, hopefully we'll have more time to talk at the reception. I must go find Edwin now. He gets all out of sorts if I go missing for too long." Priscilla walked out.

"I have to say, she's holding up very well," Alec said, watching her leave.

"She's twice your age," I said.

He shrugged.

"And married," I added.

"Yeah, that one's a little trickier, especially if she's got a husband who tracks her every move."

"And you don't want any piece of that man. Just seeing him for a few minutes this morning put me in a shit mood."

"Why? What happened?"

I stopped moving around and finally sat down. "He said to her, 'Do the right thing,' but it felt more like code for 'Do what I *want* you to.'"

"What did Leah say?"

"She said, 'I always do the right thing,' but there was an undertone to that as well, as if they were having their own secret conversation."

"So you think your guy is right?"

"There's no proof yet, but I don't like what I'm seeing. I'm going to have to avoid him as much as possible today or I might kill him."

Alec jerked his gaze from the window, back to me.

"You fucked Leah, didn't you?" he said.

"I didn't 'fuck her,' if you must know." Even speaking like that about her irked me.

"You did *something*."

"I'm not discussing what I did or didn't do with Leah."

"It made it worse?" Alec groaned.

It was on the tip of my tongue to tell him it wasn't his business. Yet I felt like I was getting sucked into quicksand and grabbing frantically for any branch or twig within reach.

"It might've," I admitted.

There was a long pause as he seemed to be grasping for what to say. He should be struggling. It had been his suggestion that I succumb to my desires that had backfired. Thankfully, I'd only kissed her. How bad might it be if I'd slept with her?

"Maybe that wasn't such a good idea," he said.

Worst part of his admission was that he was fighting not to laugh as he made it.

"Stop laughing and tell me what the fuck I do now." It didn't escape me that I was asking the man who'd already steered me wrong.

"This is uncharted territory. This hasn't ever happened to me. Usually I don't care what happened after I sleep with them." At least the laughter was gone. "Thank God, too, because it sounds and looks horrible."

"You were so quick with the advice before and now this is all you've got?"

"Well, who told you to listen to me?" he asked.

CHAPTER 35

Leah

ALEC WAS LEANING ON THE RAIL, LAUGHING AT SOMETHING ON his phone. Instinct told me it was a woman.

"What's so funny?" I asked, walking over.

"Girl I've seen a few times. She's quite comical."

"Dating someone funny has its perks."

Okay, there was someone he was involved with. This boded well. Maybe we wouldn't have to have the little talk I'd dreaded. When I'd asked Kade to have him come, I must have been delirious and sleep deprived. Why would this ever be a good thing for Missy? Yes, he'd see her shining and be like, wow, maybe she was a woman that wasn't beneath his attention.

But I'd just come from the ranch after the glam squad had gotten their hands on her. Talk about a glow-up. She would put Dorothy, the OG of glow-ups, to shame, and my blunder was immediately obvious. He wasn't just going to acknowledge her being a woman. He was going to want her, and bad, because every man here would. She was knock-'em-out gorgeous.

"I'm not dating her. I just saw her a few times." He tucked his phone in his pocket, as if he had to put the woman out of his mind now that I'd labeled them as dating.

"What's wrong? You allergic to the word *dating*?"

"No," he said with a little too much force. "I'm just not dating her. I wasn't even planning on seeing her once I got back."

"You just said she was funny. And clearly you're attracted to her if you saw her more than once. I know you too well to imagine that it was platonic."

"Yeah, but the spark has started to die."

"Bloom off the rose?" I asked without even a hint of fake compassion.

"Yes. Exactly." He threw a hand up.

"You are such a dog." I shook my head.

"What? I thought you understood." Alec had the exact same smirk as Kade.

"Yes, I understand that you are a dog."

"If I was a dog, I'd be pulling you behind the bushes right now, because you outdid yourself with this getup." He threw his hands up. "But don't worry. I won't even try, because I like keeping my balls intact. But why do I feel like you've come over to lecture me with some goal in mind?"

There was no holding back now. Might as well put on my mom cap and have at it. "Missy is too young, sweet, and innocent for you." And there was no way I was letting her get added to the list of women that had been in and out of his bed.

"Missy?" He squinted, as if trying to place her name.

"The nice little redheaded gal that works her ass off here?"

He had to look off and think on it for a second before light popped into his eyes. "Oh, yeah, I got it. I know who you mean." There was a pause before he asked, "I didn't hit on her, did I?"

She definitely hadn't been on his radar. He'd barely remembered her, and now I'd brought her to his attention. Didn't matter. No way would she escape his attention after he saw her tonight.

"No, you didn't, and she's way too young to hit on, too. I just wanted to warn you off. She's not even eighteen." Okay, maybe she was twenty-one, and not seventeen, but she was still too sweet for him. If I had to lie to safeguard her, I'd do it.

"What do you take me for? I don't go after babies."

"Just wanted to make sure you realized how very young she was."

"Noted. If that occurs to me at any point, may my eyes fall from their sockets or the police haul me away."

"I'm going to hold you to that."

"Wouldn't expect anything less from you."

More and more people were beginning to make their way to the ranch.

"I've got to go get ready to walk. Don't forget you promised me."

"Yeah, yeah, I barely noticed her. You've got nothing to worry about."

I was heading back through the crowds forming when Edwin beelined for me.

"Do you have a moment?" He was smiling as he spoke, but that was just for any nosy onlookers. There was nothing pleasant underneath this surface.

"No."

I went to take a step around him, and he moved with me. "We should really talk."

"We've talked more than I ever wanted to. I'm done speaking to you."

"I don't want to make a spectacle out here, but I will."

"Whatever you want from me, the answer is no. Whatever you want to talk to me about, I don't want to hear. Nothing good comes from being around you. Now I have to go. You want to create a scene, then do so, but I have a wedding to walk in."

He looked over my shoulder, and I glanced in that direction. Alec hadn't moved from his spot, but he was staring this way as if he had Edwin's number. I took the opportunity to leave before Edwin made a move to stop me again. I wasn't delusional enough to believe this would be the last of him tonight. No, he'd find me and force the issue, because Edwin always got what he wanted. Or almost did. He'd never gotten *me* the way he wanted, and never would.

"You ready?" I asked Cassie when I got inside the ranch. She was standing beside her stepfather smiling, looking as if she were trying to hold back her tears.

"Don't you dare cry," her makeup artist said. "You'll ruin my masterpiece."

In this moment, I would've hugged Kade if he were standing beside me for giving me this moment. While it came with lots of baggage, standing here now, I wouldn't have given away this moment for anything.

———

I WALKED OVER AND TOOK A SEAT BESIDE MY BROTHER IN THE farthest corner of the tent as everyone waited for the wedding procession to begin.

"You see Leah?" I asked.

"Yeah, and then I saw her stepfather trying to corner her," Alec said, and gave me a side glance. "Don't get all worked up. I was watching."

"What did he do?"

"Nothing much. He was trying to talk to her, but she didn't seem to want any part of it. He might have pushed the issue, but he noticed me and let her be."

I wanted to break out laughing then and there. No way was that just a glance. "You just looked at him and he stopped?"

"I might've made a cutting motion across my neck as I stared."

"Oh, well, if that's all."

"Here they come."

The music picked up and slowly the wedding party began to make their way out of the house and down the curving slate walkway that had been installed just for this event. It led right to the tent. Once the tent was gone, I'd have a path to nowhere, but I'd figure that out later. I couldn't think of anything beyond the moment I spotted Leah walking across the field.

It was a good thing I'd decided to take the seat next to Alec, because I'd never be able to stay upright otherwise. Leah was always beautiful, even without a stitch of makeup and in worn-out jeans. It might've been my favorite way to see her, with her hair all tousled and pulled up into a messy ponytail.

But her walking across the field in that dress, the way it shimmered and followed the lines of her body, her hair falling in smooth waves... I wasn't sure I'd ever seen a more beautiful woman in my life.

I was going to have to throw an extra hundred into Cassie's wedding gift to show my appreciation.

"Whoa," Alec said. "She sure does look fucking—"

I elbowed him, afraid of what would come out next.

"—festive. She looks *festive*, is what I was going to say, so no need to act the barbarian."

I shushed him, continuing to watch only her as she walked closer, my eyes staying on her even when the bride made her arrival. For the first time in my life, I wondered what it would be like to be the man waiting at the altar. To be the man getting married.

There was no denying it anymore. I fucking loved Leah. I'd probably always loved her and there was no getting away from it. She could've stolen that painting and murdered five people in the process and I wasn't sure it would make a damned bit of difference.

"Oh shit," Alec said, looking at me. "You're cooked, aren't you?"

I let out a pathetic sigh. "I'm not just cooked, I'm charcoaled."

"Then you gotta just roll with it. No other choice." He shrugged.

I wasn't sure that was an option. Love wasn't a single-player game, and she might not be interested. I certainly hadn't helped my case.

And how was I going to make it through the night without killing her stepfather?

CHAPTER 36

Kade

"Where's Leah? Her ex is here," Alec said, scanning the heads at the reception, which was in full swing.

I had no idea where she'd gone. I was seated so far away from her at dinner that I'd barely seen the top of her head. Hosting her wedding might've meant all my workers got an invite, but our table was barely even in the tent.

"I'm surprised Cassie invited him. And how do you know all this?" I asked.

"He came as someone's date. Leah's mom filled me when I was feeding her shots."

"You were feeding her shots? Please tell me that you're not serious about banging her."

"I was only plying her with alcohol for info." He pointed across the room to a fair-haired, upper-crust-looking guy. We couldn't have appeared more different.

Greg wrapped an arm around his date and then leaned in to whisper in her ear, making her laugh.

"That weasel is making sure everyone in this place knows he doesn't give a shit about Leah." I took a step toward the couple.

Alec matched my movements, his hands up, ready to block me. "You can't go beat the shit out of him just for hugging his date."

"Maybe I can't beat him for it, but I can definitely fuck with him a bit."

If Alec were smaller, I would've shoved him out of the way, but as far as fighting ability, we were pretty much a draw. We'd end up wrestling here for hours until someone quit due to exhaustion. We'd done it before.

"You want to make it look like she cares? Like she's been sitting here crying for him? Then be my guest. Go start with the guy." He stepped out of my way and waved his hand.

"I hate when you're right."

"You think you would've gotten used to it by now, but you've always been a slow learner."

"But quick with my right hook, which I'll remind you of if you don't shut up. Actually, forget it. I don't have time to fight with you. I need to go find Leah."

"Don't make her feel worse."

"Why would I do that?"

"How would I know why you like being a dick to her? I don't know, she doesn't have pigtails to pull anymore?" He threw his hands up.

"Wait, looks like she's on a collision course with Greg. I have to go."

"Wouldn't dream of stopping you," Alec said.

I made my way across the crowd to where Leah was talking to her ex and his date.

I wrapped my arm around her waist and gave her a peck on the temple, hoping she wouldn't blow the game up.

She leaned into me. "Greg, this is Kade," she said.

Greg scanned me, looking like a man who knew he'd blown it. Was the bimbo his plan on getting back with Leah? Did he think trying to make her jealous was the way to go?

"Kade? The guy you grew up with?"

"Yes," I answered for her. "That's me."

"I thought you were here on a sort of work parole?" Greg asked. "You're allowed to dally with your warden?" He waved a finger back and forth, his mouth tightening.

"Why? Does that bother you?" I asked.

"Of course it doesn't. I just thought it would be against the rules to—"

"I'd watch what you say next."

Greg looked at me, trying to assess me.

"That's right. I'd tread carefully. You don't have much farther to go," I said, helping him keep his teeth. As much as I wanted to punch him, and man would it feel good, I didn't want to ruin this wedding or have to call in more favors to keep Leah here.

She tightened her grip on me, locking her arm on my forearm.

"Well, it was nice seeing you, Greg, but Kade and I have some things to handle before dinner."

"Yes, we like to handle things quite often," I said, just to stick it to him a little more.

Leah was tugging on my arm, but I couldn't make it that easy for this man or he'd be running his mouth all night. No, it needed to be taken care of now, before he ruined this event, or tried. I'd drown him in the river before I let him ruin anything for Leah.

"We good, or was there something else you wanted to say?" I asked, not budging from my spot.

"What else would there be to say?" Greg asked, playing stupid and attempting to save face.

I nodded at his floozy, giving her the benefit of the doubt that maybe she didn't realize the trash she'd arrived with.

I steered Leah toward the dance floor.

"What are you doing?" she asked.

"Dancing?" I curved an arm around her waist as I moved us around the dance floor. As if on cue, a slow Eric Clapton song came on.

"You know what I mean."

"I'm not letting that little shit think you're unhappy, sitting here alone and pining away in a depression, even if you are." I waited, watching her eyes, hoping she'd tell me she wasn't that miserable here. She smirked. It was enough that I'd take it as a win.

"By the way, I slipped an extra couple bills into Cassie's wedding gift just as a thank-you for this dress. That girl knows what works," I said.

"Don't tease me. I know it's a lot." She looked at the crowd, a pretty pink flush across her cheeks.

"There's a lot, and then there's this."

"You're not funny."

I wasn't trying to be. She had no idea how utterly captivating she was, but I didn't think she was quite in the right space to hear it, either.

"You sure? I think I'm quite funny. Maybe we should take a vote?"

"Votes don't work out so hot for you," she said.

But she laughed. I wasn't oblivious to the reception she seemed to be getting from some of this crowd, but here she was, chin up and facing them like none of it fazed her.

"I know you bribed them last time. I'm positive of it. I just haven't been able to gather proof of it yet," I said, hoping to lure more laughter out of her.

The music stopped and Leah's gaze narrowed in on a spot over by the bar.

"Oh no."

"What's wrong?" I glanced over and spotted Alec, who was staring very intently across the party at a red-haired bombshell. *Shit.* "You're the one who told me to invite him."

"I know, and I'll go handle it."

"I'll come with you."

We turned to head over, and Elijah appeared. He was dressed in a fine suit with a piece of hay stuck to his arm.

"Kade, I need you to come down to the barn for a second. Princess is acting up again."

"Go check on her. I'll handle this," Leah said, already walking off.

————

LEAH

WE HADN'T EVEN MADE IT HALFWAY THROUGH THE WEDDING and Alec was locked on to Missy like a heat-seeking missile.

He turned to me. "Leah, who's that woman?" Recognition flashed as he squinted. "Wait, is *that* Missy?"

"*No*." The word came out of me like it had been ripped out of my gut.

Alec kept on staring. And staring, as if he couldn't stop himself. As if she were the only person in the world.

"Huh?" he said, turning to me, blinking. He didn't even realize how obvious he'd been or that I'd caught him staring.

I'd wanted to give Missy a moment, but not one that would lead to what was happening here. She was too young, too sweet for the likes of Alec, whether he realized it or not.

"Not her," I said, glancing in Missy's direction. "She's not one to add to your roster—remember our talk?"

He dragged his gaze back to me. "Oh, no, I'd never. I'm just surprised." He looked back to her. "I mean, I knew she was a cute kid, but damn is she turning into one of the most beautiful—"

"You're doing it again, and no."

"Doing what?"

"Staring at her with that look you have, and don't tell me you don't know what one I'm talking about."

"I told you I wasn't going to do anything. She's a kid. I'm surprised, is all."

"If you're not going to do anything, stop staring at her. She's not a one-night-stand girl." Was it possible he didn't even realize the heat he was throwing off? Was he kidding me or himself?

He shook his head, as if he hadn't realized he'd been doing it again. "You're beating a dead horse. How many times do I need to tell you I'm not interested in that way?"

He wasn't bullshitting me. He was bullshitting himself.

"Just promise me you won't touch her if the urge presents itself." Or if he finally acknowledged it.

"She's too young and innocent for me. I don't mess with girls right out of the playroom."

Again, he *sounded* like he believed what he was saying, but I knew that look. He wanted her, whether he realized it or not.

"And I, for one, own my feelings," he said with a raised brow.

"Are you trying to insinuate that I don't?"

"If the shoe fits." He shrugged.

"I am not into your brother."

"Strange how you didn't think for a second I meant Elijah or Adam." He made a long humming noise.

"I'm not." *Was* I attracted to Kade? I was human. Were we maybe becoming friends again, or some shape of that? Perhaps. But we weren't anything more, and couldn't be.

"And I'm not angling for Missy."

"Then we're good. Nothing else to talk about." I looked down the bar, trying to wave over the bartender. I needed a shot and didn't care who saw me right now.

"Nope," he said.

"Not at all," I agreed.

The bartender stopped in front of us.

Alec looked at me, and I nodded.

"Two shots of the best whiskey you've got," he said.

"Maybe bring us that bottle," I added.

"Good thinking," he said.

We were on the same page at least on this.

CHAPTER 37

Leah

I WAS OVER BY THE BAR, WATCHING CASSIE DANCING AND laughing with her husband. Everyone was having a good time, and even with the couple of blips, it was almost like things were normal. If nothing else, she'd had a good wedding and I'd gotten to watch her laugh and cry, walk down the aisle, see her and her husband exchange vows and look at each other like they were the entire world with the mountains sprawling in the background. This had turned into one hell of a good venue.

"We need to have that talk, unless you want to do it here," Edwin said, having crept up behind me.

He'd never leave me alone until he said whatever it was he had to say. I threw back the last of my drink and turned to face him.

"Fine. Let's go," I said, even though I was reaching my limit of what I would take from this man. Ruining Cassie's wedding with a scene would be a step too far.

I waved him toward the banquet tent exit.

He took the lead, expecting me to just follow. I stared at his back, wishing I'd grabbed a steak knife off one of the tables. Would I really stab him? It was getting close enough that it wasn't an easy *no* anymore.

Edwin kept walking. He probably wanted to get me out of gunshot-hearing range and do away with me. Say it was an "accident." He was such a good con artist, he'd probably get away with it, too.

Maybe that was why I could never shake this inner tremble I had whenever he was near. No one else ever looked at him sideways, but I knew what he was capable of. He somehow walked away smelling like his expensive cologne and looking as sleek as his thousand-dollar suits, no matter what grime and muck he'd been shoveling.

"This is far enough," I said as soon as we hit the ranch porch.

He looked around and then nodded, as if he were only stopping because he'd approved.

"How are things going?" he asked, even now sounding so polished and sophisticated, no sign of the slimebag he was.

"Fine. What do you want?" I said, giving him nothing because that was what he deserved. Technically he deserved less, but that wasn't possible. How many times had I hoped I was wrong about this man only to find out he was even worse than I thought?

"You and Kade look pretty chummy," he said.

Of course that would bother him. "And?"

"I just want to remind you how bad it would be to put crazy ideas into his head. We wouldn't want pillow talk to ruin anyone's life."

Was he afraid of Kade? Was he afraid of catching a beating? He didn't need to be. Kade might be putting on a good act for my ex, but I still didn't think he'd be willing to risk the ire of the law to punch Edwin in the face. We all knew my stepfather was the type to press charges, too, even if he deserved the beating more than anyone I'd ever met.

Funny how he said "anyone's life" when it always meant mine. I'd finally thought I'd been free of this man, had spent years building distance between us, and he'd still screwed up my life.

"Don't talk to me about what might happen and what I should be doing. I've done enough. You'd be in prison if it weren't for me. You set me up, you asshole, and I don't want to hear anything else."

That would've wiped the arrogance off a weaker man's face, but that wasn't who Edwin was. Sometimes I wondered if the key to getting away with all he'd done was to act as if he was in the right. This man would never have a guilty conscience. He didn't come equipped with the ability to feel bad for anything.

"Set you up? You and your stories. You're awfully brazen for somebody convicted of a felony."

I couldn't prove my innocence the first time. I wasn't delusional enough to think a second attempt would make a difference.

"You might pretend in front of everybody else, but I'm not going to stomach it," I said.

"Pretend? That's not what the courts thought. It's not what they'd think if they found more tucked away in a warehouse in your name." He smiled.

Once I'd taken the fall for his crime, of course he'd

made sure to pile more on so I could never dig myself out unless he let me. He owned me, and there wasn't any way around it. I might be better off on this ranch for the rest of my life if it kept him at bay.

But I just couldn't roll over that easy, at least not in this setting. If he knew he had me, it was over. If I stopped pushing back, he really would own me.

"Don't press me or I will talk, wherever the chips fall."

"You'll only make it worse on yourself. The more trouble you stir up, the more will bounce back onto you after all. I mean, it looks pretty cushy here, but it was your first offense. Another offense and you probably won't be so lucky."

I wanted to rip his throat out. I wanted to scream that I'd get him if it was the last thing I did, but I couldn't. Everything he said was accurate. I was screwed, and he held all the cards, at least for now. So I hit the only soft spot I'd ever sensed in him.

"I just hope I don't slip and say something to Kade one night."

I'd hit the target if his reaching out and gripping my forearm like a vise meant anything.

"You say one word to him and your heels will leave tracks through this whole place as they drag you out of here. Do you hear me?"

Why was he so afraid of Kade? This was more than fear of catching a beating.

"You had better take your hands off her."

My stepfather's face morphed back into its normal mask the moment he heard Kade's voice. Showed how bad he was slipping that he'd even gotten caught. He used to stay more on his toes than this.

"Kade, we were just having a family chat," he said, immediately letting me go.

"We don't have those kinds of chats with women around here." Kade walked closer and stepped in between us, physically backing Edwin up another couple steps.

"I'm sure you can understand a father's frustration in a moment like this."

Kade's gaze shot to my arm, where marks were already showing.

"No. I actually don't." He walked closer, forcing Edwin to step back again. "What I would love to know is why you think you have any say in whether she stays here or not?"

"You came upon us at a very awkward moment. I'm only trying to help her not get herself in more trouble by saying foolish things or doing something crazy. Like I said, you caught us in the middle of a family squabble, is all. I know this must look horrible to you, but after what's happened, I get a little emotional if I'm afraid she might be heading off down the track again. I've cared for her like she was my own flesh and blood. It's hard to stand by while she's making such poor decisions." The veil was firmly back in place and he was calm sophistication again, expecting everyone to fall in line.

I stared at the ground, waiting to hear Kade say he understood. How could he not? Edwin was such a stand-up guy. Everyone knew it. How many times had someone said it to me over the last decade?

"Actually, I don't. Get out." Kade sounded as if he were barely holding back from ripping Edwin apart.

"Excuse me?"

"What are you misunderstanding? I'm telling you to

get off my property." Kade stood there, waiting, making it clear he wasn't leaving until my stepfather did.

"I believe it's up to Leah if she's done having this conversation with me," Edwin said, his dark underbelly showing. He wasn't used to getting any pushback, let alone what Kade was dishing out.

"This is my ranch, and she's under my protection, so this is how it's going to go. You're going to leave now. Not after you say goodbye to the bride; not after you circle a few times and work the crowd. You can go get your wife and leave, or just leave, but you need to get out of here in the next five minutes."

"I... What?" Edwin's face was so red that his flush was visible even in the dim light.

"You heard me," Kade said. "If you don't, something very bad is going to happen. I haven't decided which route to go yet, but there will be a lot of pain and humiliation and zero witnesses."

"I'm not sure what I've done to—"

"You've received your warning." He looked at his watch.

Edwin gaped at him and then tried to look past Kade to me. "Leah, how can you—"

"You don't get to speak to her. You're dealing with me," Kade said. He tapped his watch. "Four minutes."

Edwin scrambled off.

Kade turned to me. "Are you okay?" he asked, his voice soft as his hand came to my cheek.

I had a lot of emotions flowing through me, and none of them so simply wrapped up in that word.

Across the way, I could see Cassie holding court, getting ready to depart.

"I have to get back over there before she leaves," I

said, wanting nothing more than to go into the ranch and bury my head under the covers.

"We need to talk as soon as this is over," he said.

"I know." He deserved *something* at this point. But how much could I say without dragging him into it? I wasn't sure.

CHAPTER 38

Leah

THE SECOND CASSIE AND HER HUSBAND LEFT, I'D SNUCK BACK into the ranch and poured myself a glass of whiskey on the rocks. I settled onto the couch in an old t-shirt I liked sleeping in and tried to figure out what I was going to say to Kade. There was no denying that something was wrong at this point, but it came down to how much I told him and how much he'd already heard. The last thing I wanted was to get Kade messed up in what Edwin was doing.

The time sped past, and I still hadn't come up with a solution when Kade walked in.

He went and poured himself a drink before he took a seat on the other side of the couch. His eyes locked on mine as he took a heavy swig.

"We *need* to talk," he said.

"I know." There was no putting it off. Not now, after he'd heard at least some of my argument with Edwin.

"Look me in the eye and tell me you stole the painting," he said.

My throat tightened. "The situation is pretty messy," I said. I needed to know what he knew. I wasn't going to drag him into this if I could avoid it. Letting Edwin into your life was like breathing in toxic fumes every day.

"You didn't take it," Kade said, his voice firm. "You're not a thief."

I shook my head, trying to keep my voice steady. "Why do you want to stir up trouble? It would be better for you not to get involved."

"Trouble for who? You didn't take that painting." He looked away. "How could I be so stupid? I know you didn't. I should've fucking killed him tonight. I know it was him, but why? It just doesn't make any sense. Does he have something on you? Tell me what is going on." Kade's voice was softer now, almost pleading.

I swallowed hard, my heart pounding so loud it echoed in my ears. "I don't want to get you mixed up in this."

"Leah—"

"You think you want to know, but you don't."

He sat back, expression unreadable, but he didn't look away. He wasn't going to let it go—of course he wasn't. That wasn't who he was.

"Why are you taking the fall for him? What happened? Just tell me the truth. What does he have on you?"

The way he was staring at me, almost desperate for me to speak to him, was my undoing. I hadn't ever wanted this situation, or this secret. And now he knew. The only thing I could do was try to get a compromise out of him before I said anything more.

"This doesn't go beyond us. Nothing comes from this. This conversation is the end of it. I need you to agree to that."

He nodded. "Just tell me."

"I'm going to need a refill."

He nodded and topped off my glass. I got the feeling he would've let me chug from the bottle if it would get him answers.

I waited until I had another sip warming my body. Kade waited patiently, until I'd not only had one sip but three. If I didn't get the story out soon, I'd be too drunk to tell it.

"This is going to sound unbelievable, but you want to know my truth and this is the only truth I have. That stolen painting was delivered to my apartment while I was out of town. At the time, I had no idea who shipped it. I didn't know it was there and I've still never seen it in person. It was confiscated by the police before I got home from my vacation.

"I'd hired someone to put lighting in for a painting I'd bought but hadn't received yet. The contractor was doing this while I was away. The super of the building knew I was expecting a painting and put it in my apartment for me. The contractor saw the box placed there, probably close to the location of where I'd had the lighting put in, and thought he was supposed to hang that for me as well. You know the rest. The *world* knows the rest. I got home and the police were waiting at my door before I had a chance to bring in my bags."

Kade was leaning back, trying to figure out the rest the same way I had initially.

"What about the person who delivered it? Where did it say it came from?"

"The shipper's information was completely made up and the person who brought it was wearing a delivery outfit with a hat, sunglasses, and a surgical mask." I took another long sip of whiskey, thinking back to all that had transpired.

"But it was Edwin's package?" Kade asked, daring me to deny it. "Why didn't you tell them it was his?"

"I didn't know that at first. As soon as I got out on bail, he was obviously one of the first people I asked, as he is in the art field." The more I talked, the less I cared what I said. I didn't even try to deny it anymore. It felt so good to tell someone the whole story that I found myself digging up details I'd never thought I'd share.

I walked into Edwin and my mother's Upper East Side apartment, where Edwin was waiting for me.

"Did you send that painting to me? Did you set me up?"

"If you try to blame me, it won't work," he said. "I have witnesses that will testify to meeting you and negotiating the deal. The only thing you'll do if you try to blame it on me is cause inconvenience. Can you imagine what else they might find if you don't keep your mouth shut?

"Nobody will believe you anyway. I'll just have another painting show up in a warehouse with your name, and then another. There's no way out, so you should just accept it." He shrugged. "They'll probably go easy on you. I'll use my influence to get you a soft sentence."

"Why are you doing this to me?"

"I needed somewhere to park the painting for a few days and you weren't even supposed to be home. It would've been gone before you came back."

"Do you care nothing for what you're doing to my life?"

"Why? We're nothing to each other, remember?" he said, a dark glint in his eye.

I SHIVERED, THE MEMORY ALL TOO VIVID.

"I didn't even have a chance to put my bags down. They arrested me in the lobby as my neighbors walked past." I stopped talking and looked at Kade, my skin flushed with the remembered humiliation. "There it is. The whole ugly truth and sordid details. So you see, there's nothing you can do to help me. If you do anything, it will just get worse. You don't understand the kind of person he is. I mean, he's so twisted that he read my diary when I was a kid."

"Did you put what I told you about the loan in your diary?" Kade asked.

"Yes. I'm sorry. I wasn't thinking about what I was writing."

"You shouldn't have had to," he said.

His hands were clenched in front of him. He wasn't saying anything else, or doing much of anything. He just sat there, barely moving.

I got up, making my way to the kitchen to put some more ice in my glass. There was no way I was sleeping tonight without a lot of help. The options were passing out or no shut-eye at all. While I was preparing to drink myself into oblivion, Kade was still sitting on the couch.

He was too still, too quiet, and adding to my need to drink. His stillness was coming from his helplessness, reminding me of my own.

When he finally moved, he turned toward me, a raw,

DONNA AUGUSTINE

feral look in his eyes, like he were an injured animal that wasn't used to feeling pain.

"I wish I had known." His voice was raw.

"You couldn't have done anything."

I didn't move as he got up and headed toward me. Every step closer made me positive he was going to kiss me. I shouldn't want him to. I shouldn't be staring at his lips as if they didn't meet mine in the next minute I'd stop breathing. It was just a remnant of a childhood crush. That was all. They say you never forget your first love. That's all this was.

He stopped beside me, so close I could feel his heat. If I leaned an inch in his direction, we'd be touching.

His eyes went to my legs, lingering at the hem of the t-shirt.

He pulled the stool out from the island and took a seat.

I was able to breathe for a second before he grabbed the hem of my shirt and used it to slowly tug me in between his legs.

I shouldn't have moved, I could've pulled away, except my legs and body weren't agreeing with what my mind was telling me. I was undergoing a mutiny where the crew had decided that my brain should no longer be in charge.

"I could end up in prison if we mess around." My brain thought that was a really solid argument. The crew didn't agree, as my nipples hardened and my back arched.

"No one is taking you anywhere," he said. He sounded as if he actually had a choice in the matter. "Not a court, not a judge, and definitely not that bastard."

He wrapped his arm around my waist, pulling me close, his mouth colliding with mine.

I'd measured every kiss in my life up to the one I'd had with him when I was sixteen. They'd all fallen short, and that one was dulled by years and given by a boy just beginning to turn into the man he'd one day become. Even then I'd tasted the promise of the man he'd be, but nothing had prepared me for what it would be like now. For the heat and the passion I felt, from the way his calloused hands ran up my sides, or when they cupped my ass. His body was smooth hardness against my curves, and all I wanted to do was climb up his frame and then crawl inside him if I could.

His hands were running up the outside of my thighs, his eyes locked on mine, heat flaring.

They moved upward, dragging my t-shirt up to my waist. The tiny swath of lace underwear I had on barely covered me. One hand stayed steady on my hip while he trailed a finger to the top of the lace. He trailed it down the center, his thumb pressing the sensitive nub as his fingers cupped me.

The crew was cheering so loudly that my brain was about to throw in the towel and give up the ship.

"I need this. I need to touch you. Feel you," Kade said.

The desperation in his voice melted away my defenses.

I'd been telling myself for weeks that this was a bad idea, and yet I couldn't step away from him. I was an addict and he was the most addictive drug on the market. When I got near him, logic stopped being important. All that was left was an overwhelming need that didn't let enough air in for me to think of the consequences.

His hands shifted to the backs of my legs, lifting me to straddle his lap, then he pulled the t-shirt up and off me, tossing it to the side.

He cupped my waist and then slowly moved his hands up my sides until his thumbs were under my breasts.

"My God, you're beautiful," he said.

He was staring at me mesmerized, and I had a hard time dragging air into my lungs.

His mouth moved to my neck, and my head dropped backward as he continued to move against me.

"Just one time. That's it," I said.

"I'll take whatever I can get."

He ran his hand along my thigh, getting closer to the apex, until his thumb was pressed against me. He rubbed his finger in circles while his other hand gripped my hip, sliding me closer, forcing my legs open wider.

He pushed the scrap of lace I was wearing aside to thrust two fingers inside me before withdrawing them, only to grip my hips, thrusting upward, pressing against me as his tongue found mine again. All hopes of getting the crew back in order was done. It was a full-on riot inside my body.

He stood with me in his arms, his mouth not leaving mine. This wasn't flowers and hearts. This was going to be hot, hard, and savage.

He carried me to the bedroom as I pushed off his shirt, wanting to feel his flesh against mine. He dropped me down onto the mattress. I watched as he shed the last of his clothes, every hard inch of him revealed.

He gripped my panties, pulling them off my legs, continuing to gaze at every inch of me as if he couldn't get enough.

He kneeled in between my legs, running a hand along the inside of my thigh.

"Do you want me to stop? Because if we go any further, I don't know if I'll be able to stop," he said.

If I had wanted to say no, his thumb moving back to graze my clit would've stopped any attempt. Instead of saying words, I groaned and pulled him closer.

He dipped his head, running his tongue along my slit while his fingers slipped back into me.

"No, I need all of you," I said, pulling him upward.

His eyes locked with mine as he pressed into me. He was stretching me in the best way, making every nerve sing as he plunged into me. Thoughts ceased to exist as I wrapped my legs around him, meeting every thrust until I fell apart.

I was lying there, limp, sweaty, and utterly relaxed, when I realized I'd forgotten something.

"Shit. Did you..."

"Yes. Slipped it on right before."

That was the first time in my life I hadn't thought of that before having sex. Another reason this was dangerous ground for me. I lost all good sense.

I went to sit up, knowing I needed to get out of here. I could already feel this mistake hangover coming. But he tugged me closer, pulling me into him as his lips moved to my shoulder and then worked up to my neck.

"We are not even close to finished," he said, pulling me under him and moving his mouth over mine, stealing all my will to deny him.

———

KADE

. . .

LEAH WAS SLEEPING AS I DRESSED QUIETLY AND SLIPPED OUT OF the room. I couldn't chance her waking up and hearing the call I needed to make.

I left a note on the counter that I had to run into town to meet with a feed supplier and would grab some donuts on my way back.

I walked past the commotion of workmen breaking down the last of the wedding trappings and hopped in my truck. I called as soon as I hit the drive.

John answered on the second ring.

"It's the stepfather," I said.

"Yeah, that's how it's looking to me too."

"No, *it's the stepfather*." I was gripping the wheel of the truck so hard that I was afraid I'd rip it from the console.

"Well, not surprising. He might not have a criminal history or be on any police radar, but my sources have him knee deep in art robbery for decades. Word on the street is she's taking the fall for him. No one has any connection to her at all. As far as my sources say, she's as clean as the morning rain." There was the sound of papers being moved around. "And my sources? They're rock solid. If she were involved in this in any way other than as a patsy, one of them would know."

I'd never experienced a rage like this in my life, one so hot and blaring that I didn't know how blood wasn't shooting out of my ears. "I want you to get me proof. I want her name cleared and I want the dirt on him."

"I could try, but it'll be hard. My contacts won't hand anything over easily. Ratting ruins their reputations. They'd basically be retiring from the business in dishonor."

He spoke to me as if it were going to be just short of impossible. Well, he was going to make it happen, or I'd hire another fifty just like him until I found the one that got it done. I wouldn't be able to live with myself if I didn't get her name cleared.

"I'll pay enough that they'll be happy to retire."

"There's expensive, and then there's buying something like this."

"Do it," I said.

"I hope you realize the kind of money we're talking. You're going to have to really pay up."

"I thought you did your homework? My brother is in tech. They call him the Bitcoin King, and guess who decided it was a good idea to get in on the ground floor with him? Me. Now stop telling me how much it's going to cost and take care of it."

"If that's the case, I'm on it. *Gladly.*"

I pulled the truck over into the bakery parking lot, not wanting to go back empty-handed.

But I couldn't move for a minute as everything that had happened ran over again in my head.

Alec had been right, and the worst part of it was that I'd known it. I'd *known*. I just hadn't wanted to accept it. It was easier to blame her. And the pile of things I'd laid at her doorstep was so high that it was hard to even get to that door anymore. I'd wanted to blame her for my loan falling through, and my gut had said I was wrong about that too.

Edwin was lucky the wedding was over and I wouldn't be seeing him for a long while. Otherwise, I might drive until I found Edwin, beat him senseless, and leave him in the gutter like the rat he was.

The worst part of it all was last night, when Edwin

was talking and she'd looked at the ground, as if I'd turn on her. The sorrow I'd seen on her face made it feel like a sword had pierced my heart. It was still ripping me apart inside.

After a few minutes, I had enough composure to leave the truck without killing anyone.

CHAPTER 39

Leah

THE SHEETS SMELLED LIKE HIM, MAKING IT HARD TO GET OUT OF bed, but I did. There was too much to do to not get up, even if I did want to stay in bed, surrounded by his scent. It was the heart of his home. The furniture in this room was dark wood with simple but heavy lines. The walls were navy, with a suede appearance.

Everyone was on light duty today, but there were still things that had to get done, so I forced myself out of bed.

I was almost out of his room when I spotted it on top of his bureau, tucked near the base of a lamp. Almost completely hidden was a tiny horseshoe in copper.

Was it possible it was a different one? I hadn't seen it in so many years, and maybe my memory was faulty. But as I got closer, I could see the name I'd hand-etched into the metal. *Hawk Ranch.*

Maybe he'd kept it because his dreams had always been wrapped up in this ranch. It might have nothing to do with the fact that I'd given it to him. I couldn't start making more of this situation than there was. I'd be here for a year, and if I let myself start building daydreams, it would be really hard when they fell apart after the year was up.

I made my way into the kitchen, where Kade had left me a note saying he'd gone into town to meet with a supplier and would bring back donuts. He wasn't helping the daydreaming issue. I tossed the note in the garbage so no one else could happen upon it and got dressed for work. I needed to be out of here before he got back.

I walked back into the living room as Alec came in wearing the same suit he'd had on last night, just a little worse for wear.

"Hey. You have a good night?" I asked.

"I did. Greg? Probably not," he said, smiling.

"You spent last night with Lucia?" I wasn't always a fan of Alec's playboy ways, but I had to give him props for this one.

"Lucia? I thought her name was Lisa?" he said, running a hand through his hair. He shrugged. "I gotta go grab my stuff. My flight is leaving at noon. This place can go back to you and the beast in the grand castle." He winked at me.

"I'm too old for fairytales. You'd better get going."

He took off, and I ran out before Kade could get back.

IT WAS AFTER SIX, AND THERE WASN'T A SINGLE THING THAT needed to be done left, so I sat in the bunkhouse doing a puzzle with Missy. I would've mucked out some more stalls if it kept me away from Kade. Problem was that I didn't trust myself not to sleep with him again. I couldn't even stop replaying it in my head.

"I love puzzles," Missy said, pulling out some more edge pieces.

"Yeah, they're good sometimes." Especially moments like now, when I couldn't trust my attention span.

"I have to be honest, I didn't think I was going to like you so much."

"Because I was living in New York?" I asked, fitting another piece in. It was a cute little cottage scene. Missy had good taste in puzzles.

She paused with her lips open, as if she realized she'd just opened up a topic that she didn't want to.

"Yeah," she said.

Missy was officially going on record as the worst liar in creation.

"Seriously, what was it? Why did you think you wouldn't like me? Was it the conviction?" It was crazy that just a few weeks ago, I dreaded even mentioning that word. Now it slipped out like I was ordering a coffee.

"Well, that *did* make me a little nervous." She giggled.

"But that wasn't it, was it?" I asked. "I'm just curious. Not trying to make you uncomfortable. Whatever it is, it's okay. I've had to get a thick skin lately. Just tell me or it'll drive me crazy wondering, and I know there's *something*." Had it been the way I'd dressed? I'd been so scrambled that what I'd thrown on those first days had been an afterthought.

"It was the big warning conversation, wasn't it?" Adam said as he strolled out of one of the bunkhouse bedrooms.

"Warning conversation?" What the hell was he

talking about? Had they been warned about me? And by whom?

I was already getting a sinking feeling in my gut.

"It's not a big deal. Kade just said you were coming for some sort of work detail," Missy said, but she was shooting Adam a harsh glare.

"A talk?" So Kade had warned them about me.

"I mean, it wasn't a formal talk," Missy said, trying to clean up the bomb Adam had dropped.

"No, not formal at all," Adam said. "He came and said that you might not work hard, be difficult to be around, and yeah, that you were also a lying felon. He wanted us to tell him if you so much as looked at anyone the wrong way because he'd have your ass thrown in prison." Adam laughed loudly after he finished.

I couldn't speak. I thought I'd gotten the tears under control, but I was barely hanging on now.

And I'd fucking slept with the man.

"He didn't gather us," Missy said, still trying to clean this up. "We were at the bunkhouse hanging out. There was no gathering, I swear. Adam's making it sound way worse than it was. Plus I think he'd been drinking."

"Missy, it's fine," I said, stretching. "I'm pretty beat, though. We'll work again on this tomorrow, okay?"

"Shit. I shouldn't have said anything. I'm so sorry. I started all of this."

"No. You didn't start anything. It's fine." I waved her off as I grabbed my jacket off the chair.

Missy was back to staring at Adam. "You asshole. Why are you making it sound so bad?"

"Hey, I'm not lying. He said everything I just repeated," Adam said.

The guy was a troublemaker, but his words were ringing true.

The only good thing happening now was that Elijah had walked in. He could break up any fight that broke out between Missy and Adam. I had to get out of there.

I'd done some stupid things in my life, stuff that had kept me up nights, and yet nothing had made me feel as stupid as this. I'd danced with him at the wedding, laughed at his jokes. I'd probably looked like a lovestruck fool.

CHAPTER 40

Kade

John's number was flashing.

"It's done. I've got someone lined up who's going to come clean tonight. He was involved in the delivery end. Should clear her name. It's going to cost you, but by tomorrow, I expect you'll be hearing from her lawyer."

"What about her stepfather?"

"I've got a pile of dirt on him. We could bury him in some hellhole of a prison for the rest of his life. What do you want me to do with his dirt?"

"Sit on it for now." Prison might be too good for him. I was going to have to sit and think on this one.

"I got you."

"There's no links back to us?" If I did decide there was a better end to Edwin, I couldn't have it coming back to me.

"You know me better than that."

I spotted Missy heading toward the office, wringing her hands, her ponytail a mess.

"Gotta go." I hung up.

"Kade? You got a minute?" she asked. Missy's cheeks were flushed and she was breathing heavy.

"What's wrong now?"

"I screwed up bad."

"What did you do?" I waved her in and shut the door, having the feeling I wasn't going to want any interruptions if I could help it.

"I'm sorry. I didn't mean to do it." She bit her lip and then her nails while she paced across the room and then back.

"Just tell me what happened."

By the time she finished, I wished I hadn't heard. Adam was an asshole, but I couldn't be mad at him. I'd been the one who'd said those things.

I didn't even know why I'd said it to them in the first place. Like Chuck had said, I'd set them up to think the worst. Why bring Leah here and then do that? It was lousy.

Early on when we were going at each other like mortal enemies, it wouldn't have been so bad. If I'd brought it up in a joking manner before now, still not so bad. Like this, at this moment? The timing couldn't be worse.

"I'm so sorry," Missy said.

"It's not your fault. It's mine for saying those things in the first place. How did she react?"

"She blew it off like it was no big deal, but I could tell it hit hard." Missy was wringing her hands together.

"Do you know where she is now?"

"No. She walked off and then I came here."

"I'll go find her."

"Kade, I'm really sorry."

"Don't worry about it. This is all on me, Missy."

LEAH WASN'T IN THE OLD BARN OR AT THE CREEK. I FOUND HER in Princess's stall. As I stood there, I didn't know what to say. Maybe I shouldn't have rushed here until I figured it out, but I'd felt the need to find her as quickly as I could.

"I'm sorry. I know that falls short, but I am. I never should have said that."

"Why not? It's what you think of me. At least you were being honest."

"Leah, I was wrong. I should've known better."

She nodded, almost in a perfunctory way. Nothing I said was going to matter, and could I blame her?

"Please tell me how to make this right."

"Move my things into the bunkhouse."

"*I'll* move to the bunkhouse. You can take the house."

"I don't want to stay there. Either help me move my things or call the court and tell them to expect me in prison."

She couldn't possibly mean that. It would be crazy, but I felt too panicked at the prospect to push her. She was hurt, and a hurt Leah was a stubborn Leah.

"So where does that leave us?"

"There is no *us*. I'm a felon working off my sentence for a rancher named Kade. That's it."

I nodded. The wall I'd managed to knock down was firmly re-erected around her, and there was no getting through it tonight. Considering she'd be a free woman soon, I doubted there'd be time to make a crack in it going forward. I'd obliterated what we could've had. My only shot was to tell her what I'd done, tell her how I ignored her wishes not to get involved, and tell her I had a PI investigating her.

Somehow, that didn't bring me any optimism at the moment.

"You'll never know how sorry I am for this," I said.

She didn't reply, and I tried to respect her wishes, walking out of the stable and heading up to the ranch to move her things.

I'd fallen in love, and it was more gut-wrenching than I'd ever been prepared for, especially when it could've been the greatest thing in my life.

———

LEAH

I WAS ALMOST AT THE BUNKHOUSE WHEN MISSY WALKED OVER, looped her arm with mine, and tugged me with her.

"I know Kade moved your things, and I moved them again to my cabin, now our cabin."

"What—"

"Don't you dare try to argue with me. You want to see stubborn? You haven't seen anything yet."

She steered me to her cabin and then shoved me in. In the corner, she'd already gotten another bed moved in.

"You're staying here, and I don't care what you say."

I didn't say anything as I walked over and sat on the bed. Finally, with a shaking voice, I said, "Thank you."

She sat next to me, handed me a box of tissues, and then wrapped an arm around my shoulders.

"I locked the door. No one will know but me if you have another good cry."

For only the second time in my adult life, I bawled like a baby.

CHAPTER 41

Leah

I'D JUST FINISHED BRINGING PRINCESS OUT TO ONE OF THE pastures when Kade walked out of the ranch office, scanning the horizon. It was the first time we'd seen each other today. Our eyes locked.

He took a determined step toward me, and I was a big, mixed-up bag of emotions. I didn't know if I wanted to growl or purr, cozy up to him or scratch his eyes out. Probably both.

He stopped in front of me, but not as close as he would've yesterday. We were back to acquaintance spacing, and it felt chilly, like the sun had ducked behind a bunch of gray clouds. I shouldn't want the warmth he gave, but I did anyway. Logic wasn't that comforting on a frigid day. Sometimes even when you knew it was wrong, you wanted to settle into the cozy heat of delusion and what could've been.

I swallowed, waiting to hear what he'd say. Was he

going to beg forgiveness? Make a string of promises? Would I cave? Everything in me wanted to. I could already hear the excuses piling up in my head, prewritten for him. And maybe if he just put up enough of a fight, I could believe there was a chance for us.

"You had a call from your lawyer. You need to go call him back." He tilted his head toward the ranch.

My anxiety quickly found a new source. Had someone at the wedding seen Kade and me? Did they know I'd slept with him? Were they pulling me out of here? Sending me to prison? Why else would he be calling me?

I dropped my gaze to the ground, trying to puzzle through what was coming at me before I dealt with the crash. I might've said I preferred prison last night, but now common sense had fully returned. I took a few deep breaths of cool air, enough to stop me from vomiting.

"It'll be fine." Kade lifted his hand toward me but dropped it back to his side, and then crossed his arms in front of his chest, as if he needed to remind himself not to touch me.

"You know what he wants?" I asked, ignoring our feud for the moment, my anxiety overruling my current anger at Kade.

"He didn't sound as if it were bad."

"You don't know him. He might be happy if I go to prison." My lawyer would probably bust out a bottle of bubbly.

"You're not going to prison. I'd move you to some remote island before I'd ever let that happen." There was steel in his voice, as if he had control of everything and anything he wanted via sheer determination.

It was one of the things I usually loved about him and yet found infuriating right now.

"You can't fix everything," I said.

"No. Not *everything*." As he stared at me, it was clear he was talking about us.

For someone who'd fought so hard for his ranch, he was giving up awfully easy on us.

There was no point in standing there and waiting for something that wasn't coming. I nodded and then walked to the office, dialing my lawyer.

"Leah, I've got some good news for you," he said, definitely in a cheery mood. "Your name has been cleared."

"Cleared?" I repeated.

"Yes. Police happened upon an informant. He gave them all sorts of documents and evidence that clears you of the crime. Apparently that painting wasn't supposed to go to you at all, but someone else. Your entire story was corroborated. We already filed the paperwork with the court and we're just waiting on the judge to sign off. I expect you to be a free woman by the end of the day."

"I'm free?" I asked again. After the hell of the last few months, it was just over? Done? One call and I was a free woman again?

"Yes. Go enjoy your day."

I hung up the phone but didn't trust myself to stand for another ten minutes.

I was free. Just like that, I was free.

And I could leave here. I'd be expected to, even. Suddenly my legs felt weak for an altogether different reason.

———

KADE

. . .

LEAH WALKED OUT OF THE OFFICE, FINDING ME ON THE PORCH where I'd been waiting for her. She wasn't smiling. She looked more stunned than anything else.

She turned to me. "Did you know?"

"Your brother just sent me a text." I held up my phone, as if I needed proof that I'd just found out.

She didn't come over to the swing, but leaned a shoulder on the post. "They said there was an informant. They cleared my name completely."

"I'm happy for you."

She nodded, still not looking as happy as I'd expected. Was there still a chance? Could this relationship be repaired?

"I don't know what your plans are, but don't feel like you have to leave right away. In spite of what I said, all the things that happened, everyone here loves you."

I loved her, and if she stayed for a little while longer, maybe I could fix this. Find some way to repair the damage I'd done.

I could barely force myself to breathe as I waited for her to answer.

"I already called Monroe. He's setting up a flight for me tonight. Thanks, though. If I ever find myself in need of another work parole situation, I'll give you a ring."

She hadn't even hesitated. She couldn't wait to leave. She'd pack her bags and never look back, and did I blame her? No.

Just like that, it was truly over. I wasn't sure how I was going to keep going on if she was walking out of my life.

"I'll be here." I feared I'd be here until the day I died,

hoping one day she'd want to come back.

————

LEAH

I WALKED INTO MISSY'S CABIN, SHUT THE DOOR, AND DROPPED onto the bed. I was free. I could get into a car and drive off this ranch and no one could stop me. I could go wherever I wanted. Not only that, my name was cleared. I had a chance of rebuilding my career.

So why did I need to sink onto the bed, my legs feeling weak and my heart aching like I was dying?

Kade had said there was no rush to leave. He hadn't gotten down on one knee, told me he loved me, and then begged me to stay. He hadn't fought for me last night. He'd stepped away as if it would be too much to bother with. Didn't that say it all?

The door to the cabin swung open.

"I just heard! You're leaving? You're cleared?" Missy said, breathless.

"Yeah," I said, nodding, trying to mirror her happiness. "It's crazy. I don't even understand all the details, but it's over." I filled her in on the details from the lawyer, or what I could remember of them. I'd been so stunned that nothing beyond "your name is cleared" stuck very well.

"So you're leaving tonight?" she said, her smile slipping a little.

"Yeah. I have to go try to build my life back." It was the only thing left to do. I couldn't stay here, not with *him*. I was beginning to worry that I might never stop loving him if I did. And there was no denying the ache happening now. This was utter heartbreak. "You know you can come see me? You're my friend, and a good one, a better one than most. You're not getting rid of me that easily."

She nodded. "I get it. I really do. I just like having you around. I kind of think other people do as well." She gave me a knowing look.

"That's never been anything real." Or not on Kade's part, anyway.

"You sure? I've seen how Kade looks at you. I saw how he stared at you on that dance floor during the wedding. You're telling me that was casual? Because I'm not buying it. That kind of look is what I've been dreaming of my whole adult life."

I knew all about dreaming. I barely wanted to admit to myself that I'd daydreamt about how things might've been if I'd never moved away. Maybe we would've ended up married with kids? Then this morning, while I was still reeling, he said "no need to rush."

I wasn't letting any delusions take hold this time. I knew what we were. He'd had his fun and now he'd move on, and I wouldn't stick around to watch him.

There was a knock at the door and then Elijah was there, congratulating me, followed by Chuck and every other hand on the ranch, until we were overflowing out of the small cabin.

I forced a smile, tried to laugh and look happy even as my heart was dying. I was about to leave the man I loved. It didn't matter if it seemed like the right thing, or if he deserved my love. I'd given him a part of me, and I wasn't sure there were any take-backs where the heart was concerned.

———

KADE

I WAS ON THE TOP RIDGE AT THE EDGE OF MY PROPERTY, watching the sun sink. Leah would be driving away any second, and I couldn't bear to watch her.

"What the hell you doing all the way out here?" Alec asked.

"What the hell you doing in Montana?" I loved my brother but I didn't want to see anyone right now, hence coming here instead of sitting on my comfortable porch seats.

"I didn't leave after the wedding. Got holed up with a little chickee the last few days and then stumbled onto a business opportunity." He took a seat on a nearby boulder, making it obvious he wasn't leaving too soon. "Now why are you all the way out here?"

"Because I wanted some fresh air and everyone was getting on my nerves."

"Because they're all saying goodbye to Leah."

"They're all looking at me like I've been diagnosed with a terminal illness, and I'm not in the mood." I wasn't sure I blamed them, because I *did* feel a little like I was dying. Had since I'd gotten the diagnosis from Leah this morning.

"You do seem a bit morose."

"I'm fine. Nothing is different. I'm as good as I was before." I'd have to be, because what else was there to do? She wanted to leave and I had a ranch to run.

"You're really just letting her go like this? Are you even going to put up a fight? You fight like hell when it comes to the ranch, to business. But when it comes to love, man, you run faster than anyone I've ever seen."

"This isn't running. It's knowing she deserves better."

"She might deserve better, but what if she wants you?" He laughed.

"You're a dick."

"Well, we are brothers. Hard to completely escape that gene pool. But seriously, don't let her go."

I turned to him and said, "I've done the wrong thing with her for months, years if you think on it. I'm trying to do the right thing for once."

Alec nodded and then handed me a flask, which I took.

I wasn't sure what had hit him so hard, but for one of the first times in my life, I'd managed to shut him up without punching him.

CHAPTER 42

Leah

I STARED OUT THE WINDOW AT THE CITY I USED TO LOVE. THERE was a time that I'd sit in the chair by the floor-to-ceiling windows and stare out at the skyline for hours. Now I looked out and all I wanted to see was the sun rising over the mountains, or the sound of the roosters calling everyone to work instead of an alarm. I wanted to sit on the porch with the fresh air blowing through my hair instead of the HVAC kicking on.

I wanted to sit on that damned porch swing, rocking gently. Wrapped in a blanket with a hot cup of coffee in my hands, I'd watch the sun rise over the mountains.

There were other parts of that morning that I missed more than anything, but I had to stop thinking of *him*. Nothing good came from that.

When I got home, I'd spent every waking minute rebuilding my career, and it was working. My clients were slowly coming back. I was regaining people's confidence now that my name had been cleared. I could've even had my friends back if I'd wanted, but I hadn't.

I should've been happy. Things were getting back on track. But all I did was think of him, what seemed like every single minute.

The buzzer rang, signaling Monroe's arrival. He walked in the apartment a few minutes later.

"Coffee's still hot," I said, motioning toward the kitchen.

His eyes lit up and he headed to get a cup. "Man, I missed this brew. Where do you get it from?" He dropped onto my couch.

"Coffee shop around the corner sells a special blend." I'd thought I'd miss it, too. Now all I thought about was how good the brew Kade had in Montana was.

Monroe watched me intently. "Is it weird to be back after everything that happened?"

"Yeah, I guess it is. I thought I'd get some satisfaction out of walking back here with my name cleared. The reality fell a little short." Everything seemed to be falling short. I felt like I'd been living in 4K and had just been thrown back to silent movies.

"It's been a month and you still seem off, like you don't want to be here," he said, watching me in that way he did lately, as if he weren't sure who I was anymore.

"It's just jarring to be back. I'll settle in." There was no way I'd sit around and pine for that man for another month. "By the way, did you bring me those new mortgage documents? I'm still waiting on them. I don't know how you keep forgetting."

He looked at his coffee as he said, "I have to tell you something about that."

Usually when he wanted to tell me something, he just blurted it out.

"How bad is the interest rate?" I asked. I'd suspected it was horrendous but didn't even care about that. Maybe I'd just sell the place, go somewhere else and start anew.

"It's zero," he said.

"Zero? How can it be zero?" I asked, turning around to look at him.

"Okay, this is where I'm going to have to talk about a subject you said I can't."

"I told you I don't want to—"

"I know," he said. "You don't want to talk about Kade, but you *have* to know this. It's just too important not to tell you."

Even the thought of Kade made my heart rate jump, my stomach feel like it was bottoming out, and my eyes burn. How was it he could still do this to me? *Damn him.*

"Fine. What's so important? Say it. Get it out, but it better really be important, because I hate that man and I don't want to talk about him."

"I wasn't going to say anything, but you're just too miserable and I *have* to tell you. That witness who came forth? Kade paid him off, and from what I've heard, to the tune of several million."

"Who would tell you something so stupid? That's bull, 'cause Kade wouldn't have millions to throw around like that. I mean, the ranch is doing well, but I think he throws every dime back into it." To grow as fast as he had, he must've. Plus he'd kept buying more horses, cattle, and land while I'd been there.

"Alec told me. We've been talking." Monroe sipped, watching me like he was getting ready to run out the door if I made a wrong move.

"You've been talking to Alec?" I was too stunned to punch him.

"Yes. Apparently Kade is as miserable as you, and we made a decision to screw all the confidences for both of your best interests. Kade paid for that witness to come clean. He got into Bitcoin on the ground floor and rolled some of that into other tech stocks. Guy has brilliant instincts and a brother who's an insider."

I leaned forward, gaping. "Kade paid to clear my name?"

"*Yes*." Monroe stared at me, brows high, like he was wondering how many times he'd have to say it.

"There's no way this is true." It couldn't be. Why would Kade do that?

"Leah, I know it's true because he paid off this apartment too when they called your loan."

He looked too scared to be lying.

"You said Tiffany's cousin—"

"I know what I said. He made me lie. He was convinced you wouldn't accept his help or you'd feel weird."

I walked to the other end of my white sectional and dropped down onto it. "Why? Why would he do that?"

"Same reason he called me to work out a deal so you wouldn't go to prison. Same reason he called in a favor with the judge so that he'd sign off on it. Same reason he's done everything he has. The man is in love with you."

"You're saying my judge in NY owed him a favor? That's how this weird deal came to be?"

"Yes." Monroe put his coffee down and sat back on the couch. "You have no idea how good it feels to unload all of these secrets. They were killing me." His arms flopped to the side as if he'd just run a marathon.

"You're telling me Kade is the reason I didn't go to prison and *you didn't tell me*?" By the end of my question my voice had gone up a couple of octaves.

He tilted his head back to me, looking a little less relaxed. "Yes. Don't hit me. He swore me to secrecy. He never wanted you to feel indebted to him."

"But he was miserable when I got there. None of this makes sense." I fell back on the couch too, baffled, stunned, my head spinning faster than a hummingbird flapped.

"I don't know why he acted the way he did. You two are both a little crazy. I do know that man loves you. Still loves you, if Alec is correct."

"But he didn't fight for me?" Why did he just let me walk out if he cared so much?

"He didn't try to buy your love, but from where I'm sitting, he's been fighting for you this whole time. He fought to keep you out of prison, fought to save your home, and fought to clear your name. That's a whole lot of fighting. I don't know, but as far as I can see, he loves you. So the only question is, do you love him?"

"I do. I tried to be angry at him, but I can't seem to be."

"Then what the fuck are you doing? Go get your man and stop moping around this place."

————

KADE

. . .

When Leah moved into the main house from the shed, and I'd seen her on my swing that first morning, a ripple of annoyance had shot through me. This was my place of solitude to regroup every morning before the day started. But somehow I'd come to like seeing her there, and way too fast. She'd smell like strawberries and she'd tuck her little feet up underneath her, staring at the same sunrise, the corner of her lips always rising as the sun glimmered over the mountains and light the sky. She'd become part of the morning routine, the best part. What had felt complete before now felt empty.

Now I didn't even want to get out of bed because she wouldn't be there.

But I had to. So I did.

It was still a half-hour or so before sunrise when I walked out of my bedroom and the smell of coffee hit me. Chuck must've come by early for something. Every now and then if he had to go through something in the office, he'd put on a pot. I poured a cup and then walked toward the porch. It was freezing, but I couldn't seem to stop myself from hoping that one of these mornings, Leah would somehow be there.

When I did see her, for a second I thought I was imagining things. But there she was. I blinked a few times, assuring myself she was real.

"You're here? Why are you here?"

"Do you want me to leave?"

"No. Most definitely not," I said, ready to tackle her if she took my words wrong and tried to leave.

"We have some things we need to settle, and a phone call didn't feel right. You lied to me. You told me you didn't believe in grand gestures."

"I don't." I couldn't stop staring at her. Somehow she

looked even more beautiful now, and I hadn't thought that was possible.

"Then what have you been doing? You saved me from prison, called in favors to get me here. You cleared my name and even saved my home. For someone who doesn't believe in grand gestures, you haven't stopped making them. Why didn't you tell me any of this?"

"I never wanted you to feel that you owed me anything."

"But I owe you *everything*. You didn't think that I deserved to know what you did for me? That it might make a difference?"

"I wanted you to want *me*, not because I did that." I shook my head. If she'd come here to repay some debt, none of this mattered. I didn't want her like that. I wanted her heart, nothing more, nothing less.

"Kade Hawk, you are as blind as your brother says you are. Don't you know? I wanted you the day I walked onto this ranch. I have wanted you since I was that fourteen-year-old kid you teased. I watched you like you were a god. Sometimes I wonder if I wanted you since the first moment I saw you, because I don't remember a day in my life that I *didn't* want you. I don't think I could ever stop wanting you. I've loved you since before I knew what love was."

"Even after everything? The way I handled things? I was horrible. You shouldn't even want to speak to me. I should've known you were innocent."

"And I should've known you weren't an evil bastard," she said, a smile touching her lips.

"That's not your fault. I do a really good impression of one."

She stood there staring at me, and it was taking

everything I had not to walk over, grab her, drag her into the house, and lock the doors so she could never leave.

Instead I said, "Do you want to come in?" I hooked a thumb toward the door. If she walked in, she was mine. I wasn't letting her leave. Not again. The first time had nearly killed me. Now that I knew, no way would I let her go again.

She took a step toward me. Against my better instincts, I held up a hand.

She flinched, as if she were expecting some kind of rejection, and it was like someone had taken a stake to my heart.

"I thought you wanted me to come in?" Her voice was soft.

"I do. More than you know. That's the problem." I stepped closer as I fought the urge to grab her off her feet. "You come in, I'm not sure I'll let you leave."

She took another step forward, sealing her fate as she closed the distance between us. My body tensed as I watched her. We were only a couple feet away from each other and it took everything I had to not wrap my arms around her and drag her the rest of the way inside.

She stood before me, her hair cascading over her shoulders, her cheeks tinged with pink from the chill while her eyes sparkled with emotion. I'd forgo every sunrise for the rest of my life if I could look at her every day.

"What if I don't want to leave?" she said.

Those words broke the last chains holding me back. I closed the distance between us in one step and lifted her, her feet dangling as I hugged her to me.

She wrapped her arms around me, burying her head in the crook of my neck.

"I love you," I said. "I love you more than I imagined was ever possible, more than this ranch, and if you ever leave me again, I don't think I'll survive."

"I'm not going to. I promise."

CHAPTER 43

Kade

EDWIN WAS SITTING, HAVING A DRINK, WAITING FOR HIS meeting, when I walked in and took the seat across from him.

He looked up and then jerked back.

"Kade. What are you doing here?" He shifted in his seat, looking at the door and then me.

"Had some business to take care of."

"It's great to see you, but I'm actually waiting for someone who should be here any second. I'd love to catch up with you later, though."

Liar. Ten years ago I'd been instantly in awe of him. Now? I spotted a rat trying to scurry out of a trap.

He'd known I was onto him since the wedding, but he wasn't sure how much I knew. I was here to tell him exactly what I had on him, and it was a mountain of information.

"*I'm* your meeting," I said.

He laughed for a second, his hands trembling a bit as he took a sip of his drink.

"I'm not joking. I'm your meeting. Your associate won't be arriving."

His face fell, his skin blanching. "Are you having me watched?"

"No. I stopped doing that after I gathered everything I needed from you. Boy, did I learn a lot. You got the woman I love in a whole lot of trouble, and then as if that weren't enough, you tried to get them to cancel her loan?"

"You're making some pretty damning accusations. I'd watch what you say to me." He was scanning the surrounding area, frozen, stuck, not sure whether to run or stay seated. I could see the wheels turning as he tried to figure a way out of this situation, but there wasn't one.

I'd covered every base and I had documentation. The only reason he wasn't in prison yet was that I hadn't decided quite yet what I wanted to do with him.

"Or what?" I said. "You'll make me prove it in court? You'll never make it there. You'll be dead first."

He was sitting there, his eyes shooting around the room still as if he were trying to figure out a way out of his mess.

"You wouldn't."

"For Leah? Try me."

He lifted his drink with a shaking hand and downed the rest of it. "She's too good for you."

"That might be true, but you know what else is true? She's with me, and you're going to pay for what you did. Now here's what's going to happen."

———

LEAH

KADE WALKED INTO THE LIVING ROOM, WHERE I WAS GOING through the stuff in the apartment I needed to either box up or get rid of. He walked over and wrapped his arms around me, as if he hadn't seen me in days, when it had only been hours.

"How's it coming along?" he asked.

"Okay. I've got a lot sorted." It had been a month since we'd gotten together, and I wasn't sure I'd ever get used to being able to call him mine.

"When's the realtor putting it up?"

"Two weeks from today," I said.

"You sure you want to sell it? We could keep it. Stay here when you want to visit your family. I don't want you to give up something you love."

The only way that would happen was if I lost him.

"This place isn't what I want anymore," I said, smiling up at him. "How'd your secret meeting go?"

Monroe had called me the second he spotted Kade. He'd said that, from the look on Edwin's face, he thought it best to keep on walking.

"I guess not so secret, but pretty good. I think we have an understanding. How did you find out?"

"Monroe happened to walk past the restaurant you were at. He thought it best not to intrude."

"I was going to tell you, but I thought after it was done might be better."

"So what did you talk about?" I didn't like that man anywhere around the people I loved, but I'd also learned Kade was more resourceful than I'd ever known.

He tugged me over to the couch, pulling me into his

side. "He's going to be signing over all his accounts to your mother, whatever stolen art he currently has is going to show up at a local police department, and he'll be taking an extended leave for mental health on a small, isolated island no one has ever heard of."

"He agreed to all that?" Didn't sound like Edwin, but Kade tended to get what he wanted.

"It was the lesser of two evils. After all, I can't let a man like that around my wife."

"Technically I'm still just your fiancée."

"Not for long. Cassie's already been hard at work."

"Oh no."

"Oh yes. She was already calling me this morning. I'm sure whatever she plans will be perfect," he said, leaning over and kissing my head as he pulled me closer.

It didn't matter what the wedding was like, or where we lived. I was with Kade and I didn't need anything else. Life was already as perfect as it could get.

ALEC AND MISSY'S STORY COMING AT THE END OF 2025.

SCAN THE QR CODE BELOW TO JOIN MY MAILING LIST:

WANT MORE OF DONNA AUGUSTINE NOW? READ THE PARANORMAL ROMANCE Gut Deep **NOW OR ONE OF MY OTHER MANY ROMANTASY SERIES.**

FOLLOW ME ON ONE OF THESE PLATFORMS:

https://www.facebook.com/groups/223180598486878/

http://www.donnaaugustine.com

https://www.bookbub.com/authors/donna-augustine

https://twitter.com/DonnAugustine

Acknowledgments

I'm very lucky to have a group of people who have stuck with me, book after book. Lisa A., Donna Z, Lori. H, Ashleigh M., Camilla J., and Karen C., thank you for sticking with me through this new adventure!

Also by Donna Augustine

Torn Worlds (Paranormal Romance)

Gut Deep

Visceral Reaction

River of Luck

The Wilds (Post-apocalyptic Romance)

The Wilds

The Hunt

The Dead

The Magic

Born Wild (Wilds Spinoff)

Wild One

Savage One

Wyrd Blood (Post-apocalyptic Romance)

Wyrd Blood

Full Blood

Blood Binds

Ollie Wit (Urban Fantasy Romance)

A Step into the Dark

Walking in the Dark

Kissed by the Dark

Going Nowhere (Urban Fantasy Romance)

A Bridge to Nowhereland

Burning Bridges in Nowhere

Out of Nowhere

The Keepers (Urban Fantasy Romance)

The Keepers

Keepers and Killers

Shattered

Redemption

Karma (Fantasy Romance)

Karma

Jinxed

Fated

Dead Ink

Tales of Xest (Alternate Universe Fantasy Romance)

The Whimsy Witch Who Wasn't

The Nowhere Witch

The Most Wanted Witch

Witch of all Witches

www.ingramcontent.com/pod-product-compliance
Lightning Source LLC
Chambersburg PA
CBHW071849220626
47052CB00002B/29